MW01137424

The Groomer

Jon Athan

For more information on this book or the author,
please visit www.jon-athan.com. General
inquiries are welcome.

Facebook:
https://www.facebook.com/AuthorJonAthan
Twitter: @Jonny_Athan
Email: info@jon-athan.com

Book cover by Sean Lowery:
http://indieauthordesign.com/

Thank you for the support!

ISBN: 9798624417786

First Edition

WARNING

This book contains scenes of intense violence and some disturbing themes. Some parts of this book may be considered violent, cruel, disturbing, or unusual. This book is *not* intended for those easily offended or appalled. Please enjoy at your own discretion.

Table of Contents

Chapter One...1
Chapter Two...11
Chapter Three..33
Chapter Four..47
Chapter Five...59
Chapter Six...69
Chapter Seven...79
Chapter Eight...95
Chapter Nine..103
Chapter Ten...115
Chapter Eleven...125
Chapter Twelve...133
Chapter Thirteen..141
Chapter Fourteen...149
Chapter Fifteen..171
Chapter Sixteen..181
Chapter Seventeen..193
Chapter Eighteen...213
Chapter Nineteen...231
Chapter Twenty..241
Chapter Twenty-One...247
Chapter Twenty-Two...265
Chapter Twenty-Three..283
Chapter Twenty-Four..305
Chapter Twenty-Five...335

Chapter One

Want to Play a Game?

Liam Hansen sat in front of his computer, face lit up by the bright monitor. His bulky over-ear headset pulled his head down. Black bags hung under his bloodshot eyes. He blinked once a minute. He breathed loudly, but he didn't notice it because of his noise-cancelling headphones. An eight-ounce can of Red Bull stood beside his mouse pad.

He frequently tapped the W-A-S-D keys on his keyboard with his left hand while clicking on his mouse with his right hand. In the video game, his character punched a tree until a block of the trunk exploded into a smaller block of wood. The repetitive, dull *thud* of each hit was oddly relaxing. He didn't play it every day, but he enjoyed returning to his *Minecraft* world every now and then.

Liam was a ten-year-old boy. And he was already addicted to video games and energy drinks. His parents used video games to keep him busy, to keep him out of trouble—*to raise him.*

"What the hell are you doing, dude?"

Liam heard the nasally voice through his headphones. He was on a Skype voice call with a user named: *Cheese2002.* Liam didn't know his real name, so he called him 'Cheese.'

Liam responded, "I'm getting wood. What's it look like?"

"Getting wood," Cheese snickered.

"What? What's so funny?"

"Nothing, nothing," Cheese said while trying to suppress his laughter. "Just use an axe, dude. It's so much faster."

"I don't have one now."

"Make one!"

"After this. I don't need *that* much wood anyway."

Cheese cackled again. It sounded like he was rolling back-and-forth and side-to-side in his seat. Liam furrowed his brow and shrugged, as if his online friend could see him.

"Dude, seriously, what's so funny?" he asked.

As he recomposed himself, Cheese said, "N– Nothing. I mean, I can't tell you anyway. You're too young."

"Whatever, boomer."

"I'm just saying, dude. Wait a couple of years and you'll get it."

"Yeah, yeah, yeah. I don't care anyway."

Liam gathered the wood and headed back to a town over a mountain. He spent months building the town with Cheese. They built small shops and houses, a red barn for their livestock and fields for their crops, and even a mine, a library, and a guard post. But their pride and joy was the massive castle atop the mountain overlooking their town. The interior was unfurnished, but the exterior was complete.

Cheese asked, "What do you wanna build next?"

"Dude, we still have to finish the castle."

"You *actually* want to build the inside? That's gonna take forever!"

"So what?"

"I don't have 'forever,' dude."

As he directed his character to the castle, Liam asked, "Why? What else do you have to do?"

Cheese responded, "School, work, that kind of stuff."

Liam checked the clock on his phone: *1:17 AM.* He puckered his lips, then he sighed. School began at eight o'clock in the morning. He woke up at seven to eat breakfast, get ready, and arrive on time.

He said, "Yeah, I have to sleep soon, too."

"*Wait,*" Cheese said in an urgent tone. He asked, "How about a game of Fortnite? Just one match before we sleep?"

"I don't know, dude. They're kinda long games..."

"Seriously, man, you know you want to."

Liam let out another loud sigh, then he smirked and said, "Alright, one game."

He took a swig of his Red Bull and jumped into a match of Fortnite. The sound of his keyboard *clacking* and his mouse *clicking* echoed through the house. His parents—underpaid and overworked—slept with earplugs and sleep masks. His mother also used sleeping pills to aid her slumber.

He can take care of himself, they told themselves. *He's old enough now. He has an older brother and a younger sister. He has his games and his friends.*

One match in Fortnite quickly turned to two, then three, and then four. The clock on his phone read: *2:42 AM.* He was out of Red Bull, but he wasn't drowsy. The caffeine from the energy drink and the adrenaline from the video game kept him amped up. He felt his heart pounding away at his chest.

Thud, thud, thud, thud, thud!

After losing another round, Liam said, "I think I'm gonna sleep now. Thanks for–"

"Let me just ask you something real quick," Cheese interrupted.

"What's up, dude?"

"You wanna meet up this weekend?"

"Like... um... what do you mean?"

"In person," Cheese clarified. "I have some extra Minecraft Coins and V-Bucks I want to give you. I want you to get that Fortnite 'Fishstick' skin so we can wear it together."

"Okay, um... Just send it to me."

They shared a moment of awkward silence. Only their breathing and the menu music from the video game played through their headphones.

Cheese coughed to clear his throat, then he said, "I want to give it to you in person. I just thought, like... I don't know. I got you these gifts 'cause we've known each other for a while now. We play together almost every day. We've trolled a bunch of people. You remember when we raided those role-playing servers in GTA Online? Stealing their cars, running people over, trying to frame other players."

Liam smiled as he reminisced about their good times playing together. He never argued with Cheese about anything. But he was cautious because he knew Cheese was older than him. He sounded older, despite his nasally voice, and his vocabulary was extensive. He went to school, but he never specified his grade—*middle school? high school? College?*

Cheese2002—Liam guessed the number at the end of his friend's username was connected to his birth year. So, he assumed Cheese was seventeen or eighteen years old.

Cheese continued, "Let's meet at the park. I'll give you these gifts as a late birthday present, then we can play some Fortnite together if you bring your Nintendo Switch. Then your mom can stop bitching about you getting out of your room. What do you think? You down?"

Liam said, "I don't know..."

"Why, bro? Come on, it's me! *Cheese!*" Cheese said as he chuckled. "It's not like I'm going to hurt you or anything like that. And we're going to be in public. You want that Fishstick skin, don't you? Hell, dude, you can buy some Legendary Skins with the leftover V-Bucks if you want. I don't care what you do with 'em."

Liam's lips fluttered as he let out a loud, sputtering sigh. Some of his saliva hit the monitor, but he paid it no mind. He thought about his decision. He trusted Cheese, and he was always happy to receive a gift. He was also interested in buying some new skins, which changed the appearance of his character. And he never felt intimidated by Cheese. He felt more intimidated by his eight-year-old sister, in fact.

Liam said, "I can meet you at Kamala Park. It's, like, two blocks away from my school. Is Friday good?"

"Friday's good, but... let's meet at Plaza Park. They have Wi-Fi there now, so we can play Fortnite without any lag."

"Plaza Park... I guess, but... It's kinda far."

"Well, it's like we're meeting in the middle 'cause it's not so far from me. So, we'll meet there on Friday after school. Deal?"

"I mean, um… I should probably ask my–"

He stopped as he caught a glimpse of the clock on his monitor. It was now three o'clock in the morning.

Liam said, "I gotta go. I'll talk to you later, Cheese. Thanks for playing with me!"

"Hey! We're meeting on Friday, right? *Right?*"

Liam turned off his computer and jumped into bed. He thought about Cheese's invitation for a few minutes.

"I'll meet you… Friday… after school," he whispered before dozing off.

***

"Are you… Are you Cheese2002?" Liam asked as he approached a young man sitting on a bench.

The stranger fiddled with his phone before glancing at Liam. He was surprisingly attractive—lean, clean, tall, and young. His curly brown hair was stylishly messy, his brown eyes as gentle as a puppy's, and his face as hairless as a child's. He wasn't the sharpest dresser, but he wore exactly what Cheese told Liam he would be wearing: a blue button-up shirt with a gray t-shirt underneath, slim jeans, and sneakers.

"That's me," the stranger said. "You must be Liam. It's cool to finally meet you, little dude. My real name's Zachary Denton."

Zachary reached for a handshake. Liam stared at Zachary's hand for a few seconds, then he glanced around, as if he were making a drug deal in public. He shook Zachary's hand, then he hooked his thumbs under the straps of his baby blue backpack and stepped back. Zachary furrowed his brow and cocked his head to the side, as if to say: *what's the matter, buddy?*

Liam smiled nervously and said, "You, um... You sound a little different."

"Yeah? I guess it's just the mic I use when I play online. It's a piece of crap."

Liam's eyes wandered to the backpack on the bench beside Zachary. He asked, "Did you just finish school, too?"

"Oh, yeah. I drove here right after class, so I've been waiting for you for a minute."

"Oh... What, um... What school do you go–"

"Hey, check this out, dude," Zachary interrupted.

He pulled two gift cards out of his backpack—one for 3,500 Minecraft Coins and another for 2,800 V-Bucks for Fortnite. He reached out to hand them to Liam. Liam bit his bottom lip and glanced around the park again. Broad daylight bathed the park in a warm glow. Pedestrians strolled down the walkways while the homeless built tents on the lawns. He saw a police cruiser drive down the street behind Zachary, too.

He felt safe in the area, but cautionary tales— recounted by his parents and his teachers—kept stabbing the back of his mind.

'Don't take candy from a stranger.'

They never said not to take a gift card from a stranger, Liam thought.

He accepted the gift. He sat down beside Zachary and pulled his Nintendo Switch out of his backpack. He started playing *Fortnite*.

He asked, "Can I use it now?"

As he pulled his own Nintendo Switch out of his backpack, Zachary said, "Go for it, dude. It's yours. I'll get online, too."

Liam redeemed his gift card and purchased the Fishstick skin for his character on Fortnite. He saved the Minecraft gift card for home. He played a match with Zachary. Zachary taught him a few special maneuvers and tricks. Then they walked around the park and played *Pokémon GO*, laughing and chatting every step of the way.

From the outside looking in, they looked like brothers. Zachary was clearly in his twenties, but he gave off a youthful aura. He blended with his environment.

After an hour of playing and conversing, they returned to the bench. Liam put his jacket and his Nintendo Switch in his backpack.

Zachary asked, "Hey, you want me to jailbreak your Switch?"

"Huh?"

"Jailbreak, dude. You know what that is, right?"

"Um... no."

Zachary said, "It's pretty much a hack. You can make your Switch do things it's not supposed to do. Things that it will *never* be able to do officially."

"Like what?"

"On my Switch back home, I can play Gameboy Advance, PlayStation, Nintendo 64, and GameCube games. You said you liked that Mario game, right? Super Mario Odyssey? Well, if you jailbreak your system, you can play Super Mario Sunshine and Super Mario 64 and *any* Mario game you want. You won't even have to pay for it, dude."

Liam stuttered, "R–Really?"

"Yup."

"Is it, like, um… like bad? Like breaking the law?"

Zachary chuckled, then he said, "Don't worry about that. You think anyone's ever going to arrest a ten-year-old because of video games? I do it all the time and I've never been in trouble. So, what do you say, little dude? Want me to hack your Switch? I'll do it for free and it won't take more than thirty minutes. I can probably do it in fifteen."

Liam pressed his tongue against the side of his mouth and looked around. He checked the clock on his phone: *4:46 PM.* His parents usually arrived home at six o'clock. He had more than enough time to hack his Nintendo Switch. And he believed every word out of Zachary's mouth. But he couldn't get the warnings out of his head.

'Don't ever get into a stranger's car.'

The devil on Liam's shoulder said: *'But he's not a stranger, he's a friend.'*

Liam asked, "Can you do it at my house?"

"Sorry, I can't. I have to do it through my computer. I don't live so far, you know, and I can drop you off at your house right after if you want. You'd be home faster than if you started walking home now. I mean, it's up to you, Liam. I'm just glad we could meet. I had fun, little dude."

"Y–Yeah, me too," Liam said, an innocent smile blossoming on his face. He said, "Okay, I'll go with you. I just have to get home before six, okay?"

"Yeah, dude, no problem. Come on, I parked right over here."

They walked down the walkway while chatting

about their favorite Super Mario video games. Then Zachary grabbed Liam's shoulder and pulled him away from the walkway. They walked across the lawn. To Liam, it seemed like they were taking a shortcut to the parking lot. Instead, they approached a little white hatchback parked on the street.

Zachary knew the park well. He avoided the surveillance cameras in the parking lot and at the end of the walkways. Liam climbed into the passenger seat. A stack of manila file folders sat on the dashboard in front of Liam, just tall enough to block him from outside eyes—and other cameras. Liam wasn't aware of Zachary's precautions. He wasn't aware of his intentions, either.

They drove away, cruising far from Liam's home. His parents didn't see him at six o'clock—or seven, or eight.

Chapter Two

The Park

"Are you seriously drinking right now?" Holly McCarthy hissed, bug-eyed.

Her husband, Andrew McCarthy, shook his flask and said, "Don't worry about it, hun. They think it's apple juice."

"Oh. My. God. You are… a child."

"Don't be so melodramatic."

"Okay, you're a… a… I don't even know if there's a word for it. A… A wannabe college student? A poser?"

"A poser? Jeez, that's just rude."

"What? It's true, isn't it? You're thirty-four years old, almost thirty-five, and you're drinking out of a flask at a public park. I'm surprised you're not drinking out of a bottle of sunscreen."

Ha, Ha, Ha!—Andrew laughed sarcastically. Their friends, setting up lawn chairs and picnic blankets outside of a large sandbox, cackled and teased him. They sided with Holly, especially considering the circumstances. It was a sunny Saturday gathering of close friends and their families, including their young, impressionable children.

Andrew stood five-eleven. His beach blonde hair was always disheveled. His blue eyes sparkled behind his glasses. His beard was trimmed, thick but neat. He worked as a territory sales representative for a local health insurance company. He was responsible for sales profitability, growth, and market penetration as well as managing old contacts and recruiting new clients.

He lived a boring, middle-class suburban life. He wasn't macho or aggressive or violent. He wasn't a drunk, either, but he tried to add some excitement to his life every now and then.

He grabbed his wife's arm and pulled her closer to him, then he planted a sloppy kiss on her lips, tongue and all. Holly could only giggle as she tried to break away.

She said, "You're so embarrassing."

"But you love me, don't you?"

"Yeah, I guess so."

"Save it for the bedroom, you two," Matthew Baker, a family friend, said from the sidelines. "Or for your minivan."

Andrew said, "It's more like an SUV."

In unison, several of the other parents said: "*It's a minivan.*"

They shared another laugh at his expense. The couple sat on a pair of lawn chairs next to each other while holding hands. The group chatted about work, the weather, movies, and their kids while watching the children play in the sandbox. Some of the kids swung on the swings, others went down the slides, and a few hung around the jungle gym, pretending to be Spider-Man and other superheroes.

Holly was four years younger than her husband and about ten inches shorter. She worked as a fifth-grade elementary school teacher. She loved her job because it gave her the opportunity to stay close to her eight-year-old son and five-year-old daughter. *I can always keep them in the corner of my eye,* she always said. At some point, she planned on teaching them in her class.

Her brunette hair was cut short, darker than her light brown eyes. Freckles covered her well-defined cheekbones and nose. She was often mistaken for a college student—sometimes even a high school student.

Eyes glued to her phone, Monica Washington flicked her finger across the screen and said, "Jesus Christ, this is awful. Have you heard about this? Someone snatched a baby from a Wal-Mart parking lot."

"*What?* Are you serious?" Holly asked in disbelief.

Matthew sneered and said, "Crazy. How do you lose your baby in a parking lot? Bad parenting, don't you think?"

"She didn't *lose* him," Monica said. "Someone *stole* him. They picked him up from the cart and just... walked away. They said it happened in a matter of seconds, in the blink of an eye. Look, there's even a video."

Some of the parents huddled around her to watch the surveillance footage. They watched as a woman loaded her groceries into the trunk of her minivan. In one swift movement, a man in overalls and a trucker cap approached the minivan, lifted the baby from the shopping cart, slapped his hand over the baby's mouth, and walked away. He was last seen entering a beat-up white sedan at the end of the parking lot. The last few seconds of the clip depicted the mother pushing the cart aside and screaming.

Andrew didn't watch the footage, although he could hear the anchorwoman's surprise as she described the video.

Holly said, "*Wow*. It really was in the blink of an eye. I mean, what could she have done to stop that? The creep was probably watching them the entire time."

"She could have strapped him in," Matthew said. "They have seat belts on those shopping carts, you know?"

"A seat belt wouldn't have stopped him."

"It would have made it harder for him."

His eyes on the jungle gym, Andrew said, "That's right."

Holly asked, "Are you really going to blame *her* for this? She's the victim."

"It's not about blaming someone, it's about learning from their mistakes. We have kids, Holly. *All* of us have kids. We can't let our guard down, even for a second."

Holly said, "I understand that. I just feel so... so bad for her. I can't imagine what that guy is doing to that poor baby. He's probably..."

She stopped upon noticing Maxwell 'Max' McCarthy, their son, laying on his stomach in the grass nearby. The young boy inherited his mother's hair color and his father's hair texture. His eyes were brown like Holly's, too. He played Mario Kart 8 Deluxe on his Nintendo Switch. He enjoyed physical activities, but he was quiet and shy.

Holly said, "Let's just change the subject. It's a park day. We're supposed to be having fun. And I don't want our children to hear about this sort of stuff. They're too young for the real world." She beckoned to Max and said, "Max, honey, go play in the sandbox.

Look, Richie's spinning the other kids on the merry-go-round. It looks like fun, right?"

Max paused his game and glanced over at the merry-go-round. His eyes dimmed with fear. He wasn't afraid of the merry-go-round, though. He was afraid of interacting with the other kids. He thought: *what if they don't let me play with them? What if they get angry at me?* He stared at his reflection on the game system's screen. He was embarrassed about his missing front teeth.

He looked at his mother and, speaking with his shirt up to his mouth, he said, "My tummy hurts."

"Oh, *really?* So, I guess you need some medicine, huh? I have pills and water in my bag..."

Max hated medicine. He gagged at the mere thought of *trying* to swallow a pill. He stuttered, "N–No, but..."

"Max, baby, I know your tummy doesn't hurt. We've been through this before. Go play with the big boys, honey. Go down the slide, swing a little, stretch your legs. Do it for mommy, baby. *Please.*"

Max sighed in disappointment. Game console in hand, he jumped up to his feet and patted the grass away from his knees and elbows.

Andrew patted his back gently and said, "Try to have some fun, kiddo. Everything's going to be okay."

Max gave him a half-hearted smile. His sneakers sank into the sand as he stepped into the sandbox. He heard joyous laughter and incessant babbling. The children's ages ranged from four years old to twelve. Some of the kids spoke about video games, others about music, and a few played a game of make-believe.

'The sand is quicksand! If you step on it, you die!'

Max gravitated towards his younger sister, Grace, who played freeze tag under the slides with two other five-year-old girls.

Grace was different. Her brunette hair was short and straight. She was born with heterochromia—her left eye was hazel, her right brown. She was confident and energetic. She wanted to play with everyone and everything. She was trusting and curious—very, *very* curious. She wasn't afraid of people, young or old. She loved life.

Max wished he could have been more like her. He nodded at her, then he took shelter under one of the slides. In the shade, he continued his game of Mario Kart while envying his sister and her friendships.

As she ran around the poles, clearly out of breath, Grace said, "Hey... Maxie... wanna play?"

"No, I'm okay."

"You're the monster!"

"No, I'm–"

"You're the boogeyman!"

"Don't eat me!" another young girl yelled.

The girls screamed and giggled in excitement. They begged him to play with them. Max couldn't help but smile. He wasn't playing with the 'big boys,' but he felt accepted by his sister and her friends. It was enough to warm his heart. He put his Nintendo Switch in its case, then he bolted forward and chased the girls, like an Olympic sprinter chasing a medal.

Zachary Denton approached the sandbox from the opposite side. He couldn't see the group of parents on the other lawn—and they couldn't see him. He took the digital SLR camera off his neck. He snapped pictures of the grass and trees from several artistic angles, crouching, tiptoeing, and even planking around the park. He portrayed himself as an artist— a serious photographer.

He included the children in only *some* of his pictures and the kids weren't the center of attention in his photographs. They appeared in the corners and edges of his pictures—just enough to identify them but not enough for him to appear perverted or devious. He didn't want to arouse any suspicion and, if he did, he wanted to be able to downplay his actions.

His preplanned excuse went a little something like this: *'I'm just taking pictures of nature and life. It's not my fault your kids got in the way.'*

He moved forward and took a picture of the sandbox, the sun setting behind the equipment. It was a graceful shot showcasing the joy and innocence of the youth. If anyone asked, he'd call it: *Sunrise Smile at Sunset Time.* It wasn't the catchiest title, but he figured it sounded artsy enough to help him pass as an art student—or a pretentious kid with a camera.

From the corner of his eye, he caught a glimpse of Grace at a drinking fountain to his right. She was slurping and smacking her lips after each drink. Her eyes caught his attention. He had seen it in actors before, but he never saw such a phenomenon in person. He approached her slowly, eyes narrowed in curiosity.

Grace looked at him, water dripping from her mouth to her shirt. She swiped at her lips with the back of her hand, then she said, "Hello."

Zachary smiled and stuttered, "He–Hello…"

"Bye-bye."

"Wait a second, um… Your eyes are very interesting, kid."

"Intra… dest… ing?" Grace said, trying to pronounce the word.

Zachary chuckled, then he said, "It means, like… It means the opposite of boring. It means fun and cool and… and interesting, you know?"

"Okay," Grace giggled. "Thank you, mister. *Intradesting*…"

"Interesting," Zachary said as slowly and clearly as possible.

"In-ter-es-*ting*!"

"Attagirl, attagirl. Do you mind if, um… Can I take a quick picture of you? Just your eyes?"

Grace shrugged and said, "Okie dokie."

Zachary took a picture of her with his camera—a quick shot. It was a simple portrait of Grace. Her unique eyes shone in the picture. Thanks to his quick actions, no one noticed him.

He said, "Thank you. It's for my college class."

"You take pictures for school?"

"Yup."

"Take another one! Hey, take another one! Look what I can do! I'm a little princess!"

Grace grinned and posed for the camera. She started by resting her chin on her hands, palms down, and grinning from ear-to-ear. Then she leaned forward and made peace signs with her fingers, as if she were a disgraced president.

Zachary said, "You're a great model, kid, but… maybe next time."

"Why?"

"Because… where's your family, sweetie?"

"My mommy and my daddy are over there. And Maxie's playing with us. He's my big brother. Do you wanna meet my family?"

"Yeah, yeah, um… No, I can't. They look busy. Maybe next time."

"Huh? 'Maybe next time.' Why do you keep saying that? Why?"

Zachary smirked and said, "Don't worry about it, kid. It just means… It means I'll see you around." He winked at her and said, "Run along. Play with your friends. Look, your brother's waiting for you."

Max stopped chasing the girls. He watched his sister and the stranger from under the slides. He remembered his mother's frequent warnings: *don't talk to strangers.* His father's voice echoed through his head: *protect your sister, she's your responsibility, too.* He jogged forward until he reached them. He grabbed Grace's hand and pulled her closer to him.

"Leave her alone," he said.

Zachary raised his hands up in a peaceful gesture. He said, "I'm sorry, big guy. I was just leaving. You two have a nice day, okay?"

Max glared at him, as if he were about to strike him. An eight-year-old attacking a twenty-six-year-old, it was a sight to behold. Zachary walked away. He snapped more pictures of the park to bury the photographs of Grace and the other children deep in his memory card. He took dozens of pictures of a tree next to the walkway.

Grace asked, "What's wrong, Maxie? He was a nice-—"

Max dragged her away from the edge of the sandbox. He led her back to the slides. He said, "Wait here."

"Am I in trouble?"

"Just wait here."

Max jogged back to the group of parents. They planned their next gathering—a barbecue at Matthew's house. None of them noticed Zachary's inappropriate behavior.

Max tugged on his dad's arm and said, "Dad, dad, there's a guy."

"A guy?" Andrew repeated, his brow raised. "What are you talking about, Max? What's wrong?"

"Grace was talking to a guy."

"*What?*" Holly asked loudly as she leaned forward in her seat.

Andrew grabbed Max's forearms, gazed into his eyes, and asked, "Where's your sister now? Is she okay?"

"She's right there. Under the swings with Katie and Michelle."

"What did that 'guy' say to her?"

"I don't know, but he has a camera and... and Grace was doing her poses. Like her princess poses and stuff."

Behind them, the other parents chattered about Max's claim while searching for a man with a camera. They were all concerned about *every* child in that park, not only their own.

Matthew shouted, "There! Andrew! He's trying to walk away!"

Andrew stood up, practically jumping out of his seat. He stood on his tiptoes and leaned from side-to-side, peering past the equipment and the children. He spotted Zachary on the opposite walkway, a camera hanging from his neck.

"Get Grace and call the cops," he said without taking his eyes off him.

As she grabbed her cell phone, Holly asked, "What are you going to do?"

"I'm going to have a word with this pervert."

"That's not a good idea. He could be a psycho or a–"

Andrew ignored her. He marched forward with Matthew following his lead. Some of the other parents pulled their children out of the sandbox. Others watched over their kids while trying not to alarm them. Holly kept Grace and Max close to her as she called the police. A thick, dark cloud blocked the sunshine over the park. The cheerful laughter turned into concerned chatter. The mood shifted from jovial to ominous in seconds.

***

"Hey!" Andrew yelled as he jogged to catch up to Zachary.

Zachary stopped and glanced over his shoulder. He furrowed his brow and pointed at himself—*are you talking to me?* He was good at playing stupid.

Andrew said, "Yeah, *you.* I need to talk to you."

He stopped in front of Zachary. Matthew stood to the side, close enough to grab Zachary if he tried to run. They were surprised by the stranger's appearance. They expected a cliché pedophile—an old, wrinkled man with a mustache, a set of cold, dead eyes, and a disposable camera. Zachary was the complete opposite of their expectations. He was young, handsome, and charismatic.

Zachary asked, "Can I help you with something?"

"Who are you?" Andrew asked.

Zachary smiled and said, "Excuse me? What kind of quest–"

"Just answer him," Matthew said sternly. "Who are you? And what are you doing here?"

Zachary shrugged and said, "I'm just enjoying a day at the park."

Andrew asked, "What's the camera for?"

"What do you mean? It's a–a camera, what do you think it's for?"

"Don't get smart with us, kid."

"Come on, you guys are the ones who ran up on me and started asking these weird questions. I'm just here taking pictures for my website."

The fathers cocked their heads back. It was a bold admission—*I'm here taking pictures of kids for my website.* Matthew clenched his fists and gritted his teeth. Max didn't mention a thing about any other children being photographed, but Matthew's fatherly instincts still told him to defend every child in that park. Andrew wasn't the violent type. He tackled his problems head-on, but he never threw a punch. He was more like a chihuahua—all bark, no bite.

Matthew shoved Zachary and said, "For your website? You're taking pictures of *our* kids for your *goddamn* website?!"

"Whoa, whoa, whoa," Zachary said. "Who said anything about kids? I'm just taking pictures of the trees and nature and... and stuff like that. I took pictures in the sandbox, sure, but I was only capturing the sunset. I wasn't taking pictures of your kids, I swear. It's not that kind of website and I–I'm not that kind of guy."

"Bullshit. You're never that kind of guy until the police catch you with thousands of pictures and videos of kids on your computers and phones."

"It's not like that."

"*Bullshit!*"

"I swear!"

Seeing blood in Matthew's eyes, some of the parents started ushering their kids away from the park. Angry parents formed a large oval around the arguing trio. Megan, Matthew's wife, watched from the sidelines. Their ten-year-old son stood behind them, curious but nonchalant. Holly stood in the sandbox with Max and Grace. Even on her tiptoes, she couldn't see the commotion over the other parents.

Andrew said, "Okay, alright. Maybe you're not that kind of guy after all. Prove it to us. Show us your camera."

"*What?*" Zachary responded in exasperation, as if he were just asked to show them his genitals.

"You heard me. Show us your camera roll. If you're telling the truth, then we'll apologize, we'll shake hands, and we'll move on. Let's handle this like men."

"I–I don't... It's... This is my property, guys. I'm not–"

"If we were going to handle this like men, we would have been beating this clown's ass already," Matthew said as he jabbed his index finger at Zachary's chest.

Zachary staggered back and said, "Hey, don't touch me."

From the crowd, a woman yelled, "He's trying to get away!"

Matthew tackled Zachary to the ground, knocking the air out of him. He mounted his waist and pushed his arms down. Andrew was shocked by the sudden escalation. Some of the other parents cheered. A single child's statement turned them into an angry mob. They didn't need more evidence, they didn't need a jury to convince them.

"Get the camera," Matthew ordered while wrestling with Zachary.

Andrew snapped out of his contemplation. He pulled the camera off Zachary's neck. He tinkered with it, his thumbs trembling as he navigated the menus on the touchscreen. He found the gallery.

"Whoa, what is going on here?" a deep, austere voice asked.

The surrounding chatter dwindled. Some of the families walked away. Matthew sighed in disappointment while Andrew's pupils dilated with fear. Zachary felt a sense of relief in his chest and a knot in his stomach—simultaneous happiness and disappointment. They were dealing with a suspicious person, but their confrontation resembled a mugging to oblivious eyes.

Officer Michael Castillo, a beat cop, approached with his hand on his holster. He was a tall, powerful, bald-headed man with a dominant presence. He updated his dispatcher and requested a backup unit.

Castillo said, "Get up. *Slowly.*"

Matthew stood up, his hands raised over his head. Zachary followed his lead. He rubbed the small of his back and groaned in pain. He played up his injury to garner some sympathy. He played the role of an innocent victim. He took his camera from Andrew while sneering at him.

Castillo said, "Hand me your IDs. Don't reach for anything else." The men complied. After examining their ID cards, Castillo asked, "Alright, Mr. Baker, Mr. Denton, and Mr. McCarthy... what seems to be the problem here?"

Zachary said, "They attacked me and took my camera. They wouldn't let me leave. I think they're..."

At the same time, Matthew shouted, "This creep was taking pictures of our kids! He admitted it was for a website! I was just trying to..."

"One at a time," Castillo demanded. He pointed at Zachary and said, "You first."

Zachary responded, "I was out here taking pictures for my website. I'm a photographer. I do small commissions for people. I shoot weddings sometimes, too. I was just working on my portfolio when these guys accused me of taking pictures of their kids. They asked to see my camera. I said 'no.' It's my camera and I did nothing wrong. Then..." He rubbed his back, grimaced in pain, and groaned again. He said, "Then *this* guy tackled me and *he* took my camera."

Castillo asked, "And which one of you called the police?"

Andrew raised his hand, like a nervous boy in class, and he said, "That would be my wife."

"So, you're saying he took a picture of your kids?"

"My daughter. My son, he–he said... he said he saw this guy talking to my daughter and he saw my daughter posing like he was taking pictures of her.

Listen, we weren't trying to rough him up. We just wanted to see his camera to see if he was telling the truth or not. I'm sorry if we–"

"Would you mind bringing your daughter here?"

Two more police officers arrived. One was directed to watch Matthew and interview the other witnesses. The other cop was asked to interview Zachary. Andrew brought Grace to Castillo.

Castillo crouched to match her eye-level and smiled at her. In a soft voice, he said, "Hello, honey. My name is Michael Castillo. I'm a police officer with the Pinecreek Police Department. I want to ask you a few questions. Is that okay?"

"Okay," Grace said while holding her father's hand.

"Thank you very much. So, how was your day at the park?"

"It was great! I was swinging and spinning and sliding and dancing and running! I tagged my brother *three* times! I think I'm faster than him now."

"Wow, sounds amazing. I bet your faster than me, too."

"Maybe," Grace said, smirking.

Castillo gave her a sticker of a police badge. He said, "In that case, we can sure use a girl like you on the force. You want to be a little detective?"

"Really? Really-really?!"

The cop handed her the sticker and said, "Of course. So, can you help me out now, partner?"

Grace looked at the sticker, eyes glowing with wonder and excitement. She imagined herself as a cowboy, like Woody from Toy Story. She was the sheriff of her town. She wanted to protect her friends, her family, and all of the good people.

She said, "I can help."

Castillo said, "Great. Now, your brother told your father about a man. About *that* man." He pointed at Zachary. He asked, "Did *that* man ask you any inappropriate questions today?"

"Inappro... *pirate?*"

"Inappropriate, honey. That means... it means 'bad.' Like, um... Did he have a potty mouth? Did he say anything 'bad' to you? Anything that made you uncomfortable or maybe even confused?"

Grace shook her head.

Castillo nodded and said, "Okay. Did he take your picture?"

Grace glanced over at Zachary. She witnessed the tackle, but she didn't understand the situation. As far as she knew, a friendly stranger was attacked in the park for no reason. She didn't feel like he harassed or abused her, either. She saw a good man who needed help. She was the sheriff, and she wanted to help him.

She said, "He was nice. He didn't take my picture. He just said 'hello' and 'nice eyes.' Is that bad?"

Castillo gazed into her eyes, trying to read her innermost thoughts. He couldn't think of a single logical reason for her to lie. She seemed like a smart, honest kid after all.

He asked, "Did he give you anything?"

"No."

"And that's all he said to you?"

"Hello and nice eyes?"

"Yeah. Was that all?"

"Yes, sir," she said with her head down, as if she were being scolded.

Castillo padded her shoulder and said, "Well, thank you for your assistance, partner. You go back to your mom." As Grace turned to run, Castillo said, "And he's right, you know? You've got nice eyes, kiddo. Keep shining, sport."

"Thank you. Bye-bye," Grace said before running off.

Castillo beckoned to the officer with Zachary— *bring him over here.* And, as instructed, the officer led Zachary to Castillo and Andrew. Andrew kept his head down and avoided eye contact. His daughter told a different version of Max's story, painting Andrew and Matthew as violent, overprotective parents in the process. He was ashamed of himself.

Yet, he couldn't bury his suspicions. He didn't see Zachary as a child predator, though. He only knew one thing for certain: Zachary was doing something he shouldn't have been doing.

Castillo said, "So, it appears we have a misunderstanding on our hands. Now, I'm not going to call your son a liar, Mr. McCarthy, but he may have exaggerated the truth."

Andrew said, "Or maybe Grace lied. She's a good girl. She doesn't like seeing people in trouble. She could have told you what *this* guy wanted you to hear, right?"

"That's a possibility, sure."

"Then why aren't you searching him?"

Zachary said, "I know my rights. You need reasonable suspicion to search me for a weapon and you need probable cause to search me for anything else. If I'm being honest, I don't think you have any of that. You have enough to search these guys for beating me to the ground, though…"

Andrew sneered and said, "Come on, I didn't lay a finger on you."

Zachary continued, "But you don't have enough to search me. I didn't do *anything* wrong. Not one thing. But, if it'll make things easier for us, if it'll let me go home sooner, sure, *officer… you…* can search my camera. Okay?"

Regular police appreciated compliance and cooperation. Tyrannical police loved total obedience. Zachary understood that very well. He knew how to manipulate people of all ages and backgrounds—such as an innocent girl like Grace or a stern cop like Castillo. Years of practice helped him hone his skills.

He showed his camera to Castillo and the other police officer. He flicked through his camera roll—trees, grass, kids in the playground, adults drinking on the lawns, a homeless man's tent, more trees. The images were legal. The picture of Grace's eyes was buried under a hundred other photos. He stopped before he could reach it.

He said, "You see? I was just taking pictures of the environment. It's not my fault some kids ended up in my shots. And, look." He pulled his phone out and opened a website. He showed his phone to Castillo, then to Andrew. He said, "This is my site. I post pictures every day. I have clients. You can call them if you want. Go ahead, do it."

"That won't be necessary," Castillo said.

Andrew was impressed by the website. It was simple yet elegant—a minimal user interface, five or so pages, and everything in black and white. It was an authentic, functioning website centered on Zachary's photography. He noticed the name in the address bar: *Zachary Denton.* Before he could memorize the URL, Zachary pulled the phone away.

The other cop joined them. The police whispered amongst themselves, discussing the evidence while sorting through their options.

Castillo grunted to clear his throat, then he said, "Okay, so I noticed an assault and a robbery when I arrived. Fortunately, no one was seriously injured and the property was returned to its rightful owner. As far as I'm concerned, no one has to go to jail tonight. If it's okay with both parties, why don't we let bygones be bygones?"

"Let bygones be bygones?" Andrew repeated in disbelief. "My daughter was *harassed* by this man."

"Well, it doesn't look this way. According to your daughter, they had a simple interaction. We can debate about it being unethical or downright creepy, but I can say for certain that it was not illegal. My partner spoke to your wife and son and... Well, your son didn't have much to say. He saw your daughter with Zachary, but nothing really happened."

"He has pictures of *kids* on his camera, doesn't he? Isn't it illegal for him to record us without our permission? Invasion of privacy, right?"

Zachary said, "This is *public* property. My photography was within *reasonable community standards.* You did nothing to hide your actions, so I'm pretty much allowed to take pictures of *almost* anything. And it's for noncommercial use, okay?"

Andrew said, "I don't care if it's for 'noncommercial use.' I want you to delete those damn photos and leave my family alone."

"Consider them deleted," Zachary said. He looked at Castillo and asked, "Can I go?"

Andrew said, "I want to see you delete them. *Now.*"

Castillo stood between them to stop the argument. He held his index finger up and shook his head, like an annoyed parent.

He said, "Okay, here's option two. I arrest you, Mr. Zachary, for strong armed robbery and you, Mr. Denton, for being a public nuisance. How does that sound? You want to do it that way or do you both want to go home tonight with a warning?"

Andrew and Zachary glared at each other. Zachary's eyes were devious. He looked at him as if he were daring him to say something else. He hoped he would get himself into more trouble. *Go ahead, get on his bad side,* he thought, *go to jail and get out of my way.* Andrew memorized every detail of Zachary's smooth face. He didn't want to forget him if the situation escalated.

Castillo asked, "Can you shake hands and move on? And by 'move on,' I mean: stay away from each other."

Zachary extended his arm for a handshake. Andrew was pushed into a corner. He bit his tongue and shook his hand. Castillo warned them: *if I have to come out here again, everyone's going to jail.* The men split ways.

As her husband approached, Holly asked, "What happened? Did they find anything?"

"It was a 'misunderstanding,' apparently," Andrew said as he marched past his family. "Let's go home. I don't want to be anywhere near that creep."

Holly asked, "So, what happened? Was he taking pictures or not?"

Andrew didn't respond. He gathered their belongings from the lawn. Holly glanced around the park. She couldn't find Zachary amongst the departing families.

Max shook his mom's arm and asked, "Did I do bad?"

"No, sweetie, no. You did the right thing."

"Then why's dad so mad?"

"He's not mad, baby, he's just frustrated."

"Because of me?" Grace asked. "Did *I* do bad?"

Holly smiled and said, "You were perfect. Both of you were perfect. We taught you well. I think you deserve some ice cream. You want some ice cream?"

The siblings simultaneously said: "*Yes!*"

The McCarthy family went to their minivan in the parking lot, babbling about their day while discussing their favorite flavors of ice cream. Unbeknownst to them, as they loaded their van, Zachary photographed them from behind a tree. He captured the license plate clearly. He took a mental note of the make, the model, and the color of the vehicle, too. He smirked before vanishing in a crowd of pedestrians.

Chapter Three

The Soundtrack of Suffering

Plop! Plop! Plop!

Liam's eyes opened to slits, vision blurred. His head was slumped forward, chin against his chest. A string of drool hung from his bottom lip. His vision began to focus after a few blinks. It was fuzzy, but he saw himself sitting on an iron chair. He only wore his soiled tighty-whities, yellow from old urine. But he couldn't remember pissing himself.

He grimaced in pain upon hearing a shrill cry. The wailing echoed through the dark, gloomy room, bouncing off the concrete walls like ricocheting bullets. The crying stopped, replaced by loud wheezing, then it continued. He glanced to his left. A toddler—no older than eighteen months old—sat on a metal highchair. The baby boy was strapped to the chair with a custom belt.

"M–Mom, da–dad," Liam whimpered.

He tried to stand up, but he could barely move. He glanced at his arms. His forearms were duct-taped to the chair's arms. Over his belly button, his torso was duct-taped to the backrest. He was short, so his feet dangled a foot above the floor. His breathing accelerated while tears flowed down his rosy cheeks. He heard the baby crying and a liquid dripping.

Plop! Wahh! Plop! Wahh! Plop!

Liam cried, "Mommy! Daddy! Pl–Please, I–"

"Liam Hansen," a soft, nasally voice interrupted.

Liam stopped twisting and turning. He lifted his head slowly and stared straight ahead. A light dawned on him from above, creating a circle of illumination over Liam and the toddler. The light wasn't bright enough to penetrate the darkness in front of him. He could only see some blurred shapes. *A stack of cardboard boxes? A laundry machine? A refrigerator? Maybe a water heater?*–he thought.

He guessed he was in a basement—or perhaps a dungeon from a horror video game. As his vision cleared, he noticed the figure of a large, round man and a camera on a tripod. They were being recorded.

The nasally voice continued, "Ten years old. Has a twelve-year-old brother and an eight-year-old sister. Attends McBryant Elementary School. Loves Minecraft and Fortnite. Wants to be a movie director when he grows up." The sounds of heavy breathing and rustling paper followed. The voice continued, "An unnamed toddler. Boy. Approximately eighteen months old, possibly older. Captured from a Wal-Mart parking lot. Lives at..."

Liam stopped listening. He thought about the man's first description. *I only told some close friends that I wanted to be a movie director,* he thought. Then he recognized the voice. He remembered his late-night conversations with 'Cheese2002.' They spoke about everything, including their families, their classes, and their futures.

He stuttered, "Ch–Cheese... Cheese2002... You–You're Cheese2002, aren't you? Ch–Cheese, we–we–we're friends..."

The man stopped speaking. He lowered his script and stared at Liam from the darkness. The toddler whimpered and the liquid continued dripping. There was no such thing as silence in that room.

"Yes," the man said. "I'm the real 'Cheese2002.' You can call me 'Cheese,' but I go by many, many names. To the authorities who will eventually watch this footage, you've tried to catch me as '666domain,' 'niamod999,' 'dukeofdestruction,' and many more aliases. You're not getting closer. You're getting colder and colder... and colder."

Liam blinked erratically—one eye at a time, as if he were winking at his captor. He didn't understand Cheese's message to the authorities. He thought about the man he met at the park. *What happened to Zachary? What did he do to me?*–he wondered. He couldn't remember how he ended up in Cheese's dungeon. He couldn't even remember the drive after the meetup at the park.

Liam stuttered, "Ch–Cheese, wha–what did you... what's happening? Wha–What am I doing here, du–dude?"

"You're here to star in one of my special movies."

"Spe–special mov–movies?"

"Yes."

"Wha–What are you talking about?"

"It's called 'hurtcore,' Liam. I'm going to hurt you. You're going to cry and cry and cry some more... and then you're going to die. Yes, my little 'friend,' you are going to die. And it won't end there. We're going to hurt your body until... until you look like the mud we're going to bury you in... until there's nothing left. Just blood and skin and broken bones."

Liam couldn't help but hyperventilate. He attended his grandmother's funeral. He spoke about death with his parents. He didn't fully come to terms with the concept of dying, but he understood the finality of it. He didn't want to die. He wanted to live. He thought about his family and friends, about video games and movies, and his past, his present, and his future.

Snot dripping from his nose, he snorted and cried, "Why? Why do you want to kill me? We're friends! Cheese, please!"

"Why? Liam, I think you're too young to 'get it.' You don't even know what 'getting wood' means. But let me tell you. I think it's good for the video. Yeah, this is real. This is what you're here for."

"Why?!" Liam yelled as he jerked every which way. "I trusted you! Why are you doing this to me?!"

"I'm doing this to you, *Liam Hansen,* because you're a stupid little boy."

Liam stopped moving. He stared at the large, roly-poly shadow behind the camera. The baby boy on the highchair wheezed, exhausted from all his crying.

Cheese continued, "I'm doing this to you because *you* trusted *me. You* trusted a complete stranger on the internet. You were gullible enough to fall into our trap. Didn't your parents ever teach you better? They're probably bawling their eyes out right now, thinking about killing themselves for failing you. And, if they don't, sooner or later, they might watch this video. Then... *Then* they'll really want to end it. Because I'm going to hurt you, Liam. I'm going to hurt you *so* badly."

"Please don't, pl–please," Liam said, his voice breaking. "Please, Cheese, please. I'm just... I'm just a kid. I–I'm your friend. Don't you remember the–the good times?"

Cheese repeated, "The good times? I don't care about the good times, Liam. I care about the bad times." He pointed at the camera and said, "*They* care about the bad times. Now, let's give them the show they're paying for. Smile at the camera and say 'Cheese,' kid."

"No! Please! Don't hurt me! Daddy! Mommy! Chris! Tiff! Help me!"

Liam called out to his parents. In desperation, he even called out to his older brother and younger sister, as if they could help him escape from Cheese's clutches. He bounced on the chair and screamed at the top of his lungs. The toddler cried again. His thin brown hair was soaked in sweat. His soft, round head resembled a melting tomato—red and mushy.

Liam yelled, "Help! Help! Please, mom–"

A dart soared out of the darkness. The dart struck Liam's chest above his right nipple. He felt like he was punched at first, then he felt a stinging pinch. Warm blood rolled down to the tape around his body. He stared at the dart for three measly seconds. It was a normal dart for a dartboard. He remembered watching his father play darts at a friend's house during a party.

He unleashed a bloodcurdling shriek—a blurt of incomprehensible noise. His jugulars bulged from his neck and a vein protruded from the center of his brow.

A second dart grazed his left shoulder, tearing a chunk of his skin off. It bounced off the wall behind him, then *clacked* on the floor.

Liam drew a sharp breath, then he shrieked again. He watched as the blood rolled down his shoulder, across his chest and down his arm. He felt the tingle—*the itch*—of his blood moving across his skin, but he didn't feel the heat of the liquid. His skin and his undeveloped muscles were already hot. His fear boiled his blood as it ran through his veins. He rocked back and forth, but he couldn't tear the tape.

A third dart *whooshed* past his head. He heard it hit the wall behind him. Through his watery eyes, he could see Cheese throwing the darts at him from behind the camera.

Liam begged, "Please stop! Please, Cheese! It hurts! I'm scared! I..." He shrieked and lowered his head as another dart flew towards him. It missed his arm by an inch. He cried, "I want my mommy!"

Cheese snickered as he watched the scene from the viewfinder. He zoomed in until only Liam appeared in the shot. The toddler's wheezing and crying played in the background, complementing Liam's pleas for mercy as well as his hoarse sobbing—*the soundtrack of suffering*. It was exactly what his audience sought.

Fear.

Pain.

Humiliation.

Cheese hurled darts at Liam as quickly as possible. He missed the first dart. The second dart cut Liam's left ear in half. Blood flooded his ear canal and dripped from his ear lobe. The third dart struck his forehead at his hairline, burrowing deep into his scalp. The sheer force of the blow knocked his head back, causing the back of his head to hit the chair's backrest. Blood squirted out of the wound. The beads of blood glistened on the base of the dart as well as his forehead, like sweat after a race.

The fourth dart missed his right ear by a centimeter. The fifth and sixth darts struck his chest. One of the darts cracked his sternum. The seventh dart hit his right knee and the eighth struck his left thigh. Liam couldn't help but kick his feet while sobbing hysterically. And, with each kick, the wounds on his legs widened. The patella—*his kneecap*—was visible in the hole above the dart. The white of the bone shone through the blood.

Cheese cackled as the ninth dart hit Liam's pubic region. He was aiming for his genitals. His tighty-whities were anything but white. The blood soaked his underwear.

Liam, overwhelmed by the pain and sickened by the fear, urinated himself. His urine, along with his blood, splashed on the floor under the chair.

He yelled, "Mommy! Please! I'm sorry! I won't do it again! I promise!"

Cheese lowered the dart in his hand. He asked, "What won't you do again?"

"Please, mom! Help me! I'm sorry!"

"*What* won't you do again, Liam?" Cheese asked, louder than before.

"I won't go out alone! I–I won't talk to strangers a–anymore! I won't do stupid things! Please! It hurts! It hurts so much! Ow! *Ow!*"

Cheese threw a dart at Liam's stomach. The dart penetrated the duct tape and cut into his descending colon. He threw another dart. It cracked a rib, then sliced him vertically as it ricocheted. The dart landed in the puddle of piss and blood under the chair. He tossed a dart at Liam's right arm. The dart mutilated his bicep.

Nine darts stuck out of Liam's small, fragile body. He shook all over, rivers of blood flowing across his head, his torso, and every limb. And the pain was amplified with each slight movement. He felt the steel tips shifting in his flesh, stretching and widening each wound—scraping his bones, puncturing his organs, and slicing his muscles. He sniffled and wheezed, trying his best to sit still.

He was out of breath, so he couldn't scream anymore. His throat hurt from all the crying anyway. He stared down at himself in disbelief. He was used as a human dartboard. Although he witnessed it— although *he* was the victim—it seemed inconceivable to him. He knew about death, but he didn't know about murder and torture.

He looked over at the camera upon hearing a set of footsteps. Cheese's silhouette shrank as he walked to the other end of the room. He heard a *sloshing* liquid. He recoiled in fear as Cheese made his way back. He didn't look anything like Zachary. He was monstrous.

Cheese emerged from the darkness. He stood five-seven with a wide, round physique. He weighed three-hundred pounds. He grew a pair of large, fat breasts as a result of taking anti-androgen medication, which was prescribed to him after his first offense. The medication didn't work. Like most sex offenders, his sexual deviance was hardwired into his brain.

Sweat stained the armpits and collar of his dark gray t-shirt. He wore matching sweatpants and running sneakers, although he didn't plan on running anywhere any time soon. It was a casual event for him. A plain white mask covered his face. His beady blue eyes glowed through the holes, his bald scalp was visible on top, and his flabby cheeks stuck out from the sides. He held a pitcher of a yellow liquid in his gloved hand.

Weak, Liam said, "Please… don't… hurt… me…"

Cheese stood behind Liam's chair and faced the camera. He asked, "Would you like some lemonade, kid?"

"Wa… Water…"

"Bottoms up."

Cheese dumped the lemonade on Liam's body. The acidic juice aggravated every wound. It turned orange as it cascaded over his skin and blended with his blood.

Liam felt like he was set aflame, burning from the inside and burning on the outside. His overactive imagination told him he was being bathed in acid, as if he were in a video game. Although it hurt, he couldn't stop himself from convulsing. His ears popped. Everything sounded muffled. His head fell forward as he lost consciousness. The dart fell out of his scalp and landed on his lap. He awoke ten seconds later, groaning in pain.

Shuddering, he mumbled something incomprehensible. He didn't even know what he was trying to say. He watched as Cheese walked back to the camera. He heard his old friend's laughter. It was slow and distorted—*sinister*. His eyes rolled back. He lost consciousness again. The human mind could only endure so much pain. His young, ten-year-old body wasn't prepared for the torture.

No one was built to endure that type of violence.

Liam's eyes fluttered open. He breathed slowly. He glanced over at the highchair. The toddler was gone. He looked over at the corner. He could only see Cheese's back. The large man stood in front of a workbench. Another camera on the tripod was aimed at the workbench at a downward angle. The scene was illuminated by a wall sconce.

Barely above a whisper, Liam said, "Wha–What... What are you... doing? Where's... my mom?"

Cheese didn't hear him. Liam caught a glimpse of the toddler in Cheese's arms. Cheese lay the boy down on the workbench. Then he placed the toddler's arm in a vise attached to the end of the table. The crank handle made a loud *screeching* sound with each turn. The jaws closed in on the toddler's thin arm until they hugged it.

Tighter.

Tighter.

Liam flinched, startled by the toddler's sudden shriek. The workbench rattled as the baby thrashed about. Then a *crunching* sound echoed through the room. His supple bones shattered under the pressure. His wrist snapped and twisted. His puny hand dangled down at an unnatural angle, as if it were barely attached to his arm by a piece of flesh. The veins in his wrist burst, blood spraying out in geysers. A cut stretched across his elbow. Then dark, slimy blood and crumbs of broken bones came out of the wound.

The vise flattened his forearm—from cylindrical to rectangular. Cheese spun the crank handle in the opposite direction. He zoomed in on the injuries, then he recorded a close-up of the toddler's face. He captured every detail of the toddler's suffering. Then he repeated the process on his other forearm. The crank handle squealed, then the bones *crunched* and *popped.*

The toddler shouted, "No!" It was one of the few words in his vocabulary. He repeated, "No!"

Cheese smiled behind his mask—a wide, proud smile. Tears of joy glimmered in his evil eyes. He resembled a director who just pulled an awe-inspiring performance out of his lead.

As he forced the toddler's head into the vise, he whispered, "Thank you..."

Liam looked away. He lowered his head and closed his eyes. He was tired, nauseous, sad, hurt, scared, and confused. A terrifying numbness began to spread across his body. Yet, he still felt a burning pain under the darts in his flesh. He couldn't comprehend the situation. *I just wanted a friend,* he thought, *I wanted someone to play Fortnite with, that's all.*

He heard the toddler's panicked cries and the sound of blood *plopping* on the floor. He squeezed his eyes shut as tightly as possible. He wished he could plug his ears, too. He heard something crack, then he heard another loud *crunch.* The crank kept turning and turning—and turning. He didn't know the toddler's eyes were protruding from his skull, his brain was oozing out of a hole on the back of his head, his blood was shooting out of his ears and nostrils, but he saw enough to imagine it.

And he knew something awful happened because the toddler stopped crying. Only the plopping of blood played in the room. It sounded like a heartbeat—*plop-plop... plop-plop... plop-plop.*

Liam's breathing intensified as he heard Cheese's footsteps. The predator stopped behind Liam's chair. He touched Liam's shoulders gently, avoiding his deep wounds. Liam opened his eyes. His tears plummeted to his bloody lap.

Cheese said, "Liam, Liam, Liam... Do you want to know what I'm going to do to you? Hmm?" Liam let out a shaky breath. Cheese snickered, then he said, "That baby got the easy way out. *That* was the easy way. You believe that? So, what do you think I'm going to do to you? Oh, if you only knew the *true* definition of pain—the meaning of *suffering.* You'd be shitting yourself right now. But... don't worry, I'll show you the light. I'll hurt you until you can't feel anything anymore. You're going to beg for death. I promise."

Under his breath, barely perceptible, Liam murmured, "I don't wanna die... I don't wanna die, mommy... please, I don't wanna die..."

"I'll have you singing a different tune in no time, little 'dude.' Welcome to hell..."

Cheese grabbed the dart in Liam's chest and dragged it down until it sliced into his nipple. Liam's face twisted in pain. His bellow bounced off the walls and found its way up the stairs at the other end of the room. The scream stopped at a heavy door at the top of the stairs. Faint classical music and loud, obnoxious humming could be heard from the other side of the door.

But no one came to his rescue.

Chapter Four

One Week Later

"How were your pancakes, baby?" Andrew asked.

Leaning close to the table, Grace yelled, "I'm not finished yet, daddy!"

"Okay, okay. You need, uh... You need some help finishing those?"

"Nope! They're all mine. Mine, mine, mine."

"Yours, yours, yours... You sound like your mother."

Holly gently slapped his arm and smiled at him. She watched as Grace doused her remaining chocolate chip pancakes in syrup. Then the girl stabbed her pancakes with her fork and used them to mop up the rest of the syrup on her plate. The fork scraped the plate, sending a shrill *screech* through the diner.

A mug of coffee clasped in both hands, Holly said, "Be careful, hun. Don't scratch the plate. And don't use so much syrup, baby. You know too much sugar is bad for you."

"Sorry," Grace said without glancing at her mother.

Andrew nodded at Max, who sat next to Grace across from their parents. He asked, "How was your waffle, kiddo?"

Max ate a Belgian waffle with strawberry syrup. He now played Fortnite on his Nintendo Switch as he waited for his sister to finish her meal. She was a notoriously slow eater. Lost in the construction and destruction of the game world, he didn't hear his father's question.

Andrew knocked on the table and said, "Knock, knock. Hello? Is anyone home?"

"Huh?" Max grunted.

"Jesus Christ, one kid can't get off his game and the other takes an hour to finish two pancakes. We're great parents, aren't we?"

Holly giggled and said, "As long as they're happy."

"Yeah, yeah, as long as they're happy."

The couple kissed and rolled their eyes. Although they were frustrated at times, they loved being parents. It was a special experience and they shared a special bond because of it.

Grace said, "Hey, I only ate for... sixty-six minutes and... sixty-six seconds."

Andrew cocked his head back and furrowed his brow. He said, "That's still more than an–"

Shh—Holly shushed him as she giggled. She said, "You know, six is her favorite number."

Andrew shrugged and whispered, "Favorite or not, it's still over an hour." He stood from his seat and said, "I'm going to use the restroom. I'll be back in *six* minutes and *sixty-six* seconds."

"Okie dokie," Grace said before shoving the pancakes into her mouth.

As he walked away, Andrew said, "That's seven minutes and six seconds, baby. I really have to start teaching you about time..."

He smiled and nodded at a waitress balancing a tray of plates. He squeezed past her and made his way past the bar. The restaurant was bustling with the brunch rush, filled with families, couples, and lonely diners. The employees were busy, some orders were botched, but the atmosphere in the diner remained peaceful and jovial.

Andrew stopped in his tracks before he could walk past the bar. He narrowed his eyes and cocked his head to the side. He glanced over his shoulder, he looked straight ahead, then he glanced over his shoulder, as if he couldn't believe what he was seeing.

Zachary sat at the bar by his lonesome, eating a platter of scrambled eggs, crispy bacon, ham, sausage, and golden hashed browns. His digital SLR camera sat next to his mug of coffee on the counter. The lens was aimed at the other end of the diner—aimed at the McCarthy family.

Andrew thought: *how did he get here? It couldn't be a coincidence, could it? Did he follow us? Is he recording my family? Or is his camera off? Should I say something?*

"Excuse me, sir," a waitress said, carrying a coffee pot and two mugs in her hands.

Andrew stepped aside. Zachary glanced over at them. They made eye contact for a second, then Andrew walked away.

As he headed to the restroom beside the bar, Andrew muttered, "Shit, shit, shit. I should have said something. Why did I walk away? *Why?*" He went to a urinal and pissed. He whispered, "What do I do now? I can't just ignore him, can I? I mean, he's a creep, right? I need to say something. I *can't* pussy out."

Unbeknownst to Andrew, an elderly man at the neighboring urinal watched him with a raised brow.

His expression said: *why the hell is this guy talking to himself?*

Andrew wasn't concerned about him. He washed his hands, then he splashed some water on his face. He stared at his reflection in the mirror and drew several deep breaths.

He whispered, "You're a man, Andrew. So, you do what men do. You can do it." He dried his hands with a paper towel and repeated, "You can do it."

He stormed out of the restroom. He leaned back as a waiter hurried past him. He drew another deep breath, then he marched forward. He approached the bar. A young boy ran towards him, face sticky with syrup and fingers decorated with whipped cream. He stepped aside and dodged the boy. He could only smile as the boy's mother ran past him, too, embarrassed by her child's antics.

Andrew felt his chest tightening as he approached Zachary. He opened his mouth to speak, but he drew a blank. A dozen questions rattled in his mind before he entered the restroom—and now he couldn't think of a *single* word to say to him. He turned and walked away before Zachary could see him again.

At his table, Holly spoke to Max about his video game while Grace wiped her face with a wet napkin and hummed a song. She didn't finish her pancakes. Andrew sat next to his wife. *So, you do what men do,* his words echoed through his head.

Men asked their wives for advice.

He leaned close to her ear and whispered, "Holly, that guy from the park is here."

"What? Who?"

Andrew glanced at his children. He didn't want them to hear them because he didn't want to concern them. Fortunately, Max was engaged in another match and Grace wasn't paying attention.

"The guy from the park, the one who was taking pictures," he said. "We saw him last weekend. He almost got me arrested, remember?"

Holly leaned forward in her seat and glanced around. She said, "I don't see him."

"He's sitting near the center of the bar. He's by himself. His camera is pointing this way. I think... I think he's recording us."

"I don't see him."

"He's right there."

"*Who?*" Grace asked.

They ignored her. Holly narrowed her eyes and scanned the diner from left to right. A family of four, a teenage couple on a date, a family of five, an adult couple on a date, a lonely businessman, an elderly woman with a middle-aged woman... *Zachary Denton.* Her eyes widened as she spotted the young photographer at the bar. He nibbled on his sausage, like a rabbit eating a carrot.

In a hushed voice, Holly asked, "What is he doing here?"

"How am I supposed to know? He probably just got done taking pictures of kids at another park for some kiddie por–"

"*Hey,* watch your mouth, Andrew."

"Okay, okay. I'm just saying: *who knows?* Who knows what he's doing here? I mean, obviously he's eating, but... maybe he followed us."

Holly bit her bottom lip, then she said, "Maybe it's just a coincidence. The cops didn't find anything on him, right? And the cops didn't call us with a follow-up or anything like that, did they? I mean, if he had a history of doing... *that* type of stuff, the cops would have known and they would have done something about it when we were at the park. They just don't let sex offenders walk around parks with kids like that."

"I don't know. I guess not. So, what do we do?"

Holly looked at her children. Grace watched her with puckered lips. Max had stopped playing during their conversation. He overheard some words: guy from the park, camera, cops, sex offenders. He was smart enough to connect their conversation to the event at the park last week. But he couldn't see Zachary from his position.

Holly said, "Not in front of the kids. He isn't doing anything to us, so we don't have to do anything to him. Let's just go and get as far away from him as possible. If it's just a coincidence, then we'd just be asking for trouble by making a big deal out of nothing."

Andrew responded, "And if it isn't a coincidence, we'd just be letting him think that this type of *creepy* behavior is okay. We'd be... emboldening him."

"Now's not the place. We're with the kids and we're in public. Let's not scare our babies."

"I'm not scared," Grace said.

Max asked, "What's going on? Did that guy come–"

Holly said, "It's time to go home. Let's go to the car. Come on, follow me. Stay close."

Andrew grabbed the bill from the table. His family walked between the booths and tables, avoiding the bar. Grace was completely unaware of the situation. Max searched for Zachary, but he couldn't find him over the other patrons and busy waiting staff. The door chime rang through the diner as they exited the building.

Andrew walked alongside the bar, dragging his feet to the cash register at the end. His eyes were stuck on Zachary every step of the way. He walked past him. One step, two steps, *three steps*—he stopped. He couldn't bite his tongue. A voice in his head told him to be a man, to be a guardian, to be a strong, reliable father.

He turned and faced Zachary. He wagged his receipt at him and said, "You're the same guy from the park, aren't you? The cop, he called you... Denton, right? Mr. Denton?"

Zachary glanced at him, looked back at his plate, then he squinted back at Andrew, as if he didn't get a good glimpse of him the first time. He smiled and shrugged.

He said, "It's you. What are you doing here? Well, I mean... What do you want from me?"

"What do *I* want from *you?* No, no, no. We're not going to play it like that. *You* followed *us* here."

"Us? Who's 'us,' man? What are you talking about?"

"Oh, come on. Don't play stupid with me. You were watching me and my family. You... You... You're *stalking* us."

Zachary shook his head and said, "Whoa, man. We're at the same place. Okay, cool. That doesn't mean I'm 'stalking' you. It's just a coincidence."

"And it's just a coincidence that your camera is pointing at the same table we were sitting at?"

Zachary looked at his camera, then he laughed in disbelief and shrugged again. He said, "Yeah, man, *yeah.* I just put it down and started eating. There's nothing else to it. A coincidence, okay? A damn coincidence."

Andrew beckoned to him—*hand it over.* Zachary shook his head. The men were at an impasse. Zachary didn't expect Andrew to react violently. He saw the fear in him during their encounter at the park. And he was correct about Andrew. Andrew couldn't muster the courage to take the camera by force. He immediately thought about calling the police, but he remembered Holly's words.

Andrew said, "Come on, let's make this easy for the both of us. You showed the cop your camera roll last time. So, why don't you show me now? Prove to me that you weren't recording my family."

"No. I don't have to prove shit to you. No one complained about me. Your son didn't lie about me this time, did he? So, you have no reason to harass me. Now leave me alone. *Please.*"

"Show me your camera."

"Get. Away. From. *Me.*"

Andrew said, "Show me your camera or I'm calling the cops."

"Is there a problem?" a man asked from behind Andrew. "Sorry to interrupt. My name is Shawn Wallace. I'm the manager."

Andrew looked back at him, surprised by the manager's intrusion. The chatter in the neighboring booths and stools dwindled to whispers. From the periphery of his vision, he could see some of the other patrons watching the argument. A teenager recorded them with her cell phone.

Andrew sighed, then he said, "I'm sorry. It's just… This man, he, uh… It's a long story, okay? I have reason to believe he was recording my family as we ate at that booth over there. I just want to look at his camera and if there's nothing there, *if* I'm wrong, I'll leave in peace."

"I didn't record him or anybody in here. I just sat my camera down and ate my food. That's it."

"I don't believe him. Last weekend, we called the–"

"Britney!" Shawn yelled. A young brunette waitress approached them. Shawn asked, "Sorry, you can get back to it in a second. We just need your assistance."

Britney responded, "Sure, okay. What's up?"

"I'm not going to sit here and accuse anyone of anything. It's not my job. But it *is* my job to make sure everyone feels safe and comfortable. This customer is saying that this young man at the bar was recording him and his family. Did you notice anything like that?"

"Hmm… No, I didn't. He just ordered his food and ate. That's all I noticed."

"Okay, thank you. You can get back to work."

"Sure thing."

Shawn turned his attention to Andrew. He sucked his teeth and gave him a slight shrug. Andrew scowled and returned the shrug.

He said, "That's it? You're just going to believe her and ignore my complaint? That's how you run your business?"

"There's not much I can do without evidence. I asked my waitress and she didn't notice anything out of the ordinary. She has no reason to lie. And I'm not saying you do. I'm not saying that at all. If you'd like, I can call the police and all of you can talk it over *outside.* I just can't have this argument inside of my restaurant. Will that work for the both of you?"

Zachary took a sip of his coffee, then he said, "You know what? Go ahead and call the police. I'll step outside and I'll show them my camera. But if we have to do this again—'cause me and this guy just went through this last weekend—I am going to sue. I'm going to sue the police and maybe this diner." He looked Andrew in the eye and said, "And I'll *definitely* sue you for civil harassment and intentional infliction of emotional distress."

Andrew stood there with his mouth ajar in disbelief. He glanced at the manager and the photographer, cycling between them. He could see Zachary was cunning and intelligent. He was prepared. His legal threat sounded rehearsed but authentic. Andrew's outlook shifted. At that moment, he didn't see Zachary as a child predator. He saw him as a con artist, trying his best to provoke Andrew so he could sue. One question stayed on his mind: *who the hell is this guy?*

He jabbed his finger at Zachary and said, "You better stay away from me and my family, you little punk?"

"Who are you calling a punk?" Zachary asked.

Andrew walked away. He sneered in annoyance as the manager apologized to Zachary. He even offered him a free dessert. Andrew paid his bill, then he left the diner in a huff.

Chapter Five

Two Men, One Campsite

The camera recorded a forest. The footage was low-quality, fuzzy like a VHS. There was a campsite in the foreground. A campfire at the center illuminated a tent, a lawn chair, and a cooler. In the background, at the center of the shot, there was a tall, thick tree. It was so tall that only some branches from its crown were visible. The rest of the background was cluttered with the silhouettes of other trees.

Although his face wasn't clear in the footage, Liam was tied to the tree at the center with a roll of thin but durable rope. He sat on the ground with his back against the trunk. His face was swollen and bruised from a bare-knuckle beating. Part of his scalp was torn off by one of the punches. The darts were removed, leaving deep holes across his body. The scabbing around some of the wounds was yellow. There were dark bruises around his wrists and ankles. He had been bound.

Blood covered every inch of his body. His underwear was crusty with his old, dried blood. His breathing was slow and shallow—eight or nine breaths per minute.

But he clung to life. He endured so much pain, lost so much blood, but he wasn't ready to die. He kept thinking about his family. He hoped his father would rescue him. He imagined it over and over. *Dad will save me, he's my superhero,* he thought. A cool breeze caressed his damp skin. He twitched as the wood in the campfire *popped* and *snapped.* He listened to the whooshing of the wind and rustling of the leaves. The forest was tranquil.

Then he heard a crackling leaf behind him—and then another. He tried to look over his shoulder, but he could only see the tree trunk.

Another *crackling* leaf.

Another *crunch.*

From the corner of his eye, he saw a man crawl out of the darkness behind the tree. He lurked on all fours, moving like an animal sneaking up on its prey. He cocked his head left and right, as if he were searching for something. He wore navy coveralls and a white mask, like Cheese's. His mask, however, was decorated with makeup—smeared lipstick, dark eyeshadow.

Liam shivered as the man crawled in front of him. He didn't try to escape, though. He knew it was useless. He couldn't break free from the rope and he couldn't overpower a healthy man. He looked away, head shaking frantically. The man leaned closer to his face. He sniffed him through the mask, then he let out one husky breath after another.

The man caressed Liam's face with the back of his muddy fingers and said, "You're my toy today. My beautiful, precious toy. I'm going to play with you. Have you ever played with a man before? Your daddy? Maybe your older brother?" Liam's broken teeth chattered as tears welled in his eyes. The man continued, "We'll play 'house.' I'll be mommy and you'll be daddy. Should I take off your underwear, sweetie?"

Frowning, Liam cried, "N–N–No..."

"Don't you love me, honey? Or should I call you 'daddy?' My big daddy, hmm?"

"N–No... No..."

"I love you, big daddy."

"No..."

Liam couldn't say anything other than 'no.' He didn't understand the man's questions, but he already knew Cheese and his friends were evil. In their vocabulary, 'playing' was the same as 'torturing.' He pissed himself again, terrified

The man said, "Then let's play... 'Abusive mom and *stupid* son.' I'll be mommy, you'll be my son. You bled on your clothes again. That's no good, baby. I'll have to teach you a lesson."

"No... No... No..."

The man stood up. He stared down at Liam with his head cocked to the side. He pulled his leg back, then he punted Liam's face. Blood shot out of his broken nose. Liam snorted and whimpered. The man kicked him again. His boot hit Liam's jaw, ejecting four teeth out of his gums and knocking him unconscious. The man kicked him again. The bloody teeth fell out of Liam's mouth. He stomped on his chest, his stomach, and his legs. His mutilated skin made a *crinkling* sound, like shredding paper, and the muffled crunch of his bones breaking barely escaped his flesh.

During the stomping, Cheese waddled into the scene with a backpack. He sat on the lawn chair and took a frying pan out of his bag. Then he opened the cooler and took a can of ice-cold beer out. He took a swig—*ahhh!* He casually took the toddler's crushed, decapitated head out of the cooler. He used a hatchet to remove the toddler's crown above his eyebrows. It only took one swipe, as if he were cutting a cucumber with a knife. With his bare hands, he scooped the toddler's brain out of his skull.

He threw it on the frying pan, then he held the pan over the campfire. After a few seconds, the brain started sizzling.

Cheese held the decapitated head up, chuckling as he showed it to the camera. He threw it back in the cooler. He took a block of butter out of the cooler and threw it on the pan. Then he seasoned the toddler's brain with salt and pepper from his bag. He waved his hand in front of his face as a nauseating scent pummeled his nostrils. He caught a whiff of something metallic, too. But he kept laughing. He flipped the brain, like a meat patty at a fast food restaurant, then he twirled his wrist to spread the melting butter.

A little more salt.

A little more pepper.

He waited until it was cooked through. Then he took a fork out of his bag. He stabbed the cooked brain, then he twisted his wrist until he cut a piece off. He pushed his mask up to his nose and leaned closer to the fire. He wanted his audience to see his actions. He shoved the brain into his mouth. *Hmm*— the sound seeped past his lips as red juices dribbled down his clean-shaved chin. Then he started chewing with his mouth open. The brain was mushy, red and black—stuck between his teeth. He swallowed it with a grin on his face.

He knew the risks, but he wasn't afraid of prion diseases. He was only concerned with giving his audience a special show.

Cheese glanced over at his accomplice and said, "You should try this. It's delicious."

Out of breath from the stomping, the man in coveralls said, "I'll be... right there. I'm not... done with him."

"Hey, I have an idea."

"What is it?"

"You know what would go great with some brain?"

"What?"

Cheese searched through his bag. It was filled with common household items—hammers, screwdrivers, knives, forks, spoons. He took a pair of shears out. He tossed them at his accomplice.

He said, "*Wiener.*"

The other man stared at Cheese with a deadpan expression, then he chuckled. He grabbed the shears. He tore Liam's underwear off with one tug. Liam regained consciousness. He shivered uncontrollably while slimy blood poured out of his mouth. He mouthed: *mommy, daddy, mommy, daddy.*

The man said, "It's going to be a small one. Like, uh... Like one of those Gerber Meat Sticks. You ever heard of those?"

"Oh yeah. I love those. But I think this one's going to taste better. Hurry up. Cut it off."

"Alright. I'm doin' it, I'm doin' it. Hold your horses."

The shears made a loud *snip* sound. Liam's shriek echoed through the woods, sending the birds skyward and the critters into hiding.

The rest of the footage was too awful for words.

Clips of the video appeared on a website dedicated to 'hurtcore'—extreme pornography filled with degrading violence, usually featuring children. The full video was available for purchase for ten thousand dollars. And people from around the world purchased it using digital currency.

***

At sunrise, Cheese and his accomplice carried a large wooden chest through the woods. They lunged over holes, squeezed past bushes, and avoided the mud. They wore their masks as well as gloves and shoe covers. Cheese's accomplice also wore a hairnet over his wavy, grizzled hair. A duffel bag was slung over his shoulder, two shovels sticking out from the opening.

The soundtrack of suffering turned into the soundtrack of nature. They heard the chirping birds, the gusts of wind, the groaning trees, and the scampering critters. The tranquility was jarring compared to the carnage of the previous night. The men didn't say a word about it. They acted as if they weren't friends.

They reached a creek. The clashing water calmed their nerves. They remembered one of their past videos where Cheese recorded his partner drowning an infant in a sink. They could hear the baby's cries over the rushing water. They set the chest and the duffel bag down next to some wet, jagged stones beside the creek.

Cheese said, "Get ready."

They removed their masks. They put on gas masks instead. Then they walked in circles beside the creek, estimating the softness of the ground with each step. They dug a hole about three feet wide, six feet long, and nine feet deep.

Cheese said, "Open the chest. I'll get the spray."

The chest reeked of death. Liam's body was cut into six pieces—four limbs, a torso, and a head. The toddler's body was hollowed out. Most of the baby's organs were missing, cooked and consumed on camera for an audience of deviants. The pale, discolored pieces floated in a pool of bloody bleach.

"Get out of the way," Cheese said.

He shot bear spray into the chest. He closed the chest and locked it with a padlock. They threw the chest into the grave, then they sprayed it with bear spray and pepper spray. They doused the area with the chemical agents, too, hoping to keep the wild animals and any police K-9s away. The smell of the creek water also helped mask the scent of death.

As they shoveled the mud back into the hole, voice muffled by his mask, the man in coveralls asked, "How much you think we're going to make off this one?"

"I don't like guessing," Cheese responded.

"Well, how much did you make off the last one?"

"Can't remember."

"Can't remember? Or you don't want to tell me?"

Cheese stopped shoveling. He thrust his shovel into the ground and glared at him. His partner kept shoveling. He was aware of Cheese's anger, but he didn't feel threatened by him. He was leaner, stronger, and older. He could have killed Cheese with the shovel and buried him with the children—and Cheese knew that very well.

Cheese said, "I don't want to talk about money right now." He continued shoveling. He said, "If you have... any questions... email me."

"Why would I do that? We're both here right now. No one's listening, no one can track us. Let's talk about it now."

"What do you want?"

"I want more money. I *know* you're selling a shit-ton of movies. I've seen those websites. You've got a fanbase. A sick, disgusting, *rich* fanbase. You... You're the Spielberg of hurtcore. But you can't let that fame go to your fat head, motherfucker. You need to remember: we're partners. And I'm taking a lot of risks out there. Hell, I'm risking more than you. You're safe behind your computer, but I'm... I'm really out there, man. I deserve a fair cut, don't you think?"

Cheese gritted his teeth. Behind his mask, his cheeks and eyelids twitched. He had flashbacks to high school, reliving cruel moments of relentless bullying. He took out his anger on his victims. A ten-year-old kid couldn't beat a morbidly obese man after all. But he accepted the fact that he couldn't beat his partner in a fair fight. He had to endure the bullying—*again.*

Take it on the chin, he told himself.

He asked, "How much do you want?"

"Half."

"Half of what?"

"Half of whatever you're making."

Cheese nodded and said, "Yeah? You want half? Fine, then that's..." He looked at the sky and mumbled to himself, pretending to calculate the total. He said, "Then that's an extra twenty grand a month in your pocket. You happy?"

"Twenty... Twenty grand?! Shit, man, you've been holding out on me! I was expecting five or six grand, but... twenty grand extra?! *Every month?!* I'm fucking rich!"

Cheese couldn't help but smirk. He was expecting him to ask for fifty grand and he was willing to go up to thirty. *You have no idea how much we're making, do you?*–he thought. The world was filled with rich people with demented interests. He established himself as the leading producer of violent pornography. His audience was always itching for new scenes.

Cheese said, "Well, I'm glad you're happy. I'm expecting another product. Probably in a week or two. You need to be ready for the exchange."

"Oh, I'll be ready. I'll be ready with twenty fucking grand in my pocket."

"Yeah, yeah. Just don't get cocky and don't fuck it up."

"We've been doing this for a year already. I've had some close calls, the pigs are always looking to stop someone, but when have I ever fucked up?"

Cheese hit the ground with the shovel to flatten it. He said, "You've got a record. You're on the registry. You've definitely fucked up before."

"But not with you. I've *never* fucked up with you."

With the *clang* of the shovel hitting the ground echoing through the woods, Cheese said, "Well, don't start fucking up now. This one is important. This one's rare..."

Chapter Six

Not A Coincidence, A Pattern

"I want vanilla milkshake Pop-Tarts!" Max shouted.

"Mom! Mommy! Mom!" Grace yelled as she tugged on her mother's coat. "Mommy, I want Frozen 2 cereal! I can make Olaf with the marshmallows! I saw it on YouTube! Olaf marshmallows! Really!"

"No! I want Pop-Tarts!"

Holly stopped pushing the shopping cart. She closed her eyes and held her hands up—*silence.* Max frowned. He really wanted those Pop-Tarts. Grace kept whimpering and mumbling as she hopped in place and pulled on her mother's sleeve. She could only think about her favorite Disney character, Olaf.

"Vanilla milkshake... Frozen 2 cereal... What are they feeding you kids these days?" Holly muttered. She sighed and opened her eyes. She said, "Okay. You can pick the Pop-Tarts or the cereal, but you also have to eat some of this oatmeal. Deal?"

Puppy-eyed, Max asked, "How do we pick?"

"Um... You can play rock-paper-scissors."

"No way! Grace always cheats!"

"Uh-uh! I don't cheat!"

"Yeah, you do! You always go after we count! That's cheating!"

"You're lying! Liar! Liar! Lie–"

Shh!—Holly shushed her children. She smiled nervously at the passing parents. They chuckled in amusement. They were familiar with the pain and joy of raising children. The siblings' bickering was annoying to some and beautiful to others.

Holly said, "Okay, here's what we're going to do: first one to get back to me with their breakfast *without* running wins." Grace and Max locked eyes, then they dashed away. Holly yelled, "And if I even *hear* you running, you lose and you eat oatmeal for a week!"

The siblings stopped running. They walked hurriedly towards the cereal and breakfast aisles. Holly pushed her cart to the meat, seafood, and poultry refrigerators nearby. She couldn't see her kids, but she was close enough to hear them. She trusted them, and she trusted her neighbors, too. It was a naïve lapse of judgement.

Max raced to the Pop-Tarts. His favorite flavor, vanilla milkshake, was on a high shelf. He glanced around. He was too shy to ask anyone for help, so he waited until no one was watching, then he scaled the shelves. He heard them groaning under his weight.

Meanwhile, Grace faced a similar problem in the neighboring aisle. The last box of Frozen 2 cereal was on the top shelf. She tried to climb the shelves, but she immediately lost her grip. She stood on her tiptoes, then she jumped. She was two shelves away from the top.

"You can do it," she told herself. She jumped again, but her effort was fruitless. She whined, "Olaf..."

Her eyes widened as a man grabbed the box of Frozen 2 cereal. Grace pouted and stomped. She opened her mouth to scream, but she stopped her tantrum as soon as she saw the man's face. She recognized him from the park—*Zachary Denton.*

She tilted her head to the side and said, "Hey, mister, I 'member you."

Zachary wagged his finger at her and said, "And I *re*member those beautiful eyes. You were at the park a few weeks ago, weren't you?"

"Yeah..." Grace said as she lowered her head in shame.

Zachary crouched in front of her. In a soft, understanding tone, he asked, "What's the matter?"

"You got in trouble 'cause of me..."

"No, no. That wasn't your fault and I wasn't in trouble. I didn't do anything wrong. It was just a... a misunderstanding. Like an accident, you know?"

"Are you mad at me?"

"I can't be mad at you. You're a good girl. Your brother... Well, he's a good boy, too. He's a smart kid and he knows how to take care of you."

Grace clasped her hands behind her back and twirled her foot. She asked, "Are you *super* sure you're not mad at me?"

Zachary chuckled, amused by her behavior. Once again, her eyes caught his undivided attention. She was a rare girl. He knew exactly how to win her trust. He handed her the box of Frozen 2 cereal.

He said, "Take it. You were trying to get it, weren't you?"

Grace's eyes widened, sparkling with appreciation. She was always warned about taking things from strangers, but she knew the box came from the shelf and they were in public. She didn't fully comprehend her parents' warnings, either. She didn't know about the pure evil lurking within some people. She thought: *why would anyone wanna hurt me?*

She touched the box of cereal and asked, "For me?"

"Yup."

"Really? Are you sure? It's the last one."

"I'm positive. A princess like you deserves the best cereal."

She smiled as she accepted the box of cereal. She didn't know it, but her brother had already reached their mother with the vanilla milkshake Pop-Tarts.

"Thank you!" she yelled, a toothless grin on her face.

As she turned to leave, Zachary said, "Wait a second." Grace stopped and looked back at him. Zachary said, "How about a hug? I like warm hugs."

Grace's smile grew larger. *'I like warm hugs'*—it was a quote from the character Olaf in the movie *Frozen.* Those words won Grace's trust. She couldn't feel threatened by a fellow fan. As far as she knew, Zachary was a friend. She took a step forward with her arms outstretched in front of her, like a toddler asking her father to pick her up.

"Grace," Max said as he approached, his curious eyes glued to Zachary.

Zachary winked at Grace and said, "Next time."

Max grabbed Grace's hand and said, "Mom's looking for you."

Grace said, "Look, it's my friend from the park. He's nice, like daddy. His name is..." She puckered her lips and asked, "What's your name, mister? My name's Grace."

Zachary said, "It's nice to meet you, Grace. You can call me 'Olaf.' It's easy to remember."

"That's not your real name, silly," Grace giggled.

Max tugged on her arm and said, "Come on, let's go."

Ignoring him, Grace said, "Hey, 'Olaf,' do you wanna come to my tea party on Sunday?"

Max gritted his teeth and grimaced. He looked as if he were about to cry. He stared down the aisle behind him, hoping his mother would come and help him. He considered screaming, but he didn't want to cause a scene. He remembered the commotion at the park. He wasn't punished, but he saw the disappointment in his father's eyes.

He said, "Grace, *let's go.*"

"Why? I want 'Olaf' to come to my tea party. It's gonna be so fun. I'll be the princess and you can be–"

"He can't come."

"Why?"

"Because dad won't like it."

"Why?"

"Come on, let's go!"

"Why?!" Grace repeated for the third time, frustrated.

Zachary had heard enough. He won Grace's trust and he knew Andrew still harbored suspicion towards him. There was no way he could manipulate Holly, there was no way he could win over Andrew. *Plan B,* he thought. He heard the *squealing* and *rattling* of some approaching shopping carts.

Interrupting the bickering siblings, he said, "Your brother is right, Grace. You should really listen to him more often. You shouldn't invite people to your home or your tea parties or anything like that without your parents' permission. There are some bad people out

there. You're lucky I'm one of the good ones, but...
Let's just say your parents know best, okay?"

Max was awed by Zachary's nonchalant attitude.
He seemed like a decent man. He saw a potential
friend in him.

"Should I ask my mommy now?" Grace asked.

"No, no. Let's not bother her now. Besides, I have
a feeling we'll be seeing each other again soon. Now,
do you two need help finding your mother? Will you
be okay on your own?"

Max stepped forward and said, "I know where she
is. We'll be okay."

"Great," Zachary said. "Stay safe and take care.
Bye, Grace."

"Bye-bye, Olaf," Grace said, clutching the box of
cereal close to her chest.

Zachary walked away. The siblings watched him
for a few seconds, then Max pulled Grace in the
opposite direction. Before they could turn the corner,
Zachary took some pictures of them from behind
with his cell phone. There was a devilish twinkle in
his eye. Max led his sister to the checkout area. Their
mother was already in line.

Holly asked, "Grace, where were you?" She sighed
upon spotting the box of cereal. She said, "We had an
agreement. Your brother won our little game."

"I'm sorry," Grace said. "It was too high."

"Oh, did someone help you?"

"Yeah! Olaf helped me!"

Holly rolled her eyes, unaware of her daughter's
encounter with their suspected stalker. She assumed
Grace was referencing the character. Max bit his
tongue, burying his fears. *Nothing happened, nothing*

happened, nothing happened, he told himself. He flinched as two shopping carts crashed behind them. An announcement from the ceiling speakers called an employee to Register 6 for a price-check.

Holly said, "Fine, we'll buy the cereal, too. But you're going to eat some oatmeal. I don't want to hear any 'buts' from you."

"Thank you!" Grace said with excitement in her voice.

They unloaded their shopping cart, placing all of their items on the conveyer belt. Grace eyed the candy near the register, begging for some Reese's Peanut Butter Cups. Max helped his mother bag their groceries in their reusable tote bags. The small talk between Holly and the cashier was insignificant— *find everything okay? Cute kids. They grow up so quickly.*

Holly let out a short gasp before slapping her hand over her mouth. She held her breath. Her face turned ghostly pale. Tears welled in her eyes. She couldn't hear her children or the cashier. She saw Zachary at a self-checkout kiosk. He paid for a bottle of soda, a bag of chips, and a bag of Skittles. He exited the grocery store without looking back.

But Holly saw enough to positively identify him. She remembered the park and the diner. They didn't live in a megalopolis like New York City or Los Angeles, but they weren't in Bumbfuck, Nowhere, either. She didn't even see some of her neighbors that often. She felt Grace tugging on her coat, but she didn't take her eyes off the exit. Then Max pulled on her other sleeve. She snapped out of her trance.

The cashier asked, "Are you okay, ma'am?"

Holly nodded and stuttered, "Y–Yes, I–I'm sorry. What were... What were you saying?"

"Do you need any plastic bags?"

"No, no, we're fine."

"Then your total is $55.79. Will that be cash or credit?"

"Cr–Credit..."

Holly paid for her groceries, then she hurried to their minivan. Grace kept calling out to her mother, but Holly ignored her. Max could tell something was wrong. Holly checked on their seat belts, then she sat in the driver's seat and called her husband.

In his office, an Excel sheet with graphs open on his laptop, Andrew answered, "Hey, hun. I'll be home in–"

"Andrew," Holly interrupted. "Andrew, I saw that guy at the grocery store."

"Well, 'hello' to you, too."

"I'm serious. I saw him."

Andrew clicked through the Excel sheet and said, "Okay, okay. Let's rewind a little bit. Where are you and who did you see? And did you get an autograph?"

"*I'm serious*," Holly repeated, anger in her voice. "I saw that guy from the park... from the diner. Here at the grocery store, at Smart and Final. He was here. He didn't say anything to us, I don't even know if he saw us, but he was here."

Andrew leaned back in his seat. The smile was wiped from his face. He couldn't say a word. Holly looked every which way, like a paranoid drug addict. Max and Grace watched her from the backseat, baffled by her behavior. They had never seen her so scared before.

"Are you there?" Holly asked.

Andrew said, "Yeah."

"What should I do?"

"You, um… You should go home and lock the door. Lock the windows. Don't answer the door for anyone until I get there."

Holly stuttered, "Tha–That's it?"

"For you. That's it for you and the kids. I'm going to the police station to report this."

Holly said, "So, you think…" She held the phone closer to her mouth and whispered, "You think he's stalking us?"

Andrew responded, "Twice is a coincidence, three times is a pattern…"

Chapter Seven

'Friends'

PhoenixClaire21: *Hey. I saw your story. Do you need someone to talk to?*

Sydney Fox, a sixteen-year-old girl, lay in her bed, blanket over her head. Her face was lit up by the blue light from her cell phone's screen. She received the message on Instagram. Her username was: *SydFox04.* She ignored the message. Like her bloodshot eyes, her nose and cheeks were rosy. She held a wet, crumpled napkin in her hand. She flinched upon hearing a loud *thud* and a muffled shout downstairs.

She whispered, "It's always the same... Why are they always like this?"

She watched her latest update on Instagram again. The text post read: *I legit hate my life right now!! Fucking KILL me!!* The text was followed by three crying emojis and a broken heart emoji. Her cry for help was viewed by forty-two followers, but none of them responded to her update. They cared about her, but most teenagers didn't know how to handle such a situation.

Most teenagers weren't taught empathy.

Sydney's phone buzzed again. She received another message from PhoenixClaire21. It read: *I know we don't know each other so well, but I'm here if you need someone.* The message was followed by a heart emoji. She examined the account. The user went by the name 'Claire Phoenix.' In her bio, she claimed she was a nineteen-year-old art student at a local community college.

Sydney didn't know Claire. They had never met before. They followed each other because they were both interested in photography and painting. Deep down, Sydney didn't want to lose Claire as a follower, either. She cared about her follower count, so she followed everyone who followed her. The numbers— something that didn't matter in the real world— meant everything to her.

SydFox04: *I'm okay... Thanks...*

She followed the message with a smiley face, although she was frowning under her blanket. Thirty seconds passed before she received another message.

PhoenixClaire21: *I understand. Just let me know if you want to chat about anything. Seriously, I get it.* The message was followed by a winking emoji.

Sydney bit her bottom lip and sniffled. She appreciated Claire's offer. She saw her as an anonymous psychologist. They didn't go to the same school, they didn't mingle in the same social circles, so her secrets were safe with her. She heard another shout downstairs. It sounded like: *leave me the fuck alone, bitch!* A woman responded with an unintelligible yell.

SydFox04: *It's my mom and dad. They're ALWAYS fighting. Like, every day and every night! I don't even know why they're still together. It's so annoying.*

PhoenixClaire21: *Aww, I know what you're going through, hun. My parents were like that, too. So. Selfish.*

SydFox04: *Did they ever break a TV? Or a mirror? Or a plate? Or punch a hole in the wall? Did your dad ever slap your mom? Did your mom ever stab your dad with a fork??*

Claire didn't respond as quickly as before. Sydney swiped at the tears on her cheeks. She squeezed her eyes shut and whimpered upon hearing another muffled shout.

"God, what am I even doing?" she cried. "Don't abandon me. I don't know you, but I need you. Please, please, please…"

Her phone vibrated again. Through her blurred vision, she read the message from Claire.

PhoenixClaire21: *I get what you mean. When I was a kid, I saw my dad hit my mom with a belt. It was so… awful. Like, I can't even describe it, you know? He didn't hit me, but I feel like I got PTSD because of what I saw. It was just so bad.*

"Yes, yes!" Sydney said aloud. Tears of fear turned into tears of relief. She whispered, "You get me. Finally, someone gets me…"

Before she could respond, Claire sent another message. It was surprisingly frank.

PhoenixClaire21: *Have they ever hit you before??*

Sydney thought about her response. She hated her current situation, but she still loved her family. She didn't want Claire to take a screenshot of her messages and report her parents to the police. She feared her father would punish her if that happened.

SydFox04: *They're assholes to me. Like, they call me stupid and useless and bitch and all kinds of shit. They just make me feel like shit. They don't give me any rides or any money. My mom doesn't even cook anything for* me sometimes! I don't think they love me. They wouldn't cry if I died... I mean I don't think they would... My sad life. A frowning emoji and a broken heart emoji followed her message.

PhoenixClaire21: *I'm so sorry to hear that.*

She sent a frowny emoji, too. She typed for a few seconds, then she stopped, then she typed again. Like Sydney, she was thinking deeply about her response.

PhoenixClaire21: *Why don't you runaway??*

SydFox04: *No way. I have a little brother and sister. I read for them. I cook for them. I protect them. If I left, my mom and dad would hurt them next. I can't let that happen. I would die for them.*

PhoenixClaire21: *Aww, you're so strong. I'm proud of you. I ran away when I was young. You know, in Michigan, the police can't make you go home. You can leave and get government assistance. And you can probably take your brother and sister with you! It's hard, but you can do it. It's like domestic abuse, you know? You can go to a shelter for something like that. I got an apartment with a friend when I was 16. My parents couldn't do anything to stop me. Now I'm in college.*

Sydney whispered, "Maybe she's right... Maybe they wouldn't care if we all ran away... They're drunk all the time anyway. Maybe..."

PhoenixClaire21: *Btw, how old are you?* She sent another winking emoji.

SydFox04: *16. You?*

PhoenixClaire21: *19. We're almost the same. Cool, huh?*

SydFox04: *Yeah, cool.*

PhoenixClaire21: *Well, I'm here for you, Sydney. Text me anytime, okay?*

A smile blossomed on Sydney's face. For the first time in years, she felt comfortable in her home. Through a few simple text messages, a stranger reignited her hope in life. She found a trustworthy friend.

SydFox04: *Thank you so much.*

***

Sydney and Claire's relationship flourished over the next two weeks. They chatted every night, discussing their abusive households, their interests in art and photography, and their dreams and goals. Claire was always supportive, agreeing with everything Sydney wrote and understanding all of her emotions. She didn't sound like an ass-kisser, though. She dealt with Sydney with a gentle, empathetic hand, like a mother or an older sister.

Claire avoided phone calls and video chats, blaming it on her unreliable Wi-Fi and her cell phone's data limit. But they grew familiar with each other through their Instagram pictures. Claire was a curvy college student with curly hair and vibrant hazel eyes. She looked like a model straight from a magazine—or straight from Instagram. Sydney admired her beauty and confidence. Every time she looked at her pictures, she thought: *I wish I was you.*

On a quiet Saturday night, Sydney lay in bed and chatted with Claire. Her parents weren't fighting. They were knocked out cold after a night of heavy drinking.

PhoenixClaire21: *Hey, hey, hey! I have something for you!!*

SydFox04: *What is it??*

PhoenixClaire21: *You really wanna know?* She followed the message with a smirking emoji.

SydFox04: *Tell me!!*

PhoenixClaire21: *Okay. I bought you a $250 Delta gift card! And I want to PayPal you $250 for a hotel. You can travel for a few days now!! You can go anywhere, Sydney! ANYWHERE!* Three smiling emojis with tears of joy followed.

Sydney furrowed her brow. She wondered if Claire was joking or telling the truth. She had close, lifelong friends, but none of them ever spent one hundred dollars on her, let alone five hundred. She questioned Claire's intentions. Before she could type a response, Claire sent her another emoji-filled message.

PhoenixClaire21: *Where will you go??*

SydFox04: *Did you really buy a gift card? I don't know if I can accept that...*

PhoenixClaire21: *Why not? It's my gift to you, hun. You really deserve it after everything you've been through.*

SydFox04: *But it's sooo much money...*

PhoenixClaire21: *Oh, don't worry about that. It's leftover money from last year's financial aid. They give you so much.*

More emojis with tears of joy.

As she nibbled on her fingernail, Sydney whispered, "You're giving me your financial aid money... But why?"

SydFox04: *It's just too much. Besides, I don't think my parents will let me leave.*

PhoenixClaire21: *You don't need their permission, you know? Just travel somewhere in the US. Go to LA or Florida. Relax on a beach for a few days. Think of it like a... a test run. If you like it and if nothing goes wrong, then maybe you can really run away with your brother and sister. If not... then what's the worst that can happen?*

Sydney feared her parents would punish her siblings while she was gone if she ran away. On the other hand, she wanted to believe it would change her family for the better. *Maybe they'd actually miss me, maybe they'd change,* she thought. She imagined herself at a beach in California, soaking in the sun while her parents re-evaluated their actions.

PhoenixClaire21: *Live a little.* The message was followed by a winking emoji.

Sydney bit her lip and snickered. The gesture said: *I can't believe I'm about to do this.* She glanced at the door, as if her parents could somehow listen to her text messages from the hallway.

SydFox04: *Okay, so... What do you want for it?*

PhoenixClaire21: *Well, I could use some help on a little school project of mine if that's okay.*

SydFox04: *A school project? Sure. Sounds easy. What do you need from me?*

PhoenixClaire21: *I knew you'd say yes!! You're the best! So, listen, I need your picture for inspiration. Well, more like a model. I want you to be my model, Sydney.*

Giggling, Sydney sent: *I'm no model.*

PhoenixClaire21: *Are you kidding me? You're gorgeous! Your figure is perfect for my next painting!*

Sydney rolled her eyes, shook her head, and blushed. She was caught in Claire's gentle storm of compliments and empathy. Everything she wrote sounded right, as if she were a robot programed to make her feel good about herself.

SydFox04: *Okay, okay. So you need a selfie or something?*

PhoenixClaire21: *Keep an open mind, okay? I'm taking a figure painting class. We draw... nude models. So, I need a picture of your body. Naked. Okay?*

Sydney was caught off guard by the request. It sounded disgusting, immoral, and illegal. Her thumbs hovered over the screen. She tapped a letter, deleted it, tapped a different letter, and then deleted that one, too. Five minutes passed, but it felt like five hours.

PhoenixClaire21: *So...*

SydFox04: *I'm sorry. I just can't. Isn't it illegal??*

PhoenixClaire21: *It's art. And it's not like I'm going to tell my professor you're 16.* (She sent another smiling emoji with tears of joy.) *We draw nude models all the time. It's not because it's sexy. It's not porn, you know? I paint it because I think people are beautiful. I want to help people find beauty in their scars, to express themselves sexually without being judged because of their genders or age, to promote body positivity. I want to paint your body as a statement of modern beauty. You, Sydney, are beautiful. You're 16, but you've lived through enough to be 21 for all I care. And love is for everyone. Love is for YOU!!*

Sydney sighed shakily. She couldn't stop herself from overthinking. Her teenage mind was a maze, the sulci of her brain transforming into endless corridors. She weighed her options. If she rejected Claire, she feared she would lose her as a friend. If she accepted Claire's offer, she was afraid of being arrested for sharing her nude pictures. Or worse: she was afraid her parents would find out before she could leave on her vacation. She never questioned whether or not Claire would send the gift card and the payment, though. The possibility of being scammed never crossed her mind.

SydFox04: *You promise not to show anyone??*

PhoenixClaire21: *Promise! I'll only share the painting. Everyone's going to love it. I know it.*

Sydney took a deep breath. She turned on her lamp, then she tiptoed to the door. She locked it slowly so as not to make any noise. Her father hated locked doors in his house, so she hoped he wouldn't come knocking. She stared at her reflection on the full-length floor mirror beside her bed. She drew another long, deep breath.

She took off her pajamas and her underwear. She took four pictures of her reflection. In the first picture, she covered her nipples with her forearm and her crotch with her hand. Her face was visible in the picture. In the second picture, she focused on her upper body. Again, her face was visible in the picture. The third picture showcased her lower body from her waist to her feet. She didn't hide her crotch. The fourth picture depicted her back from head to toe. She figured it was an even trade for five-hundred dollars.

She dressed herself, unlocked the door, turned off the light, then climbed back into bed. Her cheeks were red with embarrassment. She second-guessed herself for a minute, then she sent the pictures.

SydFox04: *Are these okay? Please don't share them with anyone! Seriously!*

To her surprise, Claire didn't respond. Five minutes passed, then ten, and then twenty. Sydney told herself that Claire was just looking for the gift card or maybe she was so inspired that she had already started painting. She lied to herself. At heart, she knew the truth. She made an honest mistake—and she couldn't do a thing to fix it.

After thirty minutes, Claire responded: *Sorry, I almost fell asleep. I'll look tomorrow, then I'll send you the gift card. Talk to you soon! Love ya!*

As she read the message over and over, Sydney whispered, "What did I do?"

***

Sydney sat on her bed. A tear dripped from her eye as she blinked. It *plopped* on her thigh. She shuddered, but her bedroom was warm. She heard her siblings chasing each other in the neighboring room while their mother cooked in the kitchen and their father watched television in the living room. Beams of red sunset sunshine penetrated the blinds and entered the room from the window behind her.

She read a message on her phone. She read it again and again—and again *and again.* It was as if she were trying to translate it from an alien language.

The message from Claire read: *Masturbate for me in a video. Don't stop until you cum. No clothes, full face. And make sure the light is on. If you don't, I'll report you for sending those pictures. You'll get arrested, then your brother and sister will be on their own. I'll send them to your mom and dad, too. I'll send them to everyone at your school. I saved your followers, so don't try to block me. Trust me, that's the last thing you want to do. You have six hours.*

The message was followed by a winking emoji and an email address from a deep web service. It was sent three hours ago, immediately after Sydney's last class ended.

Sydney sniveled while wiping the tears and mucus off her face. She turned on her laptop and played her hip-hop playlist. It was loud enough to mask the noise in the room, but quiet enough so it didn't disturb her parents. She locked the door and undressed herself. She opened the camera app on her cell phone, then she placed it on her pillow with the screen facing the foot of the bed. She used the front-facing camera to record herself.

She sat at the foot of the bed, the small of her back against the footboard. She whimpered and looked away as she opened her legs. Tears flowing down her cheeks, she reluctantly masturbated. She wasn't producing any arousal fluid because she wasn't aroused. She was being raped by her own hand. She couldn't stop swiping at her face, so she inadvertently used her tears as a lubricant. She glanced at the door upon hearing every thud—every groan, every muffled voice.

"I'm so sorry," she whispered under her breath.

After five minutes, she faked an orgasm, sighing and shaking and curling her toes. She ended the recording, a grimace of pain twisting her face. She dressed herself, then she washed her face in the bathroom. She scrubbed her hands with soap under scalding water, too. She didn't stop until her hands were red, swollen, and pruny—until she couldn't feel any more pain. Her mother called her down to eat dinner, but she ignored her.

Sydney debated with herself for five minutes: *should I really send it? Will she stop if I do? What if I just ignore her?* Her mother called out to her again. Sydney choked down the lump in her throat. She emailed the video to Claire, hoping it would be enough for her.

But there was no such thing as 'enough' for sexual predators. The headlines never read: *sex offender caught with one picture of child pornography.* The headlines read: *sex offender caught with <u>320,000</u> pictures and videos of child pornography.* Sexual predators didn't rape one person and quit, they raped until they were caught. There was something wrong—so dangerously wrong—with their minds.

The next day, Sydney received another message from Claire: *Okay, this time, fuck yourself with a cucumber or a banana. And none of that five-minute bullshit. Make it real. Put on some mascara, too. I want to see the tears on your face. You have six hours. Don't fuck with me.*

Sydney fought with herself. She tried to convince herself Claire was bluffing. The clock was ticking— two hours, three hours, four hours, *five hours and twenty-two minutes.* She received another message from Claire. It was her father's email address.

"Oh God, oh my God," she cried.

She complied. She recorded herself masturbating with a banana. The fruit was soft, but the penetration was painful. Trails of mascara stained her cheeks. She masturbated for eleven minutes, then she faked another orgasm. She sent the video to Claire as soon as possible to avoid the deadline.

Sydney whispered, "Please stop... please leave me alone... please..."

One day later, she received another request: *take off all of your clothes, put on a collar and leash, write 'Cheese2002' on your chest with lipstick, then record yourself licking a toilet seat and drinking out of the toilet bowl.* And Sydney did as she was told.

Cheese was the mastermind behind the sextortion. He used hundreds of fake Instagram accounts to communicate with hundreds of girls and boys around the world. He had already blackmailed dozens of teenagers and kids. Sydney wasn't his only victim at the moment, either. He was good at multitasking. He only needed his victims to make one mistake to ruin their lives.

As the weeks went by, Cheese's requests became more extreme. He forced Sydney to sodomize herself with a cucumber, chew on her forearm until she bled, and whip her breasts with a belt until they turned purple and ballooned out. He asked her to write the name of his deep web message board on a sign in some of the videos. It was the best marketing he could buy—or extort.

Sydney drew the line at Cheese's most disturbing request: *bring your little brother into the picture.* She refused to hurt her family. She harmed and humiliated herself to protect them. Cheese threatened to leak all of her pictures and videos. Sydney thought about calling the police, but she didn't see a positive outcome. Her future crumbled, leaving a black void in her mind.

She couldn't face her family or her friends. She didn't want to face the consequences of her actions. She believed she was out of options.

On a Friday, Sydney ditched class. She waited until her parents went to work and her siblings went to school. Then she returned home. She made a noose out of her bed sheets. She grabbed the ottoman from her living room and carried it into the backyard, lugging it to the tree near the brick partition separating the yard and the alleyway.

She stood on the ottoman and tied the noose around a branch. She tightened the noose around her neck. She started recording herself with the front-facing camera on her cell phone. Her eyes were dim and hollow. She looked like she hadn't slept in weeks. She was ashen, like a cold corpse in a morgue. She licked her chapped lips, but she couldn't moisten them.

With a hoarse voice, she said, "This video is for my mom and my dad and the police and the... the FBI and... and anyone who can help people like me. This video is *not* for my brother or my sister. This is my... my suicide video. I'm going to kill myself because... because a woman named 'Claire' has been blackmailing me. She tricked me into sending... 'lewd' pictures of myself to her. She used those to make me do... awful, embarrassing things on video. Then she used those videos to force me to do more awful, embarrassing things. Her username on Instagram is... It was 'PhoenixClaire21.' Her email is on my phone. I know you can find it. She... or *he*... is responsible for this. I'm killing myself because of 'Claire.' I'm killing myself because... because... I'm so stupid. Because I'm so fucking stupid." Her voice cracked as tears trickled from her eyes with each blink. She said, "I'm sorry, mom. I'm sorry, dad. I'm sorry, Carlos. I'm sorry, Olivia. I hope I didn't mess anything up for you. I don't know what I was thinking, but I just... I love you all so much. I'm so sorry."

I'm so sorry, I'm so sorry—she kept repeating that sentence for a minute. Then she kicked the ottoman out from underneath her. The tree branch groaned. The phone slipped out of her hands. It spun several times, then it hit the grass underneath her. It landed on its back. And it was still recording. The footage showed Sydney swinging from the branch. She instinctively clawed at her neck at first, then she gave up. Her croaking and moaning could be heard over a bird's chirping. Some kids running down the alley could be heard in the video, too.

The video was supposed to be private. But, like everything in the twenty-first century, it ended up on the internet. Cheese used the video to promote his message board and his services. He made sure to spread it across Sydney's community, too, sharing it with her family and friends like a viral dance video.

Chapter Eight

In the Blink of an Eye

Schedules helped people organize and plan their lives. Repetition led to predictability—boring but safe. But predictable people were also the easiest to follow.

Monday through Friday, Andrew worked at Gold Standard Insurance from nine in the morning to six o'clock in the evening. Holly worked at Plaza Elementary School, a suburban school surrounded by houses, from seven o'clock in the morning to three in the afternoon. Her shift occasionally ended at four or five if she had meetings to attend. Max and Holly attended class from eight in the morning to two-thirty in the afternoon. After class, they waited for their mother near a tree in front of the school with some of their classmates.

A few teachers mingled nearby, chatting with parents while watching the children. An elderly crossing guard, Meryl Ross, helped children and parents cross the street nearby. It seemed like a safe, organized environment. There were no security guards on campus, though. Teachers could break up a fight between two eleven-year-olds. The faculty was trained to defuse situations with angry parents and watch out for prowlers during school hours. Despite the many tragedies throughout the nation, no one expected someone to shoot up the school, either.

'That could never happen to us, could it?'

Zachary strolled past the front gate. He dressed casually, an open button-up shirt with the sleeves rolled up and blue jeans. He didn't accessorize. People remembered accessories—hats, sunglasses, masks. He blended with the crowds of young parents and older siblings picking up the kids from school. He approached the large tree.

Leaves spiraled down from the branches with each cool breeze. Some kids chased each other around the thick trunk while waiting for their parents to finish talking nearby. A nice teacher helped some of the younger kids find their guardians, signaling them like a cop directing traffic. Meryl was too busy chatting with everyone at the crosswalk— *oh, she's adorable; what a cutie-pie; y'all get home safely!* No one noticed Zachary.

Max sat beside a friend, Andy, on a blue bench near the tree. He played Minecraft on his Nintendo Switch while his friend played on his tablet. Grace crouched beside the bench and used a twig to draw on the mud. She drew a family of stick figures—her family—as well as a stick figure dog. For as long as she could remember, she had always wanted a golden retriever.

Zachary entered the periphery of her vision. He stood near the gate to her right, a few meters away from the tree. She glanced at him and grinned. Before she could scream with excitement, Zachary held his index finger up to his lips—*shh.* Then he beckoned to her. Grace grabbed her blue backpack, giggled, and skipped towards him. She looked like she was approaching a sibling she hadn't seen in years.

Zachary crouched in front of her. He said, "Hello, Grace."

"Hello, Olaf," Grace said enthusiastically. "What are you doing here?"

"I take pictures of this school sometimes. For their website, you know?"

"No," Grace shrugged.

Zachary chuckled, then he said, "Well, that's not important. I just noticed you and I remembered: you owe me a warm hug, don't you?"

"Oh, yeah!"

"I'd like that hug—you know I like warm hugs—but first, I want to give you a present. I think it's something you'll really love. Is that okay?"

"Sure!"

"Great, great. It's in my car. I'm parked right across the street. Come on, let's go."

Grace puckered her lips, then she said, "Mommy is still in school. She said I–"

"We'll be back *before* your mom finishes work, I promise," Zachary interrupted. He smirked and said, "It'll be like you never left. Besides, the nice crossing guard will look after us. I think we'll be safe in her hands."

Grace moved her lips from side-to-side. She remembered her mother's recent warnings—'don't talk to strangers, don't take anything from anyone'—but she didn't feel like she was talking to a stranger. She felt safe around her classmates and she trusted Meryl to watch over her. She was interested in the gift, too.

She asked, "What's the present?"

"Come look. I'll give you a hint: *my name.*"

Olaf, Grace thought as her eyes sparkled with joy. She glanced back at her brother. Engrossed in his game, Max didn't notice her or Zachary. Zachary extended his hand forward. Grace noticed his hand was clean and smooth. She didn't feel threatened by him. So, she took his hand and walked beside him while babbling about Frozen and her other favorite Disney movies.

Wielding an LED stop sign, Meryl led another group of parents and kids across the street. Grace waved at her and Meryl returned the wave. She knew Grace and the McCarthy family, she knew Holly always took her kids home, but Zachary's presence didn't ring any alarms in her mind. She saw him for what felt like a nanosecond. And he looked like a regular young man.

Zachary led Grace down an alleyway beside a house. The residents used the alley as a shortcut to the local park. They vanished in the crowd.

Twenty minutes passed.

Eyes on his game, Max asked, "Did you catch a villager yet? I don't know how to–"

"Max, time to go," Holly said as she approached the tree, bag slung over her shoulder. She nodded at Andy and said, "Hey, Andy. Are your parents picking you up today?"

"I think so," Andy said without taking his eyes off his tablet. "Or maybe my big brother. He's probably sleeping."

"Do you need my phone so you can call your mom?"

"I have a phone."

Holly huffed and shook her head. *Eight years old and already has a smartphone,* she thought. The world was changing at a rapid pace. In a way, babies were born with phones grafted to their hands.

Max asked, "Can we give him a ride? We're not done playing."

Holly said, "Sure. I'll call your mom on the way. Is that okay, Andy?"

"Yup," Andy responded.

Holly stood on her tiptoes and looked over the bench. She glanced at the other benches surrounding the tree. Then she walked around the tree and looked at the entrance of the school. Meryl walked back onto campus, smiling. She was satisfied with her job, infected by the children's happiness. Another teacher lingered near the front office. Only a few students remained, waiting for their guardians.

Grace was nowhere to be found.

"Max, honey," Holly said while scanning the schoolgrounds. "Max, where's Grace?"

Max and Andy didn't acknowledge her. Holly fell to her knees in front of her son. She grabbed Max's arms and shook him. Max finally lifted his head and looked at his mother, confused.

Holly stuttered, "Whe–Where's your sister? Where's Grace?"

Max furrowed his brow and looked to his right, as if to say: *she's right there, where she always is.* But he didn't see anyone beside him. They saw the twig and her stick figure drawing on the mud.

Raising her voice, clearly panicking, Holly asked, "Where is she, Max?" She grabbed Andy's right arm. She asked, "Andy, ha–have you seen Grace?"

Andy shrugged and said, "She was right there."

As he stared at his sister's drawing, Max repeated, "She was right there..."

Holly staggered away from him, her bottom lip quivering. She approached every girl in front of the school—even the kids standing beside their parents. She carefully examined their faces. She didn't trust her own eyes. *She has to be here, she has to be,* she thought. She ran back into the school, ignoring her coworkers' calls.

Sprinting down an exterior hallway, she yelled, "Grace! Grace! Grace, baby!"

She slid to a stop inside of Grace's kindergarten classroom—*empty*. She checked the neighboring classroom—*empty.* She ran into the girls' restroom—*empty*. She tackled the cafeteria doors. An after-school group occupied one of the tables. The boys and girls finished their homework with the help of a tutor. Grace wasn't part of the group.

Tears gushing from her eyes, Holly collapsed and yelled, "*Grace!*"

Andrew's wristwatch read: *3:25 PM.* On his porch, he stood on top of a stepladder and checked the wiring on a security camera installed in the corner above his front door. He checked the live feed on an app on his phone. He could see himself smiling. He leaned to his side. The camera recorded the porch, front yard, sidewalk, and street. It even captured a decent image of the house *across* the street.

He muttered, "A hundred and twenty-five dollars for installation... Yeah, right. I knew I could do it myself."

The phone vibrated in his hand. The live feed was replaced by the incoming call window. The caller ID read: *Holly.*

He answered, "Hey, hun. You won't believe what I just–"

"She's gone!" Holly cried, her voice raspy and cracking. "Oh my God! She's gone!"

"Wha–What are you–"

"She's gone!"

"Holly, calm down! What's happening? Where are you? Where are the kids?"

He heard Holly's hoarse wheezing and pained groaning. He heard some concerned chatter around her, too.

Holly cried, "Someone took her! Someone took Grace! Oh God! I'm sorry! I'm so sorry!"

"G–Grace?"

Andrew heard a muffled *clack.* It sounded like Holly's phone had hit the floor. He could still hear the chatter and his wife's weeping. He was struck with a sudden sense of dizziness. He stumbled off the stepladder and leaned against the wall. He saw the ground tilting underneath him, left and right like a seesaw. The world was spinning around him.

Grace, Grace, Grace—he could only think about his precious daughter. He kept the phone up to his ear as he bolted forward. He raced to Plaza Elementary School.

Chapter Nine

What Happened?

Andrew jogged past the tree in front of the school. He noticed Grace's drawing on the mud. His heart sank as he spotted the beat cops in front of the administration building. He saw four police cruisers and an unmarked car parked on the street. Neighbors watched the school from their porches. Rumors were spreading like an Australian bushfire.

'A girl went missing. I heard it was a teacher's daughter.'

Officer Jordan Singleton stopped Andrew from running into the building. He said, "I'm sorry, sir. The school is under lockdown right now. No one is–"

"I'm Andrew McCarthy," Andrew said. "*You* called *me.* I'm here. Where's my daughter? Hmm? Is my son okay?"

"You're Mr. McCarthy? I'm sorry, sir. Please follow me."

Singleton opened the door and led Andrew into the building. The receptionist, Olivia Mendez, stood behind the reception desk. She answered phone calls from concerned parents who had heard the rumors. She frowned upon spotting Andrew. Max sat in the waiting area to the left with a female police officer and a school counselor. The cop tried to get his mind off things, but he was haunted by his failure.

He was Grace's older brother. He was the man of the house when Andrew went on his business trips. He was supposed to protect his sister and his mother.

He was told to watch his sister every morning. It was his only real responsibility. But he couldn't do that. And now he could only blame himself for his sister's disappearance.

The voice in his head repeated the same sentence over and over: *it's all your fault. It's all your fault. It's all your fault.* He sat there with a blank face and a set of distant eyes. He held his Nintendo Switch in his hands, but he didn't play any games. He didn't speak to the cop, either. He looked like he was gazing into a void, lost in the emptiness of *nothing.*

Andrew crouched in front of him. He grabbed his hand and asked, "Max, what happened?"

Max raised his head slowly. He locked eyes with his father. His blank face quickly twisted into a grimace. His eyes watered, his cheeks twitched, and his lips shook. He wanted to apologize, but he couldn't say a word.

"Max, buddy," Andrew said as he hugged him. He patted Max's back and said, "Everything's going to be okay. I'm going to... We're going to fix this, okay? Don't cry, kiddo, don't cry."

Max sobbed into Andrew's chest. Andrew fought back tears of his own. The police gave them a minute.

Singleton said, "Mr. McCarthy, your wife is waiting for you in the meeting room. Please follow me."

Andrew patted Max's head and said, "I'll be right back, buddy. Don't worry about a thing."

Don't go!—Max wanted to yell it out, but only a croak escaped his mouth. The counselor and the cop continued to try to comfort him. The cop even offered to play his game with him.

Singleton led Andrew past the receptionist. They went down a short hallway, walking past eight offices, then they entered a meeting room at the end. There was a large rectangular table in the middle of the room with eight seats on each long side and two seats at each end. Martin Booth, an older detective, and Holly sat at the closest end of the table.

Holly held a moist napkin up to her nose. Her hand trembled gently. Her eyes were wet and puffy. She was describing Grace's clothing and physical characteristics.

"Holly," Andrew said as he rushed into the room.

Holly cried, "I'm sorry. I'm sorry."

Andrew hugged her and asked, "What happened? Where's Grace?"

"I'm so sorry."

"Holly, please. Honey, talk to me. What the hell is going on?"

"I don't know, I don't know. Oh God, she's gone."

"*How?* What happened?"

Booth said, "Mr. McCarthy, I'd appreciate it if you took a seat. I understand your emotions are running high. This is a *serious* situation, an *emotional* situation, but we can't make any progress if we don't sit down and talk about it."

Andrew glared at him, but he knew he was correct. So, he took a seat to Holly's left. He dragged the chair closer to his wife so he didn't have to release her hand. Holly kept whimpering and sniffling.

Andrew asked, "Who are you? What's going on?"

Booth said, "My name is Martin Booth. I'm a detective in the Missing Persons Unit of the Pinecreek Police Department."

"Missing persons..."

"I'm sorry to be the bearer of bad news, you're apparently not caught up on the situation, but... As of now, your daughter, five-year-old Grace McCarthy, is missing."

"Grace... is missing?"

Andrew dug his fingers into his hair and leaned back in his seat. The dizziness hit him again. He smiled and shook his head—'no, you're lying, that could never happen to us.' But he saw the honesty in the detective's eyes and he heard the genuine pain in his wife's voice. It was true.

Andrew stuttered, "Wa–Was she taken?"

Booth said, "We don't know."

"What do you mean you 'don't know?' You're a detective. Holly, she–she called me thirty minutes ago. Thirty *goddamn* minutes ago. You don't have a lead or an–an idea?"

"We're looking for her now. We–"

"I didn't get an Amber alert on my phone. How... How *thoroughly* can you be searching if I haven't even gotten a damn Amber Alert?"

"We can't send an Amber alert yet."

"Why the hell not?!"

Booth raised his hand in a peaceful gesture. He had dealt with many frustrated parents before. He understood their emotions, so he accepted their anger. He welcomed it with open arms, in fact. He was willing to do anything to help the parents of missing children, including absorbing their verbal abuse.

He said, "Mr. McCarthy, as I explained to your wife here, there's a certain criteria that your case has to mcet in order for us to issue an Amber alert. First, we have to confirm that an abduction has taken place. Second, we must assess the risk of her being seriously injured or threatened. And third, we need an accurate description of your daughter and her captor or her captor's vehicle. We know what Grace looks like, what she was wearing, thanks to Mrs. McCarthy's very detailed description, but we don't have anything else at the moment. And that's because we can't be certain that she's been abducted. She could have wandered off, followed a stray dog into a different neighborhood. Or, even though you may not believe it, she could have run away."

Holly said, "She's five years old. Why would she run away?"

"I've seen four-year-olds run away from their parents. Just three weeks ago, at the Plaza View Mall, a four-year-old boy ran away from his mother because she didn't buy him an action figure. He left the mall and just... he ran as far as possible. We found him an hour later in a McDonald's parking lot just a few blocks away. You have to understand: kids are good at hiding. They're small and they can get into smaller spaces. We're looking *everywhere* for Grace. Every alley, every dumpster, every hole in the ground."

Andrew asked, "So that's your theory?"

Booth responded, "It's what we're working with right now. About ninety percent of missing children turn out to be runaways. Another four or five percent are family abduction cases. A mother or a father or an uncle... You get the idea. One percent are lost or injured. Less than one percent are nonfamily abductions. Strangers, you understand? So, aside from searching every corner, we're talking to families who were picking up their children at the time of Grace's disappearance and asking if they saw anything suspicious. We're also asking neighbors with surveillance cameras for their footage to see if we can find Grace walking alone or with someone else. That will give us an idea of her direction and... and it'll let us know whether or not she's been abducted."

Andrew nodded with a newfound sense of optimism. His new home surveillance system was effective. He remembered the clear picture on his phone's app. *Someone saw her,* he thought, *a person or a camera, someone or something saw her.*

He asked, "So... what do we do now?"

Booth said, "I still have a few more questions before I head out."

"Okay, sure. The sooner we're out there looking, the better."

"I agree," Booth said as he flipped the page on his pocket notepad. He scribbled a note, then he said, "Mrs. McCarthy, I might repeat a few questions now that your husband is present. Feel free to add anything you forgot or... or anything at all. Okay?"

"O–Okay," Holly croaked out.

Booth asked, "Does Grace have a history of disappearing?"

"Wha–What do you mean by that?" Andrew responded.

"Does Grace disappear often? Is she a fickle girl? Does she sometimes go this way or that way without telling you?"

"Um… I suppose so. If we go to a store, she might wander away for a few seconds. But she doesn't just… *leave*. She stays close enough for us to keep an eye on her."

"I see. Does she have a history of running away?"

"No."

"No?" Booth said in a dubious tone.

Confident, Andrew said, "No, never. She's never ran away before and she's never tried to."

Booth wrote down another note. He turned the page on his notepad and skimmed over his jottings.

The detective asked, "Has Grace been in any trouble recently? At home or at school?"

"No," Holly and Andrew said together.

"Nothing at all? You know, anything that might have made her upset?"

Andrew said, "*Nothing.* Look, I really don't think she ran away. She wouldn't do something like that."

"I'm just being thorough. Did she talk about anything strange or unusual lately? Maybe she was talking about an imaginary friend or perhaps someone she met on the internet?"

Andrew said, "She's not allowed to use the internet without our supervision. She has some–"

"Olaf," Holly interrupted. "Last weekend, I was at the grocery store, a–at Smart and Final, and she said she met Olaf there. Tha–That was the same time I saw that guy, *that stalker.*"

"Stalker?" Booth said, a hint of concern in his voice.

"Yes, *yes,*" Andrew said, wide-eyed. He looked like a doctor who had just discovered the cure to a deadly disease. He said, "There was a guy, a young guy... Shit, what was his name? We thought he was taking pictures of Grace and some of the other kids at a park a couple of weekends ago. Then we saw him at a diner, but we didn't really have any proof that he was doing anything other than eating there. Then... then..."

Holly said, "I saw him at the grocery store. When I asked my kids about it, they said they spoke to him for a minute. Holly said his name was 'Olaf,' like the character from that Disney movie. She said he helped her get a box of cereal from a high shelf. Maybe he did something else and she didn't tell me... and I didn't even notice it. He could have... he could have molested her. Oh my God, this is all my fault. Why didn't I–"

"I need you to stay calm, ma'am," Booth interrupted. "Breathe. I know it's the last thing you want to hear, but you can't panic now. A clear mind is more beneficial than a panicking mind. Okay?"

Holly breathed as if she were in labor. She squeezed Andrew's hand until it turned red and purple. Andrew didn't feel any pain from Holly's grip. He was numb from the fear and depression flowing through his veins. *Too little, too late,* he thought. He regretted his weak stance against Zachary at the diner. He wished he had struck him or at least tackled him, like Matthew at the park.

Booth said, "Do you have a name? A description?"

Andrew said, "A name... I saw his website and I heard his name, but I... Fuck, I can't remember it. I can't fucking remember it."

"I can't remember it, either," Holly cried. "I'm sorry. I'm sorry."

Booth said, "That's fine. It's okay. A description? You saw him multiple times, right? Can you describe him?"

Andrew nodded and said, "He looks young. Maybe early to mid-twenties. He had black, curly hair. No facial hair. Maybe... I think he has a small mole under his right eye. He dresses well, too. I mean, he looks like a college student. And he carries a camera around. He said he was a professional photographer."

Hmm—Booth made the noise as he scribbled more notes down. Holly and Andrew watched him with eager eyes, as if they expected him to identify the strange photographer on the spot.

Booth said, "So you suspected this man of stalking you and photographing your children. Did you ever call the police about this?"

"At the park," the couple responded together.

Andrew clarified, "We confronted him about it at the park. The cops came and questioned all of us. But that asshole was a smooth talker. He talked his way out of it. And I guess they didn't see anything suspicious on his camera. But they didn't search him thoroughly. They got a glimpse. That's all. He's responsible for this. I know it."

Booth asked, "Do you have a name for any of the responding officers?"

Andrew sighed, then he placed his palm on his brow and said, "No..."

"How about a date? When did this happen?"

"It was... It was three Sundays ago. Around, um... sunset. Three cops came out. I'm pretty sure they were going to write a report on it."

"Good, good," Booth said as he wrote down a date. He said, "One last question before I go: what are Grace's favorite places?"

Holly said, "She loves it here. I mean, she loves school. She loves the park. All of them. She loves the movie theater over on Main Street. It's where we watched Frozen 2. She loves the beach and... and she loves home. She really loves home."

The detective scribbled a few more notes. His mind was working on two theories: Grace wandered away from the school and lost her way, or she was abducted by a young photographer. Andrew and Holly sat there and watched. Their eyes said: *say something already!*

Booth said, "I'm going to find the responding officers and this young man. In the meantime, we're going to keep searching for Grace in the immediate area. If we don't find her in the next hour or so or if we find anything that points towards an abduction before that, I'm going to go ahead and push for an Amber alert with your kid's description."

"Tha–That's it?" Andrew asked.

"For now."

"Is there anything we can do to help?"

Booth stood from his seat. He shrugged at him and said, "Look for your girl. Keep your phone on. Take care of your son. And don't leave town."

Andrew stuttered, "Wha–What's that supposed to mean? A–Are we suspects? You think we–"

"*It means* don't leave town," Booth interrupted. "Stay close and stay available. We will find your daughter. If we don't find her in the next few hours, we'll expand our search to the surrounding woods with some volunteers. We'll spend all night searching if we have to. And you're free to join us. If you have any questions or if you remember anything else— *anything* at all—don't hesitate to call me."

Booth placed two business cards on the table in front of the couple. He nodded at them, then he exited the meeting room. The busy jabbering from the reception area wafted into the room, then it vanished as the door shut behind the detective. Andrew and Holly were paralyzed with fear. They shared the same thought: *cops search the woods when they're looking for dead bodies.* After a minute of deafening silence, they fell into each other's arms and sobbed.

Chapter Ten

The Search

"*Grace!*" Andrew yelled, his gloved hands cupped around his mouth.

He stood atop a hill, the autumn leaves crunching under his boots. His shout echoed through a vast woodland, riding the wind through the plentiful trees and bushes. Other voices joined his—men, women, and even teenagers. The community unified to find the missing girl. Some yelled her name: *Grace!* Others yelled her nicknames: *Gracie! Gray!* They worked under the assumption that she was lost.

It had been almost forty-eight hours since Grace vanished. She wasn't caught on any surveillance cameras near the school. Meryl, the crossing guard, remembered helping Grace cross the street, but she couldn't remember if she walked away from the school alone or with a stranger. She only remembered the girl's precious smile. No one came forward with any useful information.

Andrew took a deep breath, then he shouted, "Grace! *Grace!* It's daddy! Come home, baby! Please! We're here! We're right here! Show me a sign! Say... Say something!" There was no response. He only heard the other volunteers and police yelling Grace's name. He unleashed a shaky sigh, then he yelled, "We got a dog! Grace, we... we got a dog..."

His arms fell to his sides in defeat. He looked to his left, then to his right. He saw the volunteers and police walking side by side, arms-length apart while maintaining the same pace. They searched behind every bush and under every log, as if they expected her to be crushed under a fallen tree trunk. Some K-9s joined the search, too, using Grace's clothing to track her.

Andrew leaned back against a tree. He slid down to the ground. He watched as the sun began to fall beyond a mountain several miles away.

His head shuddered and he blinked rapidly. The sunset painted the sky with every tint of orange. Then the sky turned red—*blood-red*—and the clouds crimson. The berries in the bushes looked like drops of blood. Mangled animal carcasses hung from the tree branches and littered the ground. He saw an apocalyptic vision. His world was ending.

And he knew it.

He covered his face with his shaky hands and sobbed. His glasses fell on his lap. Tears soaked his beard and mucus flooded his nostrils. *Devastation*— he felt the raw, uncompromising force of true devastation for the first time in his life. He spent over thirty minutes on the hill by himself, contemplating his failures and his uncertain future.

'Why didn't I do more to stop this? What happens if she's hurt? What if I can't save her? What am I going to tell Max? Will Holly ever forgive me? Can I forgive her? Are our lives over?'

"Andrew!"

He heard a man shouting his name from behind the tree. He wiped the tears and mucus from his face. He stood up and, while pretending to clean his glasses, he walked around the tree. He saw Matthew hiking up to him.

Matthew said, "Andrew, man, we've got a little problem. Holly, she's... she's broken. She's down there by the pond crying her eyes out."

Andrew swallowed loudly, then he asked, "Did you... Did you find Grace?"

An image of Grace's drowned body flashed in his mind. He saw the headlines: *runaway five-year-old found drowned in a pond*.

Matthew said, "No, no. She's just... Holly's tired. She shouldn't have come out here in the first place. *You* shouldn't be out here. Come on, I'll take you down to her."

As Matthew turned to walk down the hill, Andrew said, "No."

Matthew stopped and looked back at him. He said, "No? Holly needs you, man. And you need her. Come on, I'll stay out here and I'll keep looking. Don't worry about a thing."

"I keep hearing that. 'Don't worry, don't worry, don't worry.' How can I *not* worry while my daughter is out there somewhere scared, confused, and alone? I get what you're trying to do, I know you care about us, but I'm not going anywhere until I find Grace. I have to do this. I *have* to do this, Matt."

"Yeah, I get it. But, Holly–"

"Can you do me a favor? Hmm? You really wanna help?"

"Of course I do. You know that. Name it and it's done."

"Take Holly home. Her parents are there with Max. She'll feel comfortable with them. I don't think she wants to see me right now and... and I can't see her. I don't think you'd understand 'cause you've never been in a situation like this, but it's just... Please make sure she gets home safely. And have a chat with Max, okay? Tell him that everything's going to be okay, tell him that dad's going to find Grace. Make sure he believes it, okay? Yeah, he needs... he needs hope."

What do you need?—Matthew wanted to ask the question, but he couldn't cough up those words. In Andrew, he saw the same thing he saw in Holly: a broken soul. But he agreed with him. He wasn't capable of understanding their pain or their struggle because he had never lost his child for more than five minutes.

He asked, "Are you going to be okay out here?"

"I'm going to find Grace," Andrew said as he looked out into the woods.

"Andrew, are *you* going to be okay?"

"I have to find her..."

Matthew gripped Andrew's shoulder and lowered his head. He didn't want him to see the tears glistening in his eyes.

He said, "I'll be back soon. Take care of yourself, man. And call me if you need anything. Really, I'm... I'm here for you."

Andrew kept staring into the woods, scanning every inch for a sign of his daughter. Matthew reluctantly walked away. He didn't want to abandon his friend, but he couldn't force him to accept his help. He went back to the pond to take Holly home.

Andrew walked in the opposite direction. He yelled for Grace until his voice was raspy.

The sun fell and darkness swept through the woods. The younger volunteers and the K-9s departed. The remaining volunteers and cops used flashlights to navigate the woodland. After an hour and a half of wandering through the dark, the search was called off.

Yet, Andrew continued walking through the woods. He spent another hour searching for Grace. He would have spent more time out there, but he lost his bearings and ended up at the parking lot at the entrance of the woods. He found Detective Booth waiting for him near his minivan.

Booth said, "I figured you'd make it back here sooner or later."

"You got some news for me?" Andrew asked as he opened the driver's door.

He pulled a water bottle out of his backpack and took a swig. He acted natural, although it was clear he was fighting an emotional breakdown.

Booth said, "No, not exactly."

"Then what are you doing here? Just, um... Just helping with the search? Shouldn't you be looking for that guy from the park?"

"We're looking into him. We've got a name, but we don't have any proof that he's involved in this. Not yet."

"What else do you need?" Andrew asked in exasperation. "We've told you everything. We told you he harassed our family. We told you he was stalking us. What? Huh? You need a picture of him carrying Grace away from her school?"

Booth sucked his lips into his mouth and shrugged. He said, "That would certainly help. We need evidence, Mr. McCarthy. We have a police report that says there was an altercation between the two of you and another party. An altercation that left *your* prime suspect on the ground with some minor back injuries. An altercation where everyone involved agreed not to press charges and, according to the officers at the scene, let bygones be bygones. And we have no calls for disturbances at any diners or grocery stores regarding this fellow. None at all. See what I'm getting at?"

The bottle *crunched* and *crackled* as Andrew clenched his fists. Water splashed out of the bottle like lava from a volcano. His nostrils flared with each deep breath. He was a passive-aggressive man, he didn't care about being macho, but he felt like punching the detective in the mouth at that moment. Booth's eyes darted down to the bottle, then back to Andrew's face. He stood his ground, hoping to get something—*anything*—from Andrew.

Andrew cracked a smile. He said, "I see what you're getting at. So, let's just get straight to the point. Give me the cold hard truth, detective. If she's out here, it's because she's *dead*, right? You think she's been abducted? Possibly injured or killed, right? What's the… the new theory? How are the brave and courageous men and women of the Pinecreek Police Department serving and protecting my family? Hmm?"

"You want the truth, Mr. McCarthy?"

"That's what I said, isn't it?"

"Fine. The truth is: we are shifting our investigation. We thought she was lost, now we believe she was abducted. We don't know if it was the man from your altercation at the park, but we're looking into him. We're already tracking some of the known sexual offenders in the area, too. Some of those bastards are locked up, waiting for myself or their parole officers to ask 'em a couple of questions. Others... Well, some of the others have been more elusive while a few of them haven't been very cooperative. But we'll find them all and we'll make them talk. One way or another, they will squeal."

Andrew saw the rage in Booth's vengeful eyes. He was comforted by his anger and he appreciated his blunt honesty. He trusted the detective. Yet, he couldn't help but feel like the police force was inefficient. *Elusive,* he thought, *how could a registered sex offender be elusive in this day and age?*

He asked, "Aren't these people tagged? I mean, don't they wear ankle bracelets so you can keep track of them? They shouldn't be *that* hard to find, right?"

Booth said, "Ideally, it would work like that. Unfortunately, it doesn't. We're not a force with unlimited resources and we're bound by the law. These guys, they're known for cutting their bracelets. And since the jails and prisons are all filled up with who knows who, they're slapped on the wrists and released again. That's the cycle our system has created. That's what we're dealing with right now. But I'm giving you my word, Mr. McCarthy: I won't rest until I hunt them all down and I find your daughter."

Andrew raised the bottle to his mouth to take a swig. To his surprise, it was empty. He tossed the bottle into his van, then he stared at the backseat. Grace always sat in the seat behind the driver's seat. He remembered watching her draw on the window with her finger. The window was clean, but he could still see her stick figures. Fresh tears filled his bloodshot eyes. He dug his fingernails into his palms as he clenched his fists again. He shared the same anger as the detective, but he didn't know how to use it—*yet.*

He asked, "Is there anything else I can do?"

Booth said, "You can take care of yourself. I'm here because your friend, Mr. Matthew Baker, called the station about you. He asked us to perform a welfare check, said your behavior was unusual. I figured I owed you a personal update, too. You got it. Now go home. Your family is waiting."

"My family... is out there somewhere," Andrew said as he glanced around. "Grace... I need to find Grace. Now tell me what I can *really* do to help. You said you were looking into that guy from the park, right? What's his name? Where can I find him?"

"I'm not telling you his name. *Don't* involve yourself in this. This is *not* your job, Mr. McCarthy."

"How could you say that with a straight face? I'm already involved in this. That's my daughter out there! And it's *my* job to protect her!"

"But it's not your job to play vigilante. Stay out of the way. Wait at home with your family. She'll be home soon. Please, be patient."

Andrew shook his head and said, "I'm tired of being patient."

"Well, you don't have many other options. I'm going back to the station now. Do you need anything else from me? Will you be okay?"

"Yeah, yeah, sure... I'll be fine. Just fine..."

Booth said, "Good, good. Take a rest, Mr. McCarthy. I'll update you soon."

Booth waited for a response, but Andrew didn't even spare a glance. The detective left in his unmarked sedan.

Andrew stood beside his van for a minute, listening to the music of the woods at night— groaning branches, rustling leaves, chirping crickets. He stared at the steering wheel and thought about driving home. He hadn't slept since Grace's disappearance. He was tired, but he wasn't ready to quit. The mere thought of facing his wife depressed him, too. He took a flask out of his coat's chest pocket. He took a swig of his whiskey, then he headed back into the woods. He spent the night calling out to Grace and drinking the pain away.

Chapter Eleven

Drastic Measures

Andrew's eyes fluttered open. He sneered and groaned in pain as a throbbing headache attacked his skull. He sat up and found himself in bed. He still wore his muddy clothing from the previous night, but he couldn't remember driving home. *I must have been crazy or suicidal,* he thought. He staggered as soon as he stood up. His hangover came with a side of dizziness.

He dragged his feet into the bathroom across the hall. As he peed, he heard muffled voices coming from downstairs. He washed his hands, then he drank straight from the faucet for thirty seconds.

"What's going on down here?" he muttered as he headed downstairs.

He found Holly and her elderly parents, Rodney and Annette Ferguson, in the living room. Matthew and his wife, Cynthia Baker, were present, too. Dozens of sheets of paper—the McCarthy's financial records—were spread across the coffee table at the center of the room. They used the calculator apps on their cell phones to make some calculations.

Holly said, "I called some pawnshops and jewelry stores. I can sell the engagement ring for three thousand. We have... We have over five thousand in our savings. Like, just a few dollars over, so let's just say five thousand. That's eight thousand from us. I can get more from our checking account, maybe. Mom, dad, you said you can lend us seven-thousand."

"*Give you*," Rodney corrected. "We're not going to have any of that 'loaning' nonsense. This is for Grace."

As if she didn't hear him, Holly continued, "So, that's fifteen-thousand in cash."

Matthew said, "Put us down for five."

"Five? Five thousand? Are you sure?"

"I'm positive. She's like our niece, Holly."

Cynthia said, "She's family. We'll do anything for family, hun."

A tear raced down Holly's cheek as she blinked. She hugged Cynthia and grabbed Matthew's hand while thanking them repeatedly.

"Okay, okay," she said shakily. "That's twenty-thousand dollars. I'm sure I can find more to sell. We have too many TVs and tablets and computers... We can make thousands from that. If not, I can get a loan. I have a *very* good credit score. We can get up to thirty thousand, I think. That's a big reward. It's big enough, right?"

Yes, yeah, sure—the quiet, unenthusiastic agreements filled the living room. They were doing their best to keep Holly's spirit alive.

Andrew walked in front of the coffee table. The living room was smothered by a tense silence. Andrew glanced through the archway to his right. He saw Max and two of his friends playing at the kitchen table. Max kept glancing at him. There was sadness and fear in his eyes. He expected a punishment sooner or later. He didn't forgive himself for Grace's disappearance.

Andrew asked, "What's going on?"

Holly, Rodney, and Matthew stared at Andrew, floored by his appearance, while Cynthia and Annette rubbed Holly's shoulders and looked away. Dirt was embedded under his fingernails and caked on his cheeks. Mud crusted on his boots and the bottom hem of his jeans. He reeked of nature and alcohol.

Holly said, "Good morning, Andrew. Well, it's..." She checked the clock on her phone. She said, "It's almost eleven. Right in time for brunch. Why don't you take a shower while my mom cooks something up for you?"

"Oh, it would be my pleasure," Annette said, seizing the opportunity to escape the tense encounter.

Andrew repeated, "What's going on?"

Holly sighed, then she said, "The search isn't working out. I'm not going to sit here and wait until it's too late. I'm... *We're* taking action *now.* We're pooling our money together. We're going to offer a reward. Maybe thirty thousand. More if I can get a loan."

"A reward? A reward for what?"

"Information. The safe return of our daughter. *Anything* that will help us find her. Hell, if–if she was kidnapped, if someone really took her, I'll even offer to drop the charges if they return her to us. They can keep the money and run as long as Grace is back in my arms, safe and sound."

Andrew cocked his head back and sneered. He said, "Are you... Are you joking?"

"No. This can–"

"No, no. Stop it, Holly. This is an *awful* idea. If any decent human being had any information, he would have come forward already. And if she was taken, a kidnapper isn't going to risk everything for thirty thousand or fifty thousand or even a hundred thousand. I don't think people even kidnap kids for money anymore! This isn't a goddamn third-world country!"

Holly closed her eyes and said, "Don't yell at me. At least I'm try–"

"You're trying to what? To embarrass us in front of the entire city? To hurt Max? Have you even thought of the consequences something like this would have on him? Huh? Have you?! We don't need a media circus right now, Holly!"

Matthew stood up. He held his arms away from him, like a teacher trying to stop two students from fighting each other.

He said, "Andrew, man, let's get out of here. I'll take you–"

Holly jumped up from her seat and yelled, "Don't tell me what we need! When Grace needed a father, when we needed a *man,* you weren't there! You let that little punk walk all over us!"

"Me? Me?!" Andrew shouted as he struck his own chest. "I confronted him when you didn't want me to. 'Oh, he'll go away. Oh, it's just a coincidence.' *You* let that man follow you around. And even if it wasn't him, *you* were supposed to be watching them. They were taken from your fucking school!"

From his seat, Rodney said, "Hey, watch your mouth, son. Now's not the time for this."

Annette heard the argument from the kitchen while she scrambled some eggs at the stove. Max's face was scrunched up as he whimpered. Concern was written on his friends' faces. Annette ushered them out of the house through the back door. Max glanced back one last time. He caught a glimpse of his ferocious parents before the door closed behind his grandmother. He had never heard them yell before. His parents often shouted when breakfast was ready or when they tried to get his attention, but they never really *yelled* in anger.

It was terrifying to him. It was like seeing two strangers in his house, fighting to the death over *his* mistake. The guilt scared him, too. He had never felt so wrong before. It made his skin tingle.

Holly opened and closed her mouth over and over, as if she were chewing the air. She was dazed by Andrew's verbal haymaker.

"I–I knew you blamed me," she croaked out.

Rodney yelled, "Oh, for crying out loud! No one's to blame!"

Holly continued, "But it's *not* my fault. You... *You,* Andrew. You weren't at work when I called you. You were at home trying to install some bullshit surveillance system. You could have picked them up from school. If you weren't so selfish with your time, you could have stopped this."

The room became silent. Andrew hadn't thought of that. He blamed himself for Grace's disappearance, any parent would have done the same under the circumstances, but he didn't really know why. The answer finally dawned on him.

Because it was all my fault, he thought. *She's right. I could have picked them up. I could have stopped Grace's kidnapper. It was always my fault.*

He locked eyes with Holly. They felt each other's suffering. They saw shame, guilt, and self-hatred within each other. In the living room, their daughter torn out of their arms and their lives turned upside down, they loved each other as much as they hated each other.

Andrew marched out of the house through the front door. Matthew and Rodney called out to him while Cynthia tried to comfort Holly.

Holly said, "Let him go, just let him go..." She sat on the sofa, head down with her hands over her brow. She sniffled and trembled, then she snorted and asked, "Can someone find me some numbers for the local news? I have to make some calls."

Andrew cruised through the city in his minivan. He felt anxious with every child he saw on the street. He was worried about them just as much as he was worried about Grace. He drove past Plaza Elementary School. The school was closed out of respect for Grace and the McCarthy family. (The faculty was also preparing their teachers and counselors to help the students understand Grace's disappearance.) He drove past the park where he first encountered Zachary. He didn't see any photographers out there.

"Goddammit," he muttered. "Where are you? Where did you take her? What did you do to my daughter?"

He drove to the woods at the outskirts of town. He parked in the parking lot. He raised his flask to his mouth—*empty.* He held it over his head and pointed it downwards towards his mouth, then he hit the bottom of the flask, like a parched man in a desert trying to get one more drop out of a bottle of water. The flask was dry. He threw it at the windshield and yelled, then he slammed his fist on the steering wheel and continued to scream. The horn echoed through the woods.

He stumbled out of the minivan, then he lurched to the front of the vehicle. He yelled, "Grace! Grace, come home! Please, baby! I'm sorry! I'm… I'm sorry!" There was no reply. He fell to his knees and cried, "Grace, sweetheart… I'm sorry. It's all my fault. I don't know what to do. I don't know how to save you. Oh God, what am I supposed to do?"

His cries danced through the desolate woods, serenading the woodland critters with a melancholic tune. He spent his day there, retracing his steps, traversing new land, and searching under every leaf.

Chapter Twelve

Limited Resources

Andrew awoke to pounding at the front door—and a pounding headache. He sat up in bed, vision fuzzy from the light. His mouth was dry, lips cracked and bloody. But he was prepared this time. He grabbed a half-empty water bottle from the nightstand and chugged it. A bottle of whiskey, his flask, a cracked shot glass, and bottles of sleeping pills and antidepressants surrounded the lamp. He tried to block the pain with alcohol and sleep.

The knocking stopped. The front door swung open, followed by a muffled welcome. There was no excitement in the voice, so he knew Grace didn't show up on their porch.

The week flew by without a single sign of Grace—without a sign of life. Holly appeared on several local news channels to announce a reward of thirty-five thousand dollars for information regarding Grace's location. She begged the public for help, sobbing her eyes out during each appearance. Grace's disappearance was also discussed on several national news networks for a few minutes before cutting back to the everyday fear-mongering and political divisiveness.

Andrew staggered into the hall. He leaned against the wall to find his bearings. He peeked into his son's room. He found Annette sitting with Max. She watched him play Minecraft on his computer, asking question after question: *what does that do? Can you build this? Why'd you kill that poor pig?* She would do anything to get his mind off his sister.

Andrew didn't know how to comfort Max. He feared he would snap at his son like he did at Holly, so he kept their communications at a minimum. As he headed downstairs, he heard some familiar voices: Holly, Rodney, and Booth. Holly sounded surprised and angry. Andrew found them sitting at the kitchen table, a mug clasped in Booth's hands. Holly glared at the detective.

"Detective Booth," Andrew said from the kitchen archway.

"Mr. McCarthy," Booth responded. "How are you holding up?"

Rodney nodded at Andrew—*good morning*—then he moseyed over to the stove. Andrew took a seat beside his wife. They didn't look at each other.

Andrew asked, "What are you doing here?"

Booth said, "Let me start from the beginning. I've got good news and bad news. The bad news is–"

"They're ending the search," Holly interrupted. "It's barely been a week and they're already ending the search."

"That's not exactly true. I said we're going to dial it back."

"What's the difference? Hmm? What is the goddamn difference?"

"I'll explain if you–"

"Please do," Andrew interrupted.

Booth sensed the rage in the room. He saw desperation in Holly's eyes and murder in Andrew's.

Rodney returned to the table. He placed a mug of coffee in front of Andrew, then he sat beside his son-in-law. He gave the detective a nervous smile, as if to say: *sorry, but what can you do?*

Booth explained, "We're going to continue conducting broad community searches every weekend. Due to our limited resources, we cannot continue searching every day from sunrise to sunset. It's just not something we can maintain at the moment."

"Limited resources?" Andrew repeated. "What? Are your cops too busy busting pot-heads in parking lots to look for my daughter? Busy stopping teenagers from stealing clothes at the mall? 'Cause, last I heard, there really isn't any *serious* crime in this city. I mean, we're not in Chicago for crying out loud. People aren't getting gunned down in the streets every day."

"I understand your frustration, but I need you to understand me, too. There's a lot going on out there, a lot you probably don't pay attention to. We have an elderly woman who was beaten to death in her home in what we initially thought was a home invasion. Turns out, her two granddaughters attacked her with hammers just to steal forty dollars from her purse. And one of them is on the run. A young teen was shot on a basketball court for his sneakers—and no one has said a thing about it. A baby was taken from a Wal-Mart parking lot, and we're still looking for him. We don't have the resources to tackle all of the evil out there head-on. That's just a fact. That's the cold hard truth."

Booth took another sip of his coffee. Andrew and Holly were rendered speechless by the detective's bluntness. Rodney stared down at his own coffee. He didn't think it was his place to speak, but he wanted to support his family so he couldn't leave. They sat in silence for fifteen seconds.

Andrew asked, "What's the good news?"

Booth said, "Since we're dialing back the search, that frees up some of our resources. It gives us a chance to shift our investigation. You see, we've been talking to the feds. They've shown a keen interest in your daughter and this case. They don't believe she's lost in the woods or dead in a ditch. They believe she was taken. And they've had their eyes on several suspected human traffickers in the area."

Lips shaking, Andrew stuttered, "A–And how is that good news? What? You think she's in some five-star hotel? Don't human traffickers... Don't they..." He paused to swallow the lump in his throat. He asked, "Don't they ship girls out to Mexico or China? Don't they turn them into prostitutes? Or ha–harvest their... their organs?"

Holly held her hand over her mouth and sobbed. She remembered all of the horror stories she read on the news.

Booth said, "It's good news because we have reason to believe Grace is still alive. It's good news because the feds are helping us investigate several suspects. It's good news because we're moving in the right direction now. To be frank, the chances of finding Grace alive were slim to none yesterday. The case was getting colder by the second. Today, there's hope."

Andrew said, "Human traffickers... Do you have any idea if that guy from the park is involved yet?"

"I can't say."

"You can't or you won't?"

"*Both*. I can't say because we're not a hundred percent sure yet. I won't say because it's against our guidelines. We don't want a case of vigilante justice on our hands. We don't want his name spreading through the news. If he's not involved, we'd be putting him in danger and we'd be assassinating his character."

Holly asked, "If he is involved, we might just be saving our daughter."

Booth responded, "Like I said, the feds are looking into him right now. They have a list of suspects. I'm feeling optimistic."

Breaking his silence, Rodney said, "Well, I think that's great. We can keep searching on our own, right? Y'all can handle the–"

"Should I offer more money?" Holly interrupted, ignoring her father.

Booth shrugged and repeated, "Money?"

"We–We're doing the reward thing, remember? You said this might be a human trafficking situation, right? You said my baby is still alive, right?"

Booth nodded and said, "That's what I've been told."

Holly's lips twitched as she smiled. She said, "Human traffickers do it for money. So, if I offer fifty thousand or... or a hundred thousand, I can buy Grace from them."

The men looked at each other. The truth was bleak and depressing. Human traffickers abducted people and sold them for money, used them for labor, or dissected them for their organs—which they then sold for money. That was true. But some human traffickers kidnapped people to produce pornography and snuff films. And that sect of traffickers was especially fond of children.

Booth suspected Holly knew that very well, but she was in denial. He wasn't willing to extinguish her spark of hope.

He said, "I'm sure we'll find her safe and sound. If it helps you sleep better at night, feel free to increase your reward. But do *not* attempt to contact anyone without us. We'll let you take the lead on this little bounty program of yours, but we can't let you do it alone. I'll assign someone to help you out. I'll also reach out to some of my sources to help you get the word out. Does that sound good to you?"

Holly said, "Sure, sure. I'll start, um… I'll start organizing some more money. Maybe we can do a GoFundMe or something like that. I can print some fliers, too. And, um… We can do some milk carton stuff. Do they still do that?" She stood up and glanced around. She muttered, "Pen, paper, phone… Yeah, we can offer more. I just need to call some people. Where's my phone? Oh God, what if someone called?"

She went into the living room. Rodney nodded at the men, then he followed his daughter. He yammered about the good news, trying to get her to forget about the cancelled search parties.

Booth asked, "So, you got anything for me?"

"Like what?" Andrew responded, a cold look in his eyes.

"Questions. Information. *Anything.*"

Vigilante justice—Booth's words echoed through Andrew's head. His hand trembled, causing the coffee in his mug to ripple. He breathed deeply through his nose. He wanted to ask for information, but he didn't want to arouse any suspicion.

He asked, "So, you... you think she's alive?"

"I do."

"Then that's all I needed to hear. Thank you for visiting, detective."

"Thank you for your time, Mr. McCarthy," Booth said as he stood up.

He gestured with his mug—*what should I do with this?*

Andrew said, "Leave it. It's fine."

"Thank you," Booth said. He stopped at the archway. He looked back at Andrew and said, "Mr. McCarthy, I should warn you about taking matters into your own hands. That's not something you want to do. If I find out you're interfering with our investigation, especially when we're *this* close to breaking new ground, I won't hesitate to have you arrested. Understood?"

Without glancing back at him, Andrew asked, "Do you need me to walk you out?"

Booth sighed in disappointment. He said his goodbyes to the rest of the family, then he was escorted out of the house by Holly. Andrew sat in the kitchen and stared at his coffee. Holly walked in and out while talking on the phone. Annette took Max into the backyard to play. Rodney came in for another cup of coffee. He tried to start some small talk, but he didn't get a response.

Andrew just sat there for an hour. He thought about his other 'options.' He was determined to find his missing daughter—*by any means necessary*.

Chapter Thirteen

The Usual Suspects

Andrew trudged through the living room where the McCarthys gathered with the Bakers and another couple, the Garcias. Fliers with Grace's picture—*in color*—covered the coffee table as well as receipts and letters and a stack of printer paper. Their eyes were glued to the television, waiting for Channel 9 News to play an interview with Holly. She managed to raise an additional fifteen-thousand dollars from her friends, family, and complete strangers on the internet.

The interview started. The headline read: *$50,000 reward for information on missing Pinecreek child, Grace McCarthy.*

The audience in the living room cheered as they listened to Holly's emotional speech. They hoped to keep her motivated with their optimism. Matthew and Rodney called out to Andrew, but Andrew just shook his head and kept moving. He went upstairs. He could hear Max and his friends in his bedroom. He didn't bother checking up on them.

Andrew entered the master bedroom and locked the door behind him. He sat at a desk in the corner of the room. He cracked his knuckles over his laptop's keyboard.

He muttered, "I can do this. I don't need a badge to investigate. Private investigators investigate every day. I mean, maybe I need a license, but who's going to check? I'm not on official business. It's just research, right? Yeah, just research." He spoke as if he were trying to convince himself to move forward. He said, "So... where should I start?"

He stared at the screen, his web browser open to Google. His eyes widened a bit as an idea popped into his head. He opened a private window on his web browser. He thought: *that should stop them from tracking me, right? Well, it should buy me some time at least, shouldn't it?* He guessed a warrant and a call to his internet service provider would expose his misdoings, but at least he wasn't handing all of his information to the authorities on a silver platter.

He opened a notebook and grabbed a pen. He wasn't going to save anything on his hard drive. He started writing a list of potential suspects.

He whispered, "Human traffickers... maybe a cartel... No, no, that's crazy. Cartels don't kidnap Americans... do they?"

He searched for any news about Americans kidnapped by Mexican drug cartels. He found articles reporting the kidnappings of Americans *in* Mexico, but he couldn't find anything about Americans being kidnapped on American soil. He crossed 'cartels' off his list. Underneath it, he wrote: *Chinese organ traffickers?* He searched it on the internet. Again, he didn't find any news about organ traffickers kidnapping Americans on American soil.

"It's obvious," he muttered. "It's always the usual suspects."

He wrote: *convicted sex offenders*. He visited the California Megan's Law website, which provided information on registered sex offenders. He was met with a disclaimer. It warned him of the legal limits on disclosures, potential errors and exclusions, mistaken identities, and the possible legal consequences of using the website's information to commit a crime or harass an offender.

He ignored it.

He used his zip code to search for convicted sex offenders in the area. He found ninety-seven offenders. There were a dozen transient sex offenders in his city, too. He disregarded the homeless offenders since he didn't believe they were capable of kidnapping and hiding a child for over a week. He set his sights on violent repeat offenders—specifically, those who targeted minors.

As he scribbled some notes, he read a criminal's profile aloud: "Edgar Chance... Thirty-nine years old... Five-foot-four... 119 pounds... Lewd or lascivious acts with a child fourteen or fifteen years of age and offender ten or more years older than the victim... Annoyed or molested a child under eighteen years of age..." He wrote down his last known address. He underlined his name and muttered, "You're bad, but you're not the worst."

He searched through the offenders, jotting down their names, offenses, and addresses. After a few searches, the website asked him to complete another CAPTCHA. *I can't search too many people or they'll be on to me*, he thought. He focused on the area around Plaza Elementary School. He went through five more profiles.

"Lewd or lascivious acts... lewd or lascivious acts... oral copulation by force or fear... rape by force or fear... lewd or lascivious acts," he read their offenses aloud.

He looked over his notes. His writing was sloppy, the jottings of a madman, but every word looked like a piece to a puzzle to him. He read it, then re-read it, and then read it a third time. He saw a connection. He circled a name: *Diego Cavazos.* Diego was a forty-seven-year-old man convicted of rape by force or fear and lewd or lascivious acts with a minor. He had a history of violent crimes involving children.

Andrew tapped the notepad and said, "You've hurt kids. You're a repeat offender. You can't stop, can you? You took Grace, didn't you? You monster... *You fucking monster*, I'm coming for you."

He changed his clothes. He wanted to look casual and forgettable—*inconspicuous.* He wanted to appear strong, but he didn't want to intimidate anyone. He wore a gray button-up shirt with a burgundy tie, black slacks, and dress shoes. He wrestled with the idea of wearing gloves. It was chilly outside, but it wasn't cold enough to warrant gloves. He wasn't making a fashion statement, either.

I need something to hide my fingerprints, he thought. *I should try to hide my hair, too, right? A baseball cap? It won't match, but it's something.*

He put on the gloves and tossed on a baseball cap. He looked like a father hiding his palmoplantar hyperhidrosis under a pair of gloves while rushing to his son's baseball game after work to catch the last inning. It wasn't as inconspicuous as he had hoped, but he didn't look like himself, either. If someone spotted him and described him to the police, he assumed no one would suspect him.

He grabbed his backpack and went to the door. He poked his head out and peeked down the hall to his left and right. The coast was clear. He crept downstairs. The guests in the living room were busy, chatting about the reward and Grace, so no one noticed him. He went down another hall and found himself in the garage.

For the first time in his life, his workbench looked like an armory. He didn't see home improvement tools used for fixing broken things anymore. He saw weapons of destruction used to *break* deviant men.

As he ran his eyes over the tools, he whispered, "A gun would make this easier, but guns are easy to track. I don't need one now. I *can't* use one. Improvise, Andrew. This is for your daughter."

He grabbed a slotted screwdriver and he gazed at it, like an artist marveling at his magnum opus. *What can I do with this?*–he thought. He threw it into the bag before his mind could run wild. He didn't want to be dissuaded by thoughts of extreme violence. He didn't really have a plan after all. He only knew he was going to hurt someone.

He filled a bag with a claw hammer, a wrench, a tape measure, and a small bottle of motor oil. He went to a locker in the corner. He took out a hand cultivator, a pair of titanium shears, a box cutter, and some rolls of duct tape. He rushed to the minivan, then he stopped. He took a step back and looked at the workbench again. He stared at a hacksaw on the wall above the table.

He thought: *what can I do with that? I can scare him with it. Yeah, if I can pull it off, I can make him talk without touching him. And if I have to use it, if he knows something and I HAVE to use it... I can cut him. I can...*

His thoughts were interrupted by the sound of the door hinges squealing behind him. He found his son standing in the doorway.

"Dad," Max said.

Andrew looked away from him. He couldn't face his son knowing he was planning on hurting someone to find Grace.

"What is it?" Andrew asked.

"Mom is... she's looking for you."

"Yeah? Um... What does she want?"

"We're gonna make a video. She said it's for the news. Like, to ask for more help and to... to find... to find..."

Max couldn't say his sister's name. He sniffled and trembled. A vein stuck out of his forehead. *Say something, idiot!*–he yelled at himself in his head.

Andrew said, "I'm busy, Max. Ask me again tomorrow or the next day. I have to go now."

"Whe–Where?"

"I'm going to look for your sister."

"Can I... Can I come?"

Andrew glanced over his shoulder, but he still avoided eye contact with his son. He started to shudder, too. He couldn't find his daughter and he couldn't help his son. He felt like the worst father on earth.

He said, "You can't."

Tears sprinkling out of his eyes and voice cracking, Max asked, "Because you hate me?"

"No... *No,* Max, I don't hate you. I could never hate you. Please don't talk like that. Don't... Don't blame yourself for any of this. I love you, buddy."

"Then why... why... why aren't you looking at me?"

Andrew grunted and coughed as his throat tightened. He looked away and breathed shakily. He heard the tools *clinking* in his bag. *For Grace,* he told himself.

He said, "Be a big boy for me and take care of your mother while I'm gone. She needs you, buddy. I love you."

"I–I love you, too," Max stuttered.

Andrew climbed into the minivan. He threw his bag on the passenger seat, then he reversed out of the garage. Max watched his father leave while contemplating the sincerity behind his words. He wiped the tears off his face and headed back into the house.

Chapter Fourteen

For Grace

The sun set behind the two-story apartment building, which resembled a roadside motel, setting the sky ablaze with reds and oranges and purples. Some children ran around in the parking lot, lost in their world of make-believe, while a few teenagers loitered at the corner near the building. A driver honked at the kids, eager to get home after a long day's work.

Diego Cavazos got off a bus down the street, a plastic bag with an oyster pail, a fortune cookie, and a bottle of Coke in his left hand. His wrinkled face, peppered with a few days' worth of stubble, drooped down. He was always frowning—always depressed. His navy coveralls were loose over his lanky figure. He ran his fingers through his thinning, graying hair, then he trudged down the sidewalk.

"It's you," Andrew said as he watched him from his van from across the street. "Yes, yeah, it's you. I remember your picture, you fucking pervert. You're Diego Cavazos. You're a *fucking* rapist, walking around like you own the place. Don't you dare touch any of those kids. I'll kill you right in that parking lot if you do. I'll really do it, man. Don't test me."

He leaned forward to get a better view of him. Diego lumbered into the parking lot. He ignored the kids—and they avoided him. He waved at an older woman on the first floor. She stood near her open front door, phone to her ear. She was gossiping with an old friend while watching the kids. The woman just gave him a nod—*hey.* She watched him with a set of cautious eyes for a few seconds, then she continued her call.

Diego's neighbors knew about his past because he was required to tell them about his crimes when he first moved in. He wasn't forgiven for his crimes, but many of his neighbors learned to accept him. It had been fifteen years since he was released from prison, and he hadn't recidivated since then. They were cautious around him, but they weren't going to surround his apartment with pitchforks or throw molotov cocktails through his window.

Diego went up the stairs. He entered the first apartment—*201.* He had a neighbor to his right and a neighbor below him. The woman on the phone stood in front of the apartment below Diego's. She liked to gossip, but she didn't seem like the nosy, intrusive type. She wasn't going to bang on his door if she heard a loud noise. She was friendly, it was part of her nature, but she really didn't want anything to do with him. Diego's next-door neighbor wasn't home, either. In fact, the apartment looked vacant.

Andrew said, "Okay, okay. I can't let anyone see me. I have to wait until the kids go inside. I'll go out there as soon as they go inside. I *will* do it. I will... I will..."

He kept saying it, hoping it would build up his courage. In the span of forty-five minutes, the oranges were replaced by the reds, then the reds by the purples, and then the sky was pitch-black. The stars weren't visible, just a waxing crescent moon— a white slit on a black canvas. Only the lampposts illuminated the street. One of the crosswalks down the street was completely obscured by the darkness.

Andrew sat motionless, eyes glued to the bag on the passenger seat. He questioned his intentions, his goal, and his morals. One questioned dominated his mind: *how far can you go, Andrew?* He once shoved someone in college, but he never caused bodily harm to anyone and he never tried to kill anyone before. He wasn't a violent man.

"Your daughter needs you," he said. "You're supposed to protect her from the bad guys. *He* is one of those bad guys. He's a rapist, a child molester, a monster. You have to do this."

He grabbed his bag and climbed out of the car. He jogged across the street. From the parking lot, he could hear loud Spanish music and children screaming with excitement from the apartment below Diego's. The noise calmed his nerves. He made his way upstairs. He stopped in front of the door. He adjusted his cap, then he drew a deep breath.

He pressed the doorbell. He heard the muffled ringing in the apartment from outside. A set of footsteps followed. Sweat seeped past his cap's sweatband, rolling down to his eyebrows. He felt lightheaded and nauseous. He held his breath without realizing it. He counted the passing seconds, but he lost count after three.

The door swung open.

Crumbs of a fortune cookie stuck in his goatee, Diego asked, "Can I help you?"

Andrew exhaled slowly through his nose. Lying through his teeth, he said, "My name is Michael...

Johnson. I work for Fred's Insurance. I was wondering if you could spare a minute to talk about your insurance plan and a couple of offers I might have lined up for you."

"Insurance?"

"Yes, sir. Are you happy with your current insurance?"

"What are we talking here? Health insurance? I get that from my employer. Car insurance? I don't got a car, pal, so I don't need it."

"How about life insurance?"

Diego shrugged and asked, "What about it?"

Andrew could tell he wasn't convincing him with his lies. He regretted his slapdash actions. He barreled towards him head-first without a thorough plan.

He said, "For just two dollars a day, more or less, you can get yourself a *$250,000* life insurance policy. Now, I'm not a pessimist, but on the off chance of a premature death, a death benefit would greatly help your family."

"Don't have one," Diego said.

"Oh, you, um… you live alone?"

"I live alone and I want to be left alone. I ain't buying what you're selling, pal."

Just as Diego went to shut the door, Andrew put his foot in the doorway. Diego cocked his head back. He ran his eyes over Andrew's body. The baseball cap caught his attention—*interesting fashion choice*. He finally noticed the gloves and the bag slung over his shoulder, too. Andrew could have passed as an unprofessional insurance salesman, but Diego was put off by his pushiness.

Andrew said, "Just one minute."

"I told you: I don't need your damn insurance."

"Let's just talk about–"

"You take one step into my home and I'm calling the cops. Now, we're both grown men, I'm not trying to disrespect you or your job or nothing like that, but I'm only counting to five and then I'm making that call. One, two…"

Andrew stuttered, "I–I have an o–offer you should–"

"Three… four…"

An image of Grace's smile—wide, toothless, genuine—flashed before Andrew's very eyes. With a twitchy blink, the image changed. He saw Grace, bound and gagged, in a closet with a set of empty, lifeless eyes. He blacked out for a second. He only heard his daughter's voice in his head.

'Daddy, help!'

He thrust his head forward and smashed his forehead against Diego's chin. Diego's jaw *popped* and Andrew's hat spiraled into the air like a leaf falling from a tree. His glasses snapped in half and fell to the floor. Luckily, he didn't have the perfect vision, but he wasn't blind without them.

The men teetered away from each other. Diego staggered into his living room, legs wobbling underneath him with each step. Andrew fell back against the handrail behind him. He leaned to his left, then he lost his balance and fell to the floor. He grabbed his hat and put it on while muttering to himself—*oh fuck, oh shit.* He grabbed his broken glasses and shoved the pieces into his back pocket. He quickly struggled to his feet, lurching his way into the apartment.

He found Diego leaning against his sofa, rubbing his jaw and mumbling incoherently. A string of slimy blood hung from his bottom lip. An episode of *Breaking Bad* played on the flatscreen television, Walter White begging for his life at gunpoint. Andrew closed and locked the door behind him. He leaned back against it to stay on his feet. He swung left and right while the world thrummed around him.

He stuttered, "I–I need answers. I'm looking for–" Diego stumbled around the sofa. He reached for the cellphone on his coffee table. Andrew yelled, "Stop! Don't move!"

He ran forward. His bag got caught on the lamp on the end table. It opened and the tools spilled out, landing on the sofa and floor with *thuds* and *clanks.* Diego dived towards the coffee table. He landed on his knees beside it. He hit it with his chest, causing it to glide across the floorboards. The empty oyster pail fell from the table. He grabbed his cell phone.

Andrew grabbed Diego's shoulder in one hand and swung down at the back of his head with the other. He threw five jabs, but it wasn't enough to daze him. Diego unlocked his phone and opened the 'phone' app while trying to crawl away. Andrew hit the side of his head with a hook, throwing all of his weight behind the punch.

Diego heard a *buzzing* sound in his right ear. He dialed 912. He deleted the 2, then he tapped 4 by accident—914.

Andrew yelled, "Stop it, damn it!"

He struck him with another hook. Diego's right ear turned crimson. He screamed and tried to pull away, then the collar of his coveralls squeezed his neck, causing him to retch. Andrew hit him with a third hook. His fist landed on Diego's temple. Diego hit the floor face-first. His nose shattered on the floorboard. Blood dripped out of his nostrils, joining the blood on his lips. He snored, knocked unconscious. Andrew kicked his cell phone away. It slid until it reached the kitchen archway.

"Tape, tape, where's the tape?" Andrew muttered, out of breath. The apartment was only lit by the television. He turned on the lamp and scanned the sofa. He whispered, "I put it in the bag, didn't I? Shit, oh shit… I need something… Fuck!"

He glanced around the room, pupils dilated with fear. The apartment was drab and depressing. There were no decorations on the walls—not a single photograph of Diego, his friends, or his family. The furniture was old and damaged, dusty and dirty. The floorboards were scuffed with splinters protruding every which way, like thorns on a rose. It looked like Diego hadn't dusted or broomed since he moved in *years* ago.

Andrew stared down at himself. He took off his tie. He hopped and gasped upon hearing Diego's groan. Diego pushed himself up on all fours.

As he crawled towards his phone, he shouted, "Help! Help! There's a–"

Andrew stood over Diego, one leg on each side of his torso. He threw the tie over his head, then he pulled it back against his neck, using it as a makeshift garotte. Andrew couldn't help but smile, impressed by his actions. *Where the hell did I learn how to do this?*–he thought. The smile vanished as he lost his balance and fell back.

The floorboards rattled as he landed on his back. The wind was knocked out of him, leaving him gasping for air. Diego tried to squirm away, but Andrew pulled back on the tie and choked him again. Diego clawed at his neck while kicking at the furniture. He hit the sofa with enough force to push it a couple of inches. He kicked the coffee table, too. The furniture *screeched* on the floorboards while their bodies *thumped* and *banged*.

Andrew looked back at the floor under him. He thought about the woman and the children in the apartment below them. He glanced at the door. *Please don't knock, please don't knock, please don't knock,* he thought. He placed his legs on top of Diego's shins to stop him from kicking, then he pulled on the tie with all of his might. Diego scratched his neck until he bled from the thin lacerations. He clawed at Andrew's forearms, too, staining his sleeves with his blood.

Through his gritted teeth, Andrew muttered, "Why... won't... you... sleep? Stop it... Stop fighting me, motherfucker. Please... *stop*..."

He tugged on the tie again. Red blotches spread across Diego's neck. His gasps were short and raspy. His eyes bulged from their sockets while his jaw moved from side-to-side, as if he were trying to *pop* it. Gurgling and crackling sounds came out of his throat. The back of his head rested on Andrew's firm chest. He stared at the ceiling, vision invaded by the orange glow of the lamp and the flashing blues from the television.

It felt like an hour had passed since Andrew first wrapped the tie around Diego's neck. In reality, it had only been four minutes and thirty-two seconds.

Andrew couldn't tell if Diego was awake, unconscious, or playing possum. He felt him twitch every few seconds. He heard him breathing, too.

Thirty-three seconds, thirty-four seconds, thirty-five seconds, thirty-six seconds... *Five minutes and seven seconds.*

Andrew released his grip on the tie after five minutes and seven seconds. He rolled Diego off him and wheezed to catch his breath. *Shit, Hollywood really makes it look easy,* he thought. He gazed at the ceiling with a look that said: *what am I doing here?* Then he heard Diego's weak coughing and gasping. There was no turning back.

He spotted a roll of duct tape under the end table beside the sofa. He grabbed it and rose to his feet. He towered over Diego, watching him squirm and groan between the sofa and the coffee table. He taped his legs together at the ankles and shins, then he taped his arms together at the wrists—*five* times over. He slapped a strip of duct tape over Diego's mouth.

He slapped Diego's cheek and, still out of breath, he said, "I'll take... it off after you... after you agree to cooperate. I need cooperation, o–okay? Do you understand me?" Diego snorted as he struggled to breathe through the blood leaking out of his nose. Andrew said, "You need to... to sit up so you won't suffocate. Don't fight me, okay? Don't do it."

He sat him up and pushed him back against the sofa. Then he hooked his arms under Diego's armpits and lifted him from the floor. He threw him onto the sofa. Diego found himself sitting in the middle seat. Due to the auto-play feature on Netflix, the next Episode of Breaking Bad played on the television— *Box Cutter*.

Andrew raised the volume until the voices on the TV *boomed* through the apartment. He hoped it would mask the noise in the room. Then he lowered it as he thought about the neighbor downstairs. He didn't want her to complain about the noise. It seemed likely since the clock was ticking towards ten o'clock and there were kids in her home.

He rushed to the front door and peeked through the peephole. He didn't see anyone in the exterior hallway or the parking lot below. He breathed a sigh of relief. He went back and sat on the coffee table in front of Diego. Andrew looked desperate, scared but determined. Diego looked drowsy, eyes wandering every which way.

Andrew said, "I know who you are. Diego Cavazos. Forty-seven years old. Rapist. *Child molester.*"

Diego finally looked at Andrew, his head shaking in disbelief. He tried to say something, but his voice was muffled by the bloodstained tape. Tears glistened in his eyes. Andrew thought: *does he feel regret or is it just the pain?* He was sickened by his thoughts. He didn't want to feel bad for him, but he did. Tears materialized in his eyes, too.

Andrew said, "I can take the tape off your mouth as long as you *don't* scream. Okay?"

Diego nodded reluctantly. Andrew glanced at the front door again. He leaned forward and pinched the corner of the tape. After another deep breath, he slowly pulled it off. He left it dangling from his cheek. Diego shuddered and panted, like a sick dog. A coat of sweat covered his face and neck. He was afraid his worst nightmare came true: *vigilante justice.*

And he was right.

Diego stammered, "I–I–I did–didn't... I was–was... Pl–Please don't do this. It was a–a long time ago. I–I apologized and they forga–"

"I'm not here to talk about your past," Andrew interrupted. "I'm here to talk about the present. My da..."

My daughter, Grace McCarthy—he stopped himself from saying those words. He didn't plan on killing him, so if he wasn't involved in Grace's abduction, he didn't want Diego to report him so easily.

'It was Grace McCarthy's father! He broke into my home and did this to me!'

Andrew asked, "Do you really live alone?"

"Y–Yes."

"No one else is in the apartment?"

"N–No..."

"You're not hiding anyone, are you?"

Diego shrugged and asked, "What are you talking about?"

Andrew walked over to the archway and peeked into the kitchen. There was a stack of dirty dishes in the sink. He looked down the hall behind the sofa. He counted three doors. He threw his tools into his bag, but he kept the hammer in his hand. He slapped the tape over Diego's mouth before he could scream.

He hissed, "*Don't move.* If I hear a floorboard, I'm going to... I'm... You don't want to know what I'm going to do to you. Okay?"

Diego swallowed loudly and nodded—*uh-huh*.

Andrew hurried down the hall. He checked the room to his left. It was a bathroom. He turned on the light and pushed the shower curtain aside. The bathtub was empty. He went back into the hall. He could see Diego sitting on the sofa in the living room. He opened the door at the end of the hall. Cardboard boxes and old, tattered coats filled the storage closet. He checked on Diego again. The sex offender trembled and whimpered, but he didn't move.

Andrew entered the room to his right—*the master bedroom*. There was a bed, a nightstand, a dresser, and a desk with an old computer. His internet usage was routinely monitored, so Diego rarely used the computer. There was a pair of rolling closet doors to the right. Andrew remembered the image of Grace he saw before he forced his way into the apartment. He felt his heart pounding against his sternum, climbing up to his throat and suffocating him.

"Grace?" he whispered.

He rolled the door open—shoeboxes, jeans, shirts, coats. Grace wasn't there, but he was alarmed by his discovery. He crouched and squinted at the floor in the closet. He saw something pink sticking out of one of the shoeboxes at the bottom of a stack. He cleared the way, then he removed the lid from the box at the bottom. He found a small pink t-shirt with a faded logo. The child's shirt was covered in black and white stains. It hadn't been washed in years. Under the shirt, he found a pair of blue underwear—*a girl's underwear*.

Andrew whispered, "Christ..."

"Help!" Diego roared from the living room. "Help me! Please!"

"Shit!"

Andrew barreled out of the bedroom. He rushed into the living room. Diego bunny-hopped his way to the front door, tape dangling from his cheek.

"Help!" Diego shouted upon spotting Andrew.

Andrew yelled, "Stop!"

He swung the hammer at him, flailing his limbs as if *he* were under attack. He struck Diego's shoulder two times. He hit his elbow once as Diego recoiled in pain. The blow sent a tingly sensation across his entire arm. Andrew swung the hammer at Diego's head. He struck the right side of his face, shattering his cheekbone while tearing off a chunk of skin. Unconscious, Diego fell against the wall next to the door.

Andrew dropped the hammer and grabbed Diego before he could hit the floor. He dragged him back to the sofa. He looked out the peephole, then out the window. He saw a car driving out of the parking lot. He thought: *Did they hear us? Are they going to the police? No, no, they wouldn't do that. They would have just called them, right?* He sat on the coffee table across from Diego. He examined him while thinking about his mistake.

He realized he would have to hurt Diego and any other suspects to force them to comply. He couldn't intimidate them with his words. His voice wasn't strong enough—not yet. The duct tape around the ankles was effective, but he failed to properly restrain his suspect's arms. He took a mental note: *like the cops, tape their arms up behind their backs so they can't reach for anything*. He stared at the wound on Diego's face. He could see his cheekbone under the dark blood and mushy flesh.

Diego's eyes flickered open. He mumbled and groaned. He reached for the tape over his mouth, but Andrew pressed the hammer against his hands and stopped him.

Andrew said, "Look at me. Look at me, you punk." Diego looked at him, eyes barely open. Andrew said, "You... You are... I saw the shoebox in your closet, Diego. I need you to explain that to me. And I need you to help me find a girl. She's missing now. I'm sure you've seen her on the news. Her name is Grace McCarthy. I was hired to find her. I want you to tell me where she is or what you've heard. I'm going to take the tape off your mouth again. If you scream, if you don't answer me, I'm... I'm going to hurt you."

Andrew removed the tape from Diego's mouth. Diego grimaced in pain as a stabbing headache attacked his temple.

He mumbled, "I didn't... What are you... I can't..."

"Okay, let's start with the children's clothing in your closet. Who does it belong to? And where did you get it?"

"Th–The clo–clothing?"

"The shirt. *The underwear.*"

"N–No, no... That's not what it looks like."

Andrew tapped Diego's hand with the hammer. He asked, "Did you take someone? Did you *hurt* someone?"

"No! It's not what it looks like!"

Diego leaned forward and tried to stand, but Andrew pounced on him. He pressed the tape over Diego's mouth, smothering his screams. He lost control of himself. He swung the hammer down at Diego's hands—*thump, thump, thump!* His bones broke with a loud *crunching* sound. On his left hand, a cut stretched across his knuckles, exposing his bones to the dirty air. Geysers of blood shot out, spreading across his hands and the tape.

The hammer slid out of Andrew's hand. It landed on the floor between the sofa and the coffee table. The sofa moved another inch as they wrestled.

But Andrew wasn't finished. Hungry for blood, the beast within him awoke. He grabbed Diego's index and middle fingers, then he pulled them back until his fingernails touched the back of his hand. The cut across his knuckles widened and blood sprinkled out in every direction. Some of the blood landed on Andrew's shirt and neck. Diego unleashed a long, muffled shriek, then he fell back against his seat. He was conscious but lightheaded.

Andrew stood from the seat. He pulled the titanium shears out of his bag. He wagged the tool at Diego, showcasing his next instrument of torture.

He said, "I'm going to give you another chance. Why do you have a girl's underwear in your closet? Where'd you get it?" He pulled the tape off Diego's mouth. Diego gasped for air while groaning in pain. Andrew slapped him and said, "Answer the question, you sick fuck. Where'd you get that underwear? Did you take a girl? A girl with heterochromia?"

Diego stuttered, "He–He–Heter…"

"Two different eye colors. Did you take her? Did you take her?!"

Diego squirmed on the sofa and sobbed. His face contorted, twisted with guilt and shame and pain. Andrew felt a combination of fear and hope. He feared Diego took Grace from her school to molest her. He hoped Grace was alive and healthy. There was a childish eagerness in his eyes—*tell me what I want to hear.*

"Help!" Diego shouted. "Ple–"

Andrew slapped the wrinkled, bloody tape over Diego's mouth. He hit Diego's stomach with his knee. Diego struggled to draw a satisfying breath. Andrew opened the shears over Diego's right ear. He hesitated for a second, then he squeezed the handles. The blades cut through his ear with ease. The severed ear rolled over Diego's face and landed on the cushion in front of him.

Diego clenched his eyes shut and whimpered. His face turned red, just a shade lighter than the blood cascading over his skin. Blood flooded his ear canal, too, deafening him from one side.

"Why won't you talk?!" Andrew barked.

He grabbed the slotted screwdriver from his bag. He thrust it at Diego's right eye. It sliced his eye horizontally, then it slid into his eye socket, wedged between his eyeball and his nose. He wiggled it inside his eye socket, as if he were beating some eggs with a fork. Diego's eyelids snapped shut over the screwdriver's shank. Tears, blood, and a clear slime oozed out. His eyelids turned dark red, dyed by the blood. The tape wrinkled and fluttered as he tried to open his mouth.

The muscles attached to his eye tore with a *shredding* sound. A piece of his severed eye slid out from between his eyelids. It looked like hard-boiled egg whites covered in hot sauce. Jolts of pain surged through Diego's skull. He felt like his brain was about to explode. He was deaf and blind on one side. He couldn't see anyway because he couldn't open his eyes. His survival instincts told him to keep his eyes shut.

'If you can't see it, it's not really happening.'

Andrew staggered back until the back of his legs touched the coffee table. He felt like his intestines were twisting and turning over each other. He covered his mouth with his forearm and breathed deeply through his nose. He looked away and dry-heaved, but it wasn't enough. Diego's cries of agony made him sick. He couldn't hold it. He puked in his mouth, but he swallowed it before it could burst out.

"God, what am I doing?" he whispered.

He was desperate, he would do anything to rescue his daughter, but he wasn't a sadist. It was impossible to ease into something like that. He examined his victim's injuries, disgusted by the gore—and himself. From his severed ear to his mutilated eye, from his broken cheekbone to his shattered nose, Diego's entire face was covered in blood. He was unrecognizable. His hands were broken and swollen, red and blue.

I did that, I'm the monster, Andrew thought. He imagined Grace in the same position, bloody and beaten. He was running out of time. He inched forward and leaned over the sofa. He grabbed Diego's chin and moved his head, forcing the sex offender to face him. The screwdriver still stuck out of Diego's eye socket.

Andrew said, "We can end this. I don't have to... I don't have to hurt you anymore. Tell me about the underwear. Tell me about Grace. Then I'll let you go. I'll call an ambulance and I'll walk out of here. Okay? Can you please—*please*—do that for me, Diego? I–I'm... I'm begging you here, man."

Diego didn't respond. He shivered, overwhelmed by the pain. Andrew removed the tape from his mouth. He didn't take his fingers off it, though. He expected Diego to scream. Only the voices on the TV continued to play through the apartment.

Diego stuttered, "A–A guy... A guy sold 'em to me on the... the internet. They came from a... a girl. I didn't do it. I didn't take nothing... from no one. Not me... I didn't take no one..."

"Which girl? Which girl did this 'guy' get that clothing from? *Answer me.*"

"I–I don't know."

"You do know. Which girl, Diego? Was it the girl from the news? Was it Grace McCarthy?"

"I–I don't... know," Diego said with a weak voice.

Andrew shook him and said, "Hey, don't sleep. Don't sleep, you bastard." Diego fell unconscious. Andrew slapped him and yelled, "Don't sleep! Was it my girl? Was it my girl?! Answer me!"

Diego didn't awaken. Andrew slapped him again. The whack was so loud that it could be heard in the neighboring apartments. The blood on his face splattered on Andrew's shirt and jeans. He slapped him a third time. He hit him with so much force that he feared he broke his palm. Blood foamed out of Diego's mouth. He remained unconscious.

"Goddammit!" Andrew yelled.

He looked at the door, then at the floor. It was only a matter of time before a nosy neighbor or a cop showed up. He glanced back at the television. In the scene, Gus Fring, a ruthless drug kingpin, slit a man's throat to set an example. It was a bloody, grotesque scene. Andrew looked back at Diego. He stared at his bloody face first, then his eyes wandered down to his neck.

Teary-eyed, Andrew whispered, "He's a pedophile. He's a rapist. He has a girl's clothes in his closet. His friend could have touched Grace. He could have her locked up in a basement or an attic or a closet. They're still hurting kids. They deserve to die. No witnesses… No witnesses until I find Grace…"

He took the box cutter out of his bag. The blade shot out with five *clicks.* He knelt on the couch beside Diego's body. He watched him snore for a few seconds. He held the blade up to Diego's neck. His hand trembled, so the blade nicked his neck. His tears plopped on the cushion. He doubted himself, then he thought about his daughter and all of Diego's victims.

He repeated, "They deserve to die."

Andrew pushed the blade into the side of Diego's neck. Diego grinded his teeth under the tape, his face twisting in pain. Andrew's teeth chattered as he slowly dragged the blade towards the center of Diego's neck—*millimeter*-by-*millimeter.* He was shocked by his own actions. Like an out-of-body experience, he felt like he was standing in the corner of the room watching someone else slit Diego's throat.

Unable to control his trembling hand, Andrew inadvertently widened the cut. Deep in the wound, the blood looked black.

Andrew pulled the blade out as a column of blood sprayed out of Diego's neck. Then the blood shot out in spurts, slower but plentiful. It was more blood than he had ever seen in his life. He had nicked Diego's external jugular. Death was certain without proper medical attention. Andrew thought about using his tie as a tourniquet, but he couldn't leave any evidence behind. He ran into the kitchen. He yanked a small towel out from under a stack of plates, then he ran out.

The plates shattered on the floor, but the explosive noise didn't bother him. He *wanted* the neighbors to hear it. He didn't want Diego to die anymore.

He slid to a stop in front of the sofa. He wrapped the towel around Diego's neck with enough pressure to slow the bleeding but not enough to suffocate him. He grabbed the handle of the screwdriver, but he hesitated. He feared Diego would go into shock if he endured anymore pain. But he couldn't leave any evidence behind. That was out of the question.

He said, "I'm sorry. I should have never come here. I'm so sorry."

Andrew pulled the screwdriver out with one tug. Bloody slime dripped from the blade. He threw it into his bag with his other blood-soaked tools. Laying on his side, Diego rocked back and forth, moaning and snorting. Andrew gathered his supplies. He scanned the floor once, twice, and then a third time. He didn't see any of his belongings. He could see the bill of his cap, but he still touched it to make sure it was on his head. He was ready to go.

He pulled the TV off the entertainment center. The living room floor—from wall-to-wall—rumbled as the TV crashed into it. *That's enough noise,* he thought, *but I have to be sure.* He yanked the tape off Diego's mouth, tearing some of his facial hair off in the process. He hoped he would regain consciousness and scream at some point.

Andrew exited the apartment without closing the door. He slipped and slid in the exterior hallway due to the blood on his soles, unwittingly leaving a trail of bloody footprints behind him. He stumbled down the stairs, then he sprinted through a patch of grass. The moist lawn and mud wiped the blood off his shoes. He took off his gloves before getting into the van, then he sped away before anyone could see him.

Chapter Fifteen

The Aftermath

At half-past eleven, Andrew arrived home. He sighed in relief. He didn't see any cars parked in the driveway or in front of his house. *The in-laws are gone,* he thought. He parked in the garage. He opened the driver's door, then he stopped. The dome light in the van illuminated the blood on his shirt. There were crusty, crimson specks on his slacks, too.

"Oh shit, oh no," he muttered. He looked at the garage door through the windshield. He whispered, "Don't come out. Please don't come out."

He undressed himself in the driver's seat, his knees hitting the steering wheel and his elbow hitting the door. He took off his shoes after spotting some drops of blood on them. He wrapped his shirt and pants around the shoes. He sat there in a tank top, boxer briefs, and socks, trying to think of an excuse for his missing clothes if someone saw him.

'I spilled some coffee, so I went to the dry cleaners. I was robbed. I'm too hot for clothes because I'm on drugs. I'm having an affair and my mistress took my clothes.'

He climbed out of the van with his clothes and his bag of tools. He hid the bag in a storage container next to the washing machine in the corner of the room. He considered washing his clothes, but he didn't want to make any noise and he was afraid it didn't matter. *Technology is getting better,* he thought, *even if I get the stains out, they'll still find his DNA.*

He stuffed the clothes in a plastic bag. He entered the house through the garage door. He stood in the hallway, waiting for Holly to march towards him and berate him for his absence. But he didn't hear anyone in the house. All of the lights were off, too. He crept down the hall and made his way into the living room. There was no one there.

He looked up at the ceiling and listened for any creaks or howls from the floorboards. *Silence*—dead silence smothered the home.

He tiptoed up the stairs, the bag rustling in his arms. He peeked into each room until he reached the end of the hall. The bathroom, Grace's bedroom, Max's bedroom, and his home office were empty. He went into the master bedroom. He approached the closet. *No, too obvious, she always goes in there,* he thought. He opened a drawer on the dresser. *No, no, what if she opens one of mine and finds it?*—he thought.

He glanced around the room and searched for the perfect hiding place. His eyes stopped on the bed. Since Grace's disappearance, Holly slept for about four hours a night—six with medication. She spent most of her days searching for Grace, calling investigators, and contacting the media about her reward. Andrew couldn't remember the last time Holly checked under the bed for anything. It was the perfect hiding place.

He hid the bag of clothes under his side of the bed. He planned on moving it as soon as the opportunity presented itself.

Andrew went to the bathroom. He stared at his reflection in the mirror, awed. Blood was smeared on his cheeks and neck, pinkish-red against his pale skin. Some blood crusted over on his beard, too. He smiled, amused by the thought. He took off his clothes in hopes of hiding his actions from his family if they were home, but the blood on his face told tales of violence.

He climbed into a hot shower. He used a shower scrub to wash the blood away. He scrubbed himself until his neck and cheeks turned red. He shampooed his beard once, twice, *thrice.* It wasn't good enough. He increased the heat. The scalding water burned his skin, leading to rosy, painful patches across his body, but he didn't feel it.

Instead, his palms turned numb while his knuckles ached. In his right ear, his hearing faded in-and-out. His right eye stung and his eyelids twitched. He felt his brain *thumping* against his skull. Projectile vomit, orange and chunky, burst out of his mouth and splattered on the wall in front of him. It cascaded slowly to the bathtub faucet.

Andrew fell to his ass and stared vacantly ahead. He held his hands over his face and sobbed as the scalding water rained down on him.

"What did I do? What did I do?!" he yelled with his hands over his face. He dug his fingers into his thick hair, then he started tugging on it. He cried, "I killed him! I killed him and I didn't find her! Oh God, I couldn't... I couldn't find my baby... I'm useless... I'm a fuck-up... I fucked up! I killed him for no reason! God, why did I go there? Why?! *Why?!*"

He spent ten minutes screaming and weeping in the shower. Then he sprayed the vomit off the wall with the showerhead. A thick clump of vomit blocked the drain. He picked it up with a piece of toilet paper and flushed it down the toilet. He put his clothes in the laundry hamper next to the shower. He covered his body in a bathrobe.

He looked at himself in the mirror again. He was red from head-to-toe, like a newborn baby. His eyes were bloodshot, shining with tears. And his nose was as red as a cherry, like Rudolph's. He saw a fragile, submissive, cowardly man in the mirror. He saw a violent, psychopathic killer, too. He saw a man standing at the crossroads.

Andrew walked out of the bathroom. He took two steps to his left, then he stopped. Holly came out of Max's bedroom. She closed the door behind her. Their eyes met, then they looked away. Andrew thought: *did she hear me screaming? Does she know what I did?* Holly crossed her arms and looked at the floor.

Andrew asked, "When did you get in?"

"Just a minute ago."

"A minute ago? Like... Like an actual minute ago?"

Holly furrowed her brow and said, "Yeah, like an *actual* minute ago. I just tucked Max into bed and kissed him goodnight." She stepped aside and beckoned to him. She asked, "You want to see him?"

"No. I mean, *yes,* but... no, he should sleep. He's been through a lot. He needs his rest, you know? We all need some rest."

There was a long silence.

Holly said, "I'm going to be on TV again. Radio, too."

"Yeah? How's that going?"

"Well, we don't have to pay anyone yet, but Detective Booth tells me they've been getting more tips since we started talking about the reward. I'm trying to be… optimistic."

Andrew held his tongue. Tips were great—when they led to results. Otherwise, an inaccurate tip was nothing more than a distraction. He saw his wife as an interference to the official investigation, but he appreciated her effort. He didn't want to extinguish her optimism. He forced a smile and nodded—*good for you.* He tried to move past her, but Holly stood her ground.

She asked, "So, where were you?"

"Wha–What?" Andrew stuttered.

"Earlier today, I asked Max to find you. He said you went out to look for Grace. He looked like he was–"

"So, Max already told you what I was doing. Why do you have to ask?"

Holly could see he was feeling defensive. She said, "I didn't ask *what,* I asked *where.* Where were you, Andrew?"

"I was just… I went out there and I searched for Grace. I went downtown, I visited the parks, I searched the woods. I'm sorry I couldn't stay for your video. I think it's a great idea, I'm glad you're optimistic, but I feel like I need to be out *there*, Holly. I don't want to talk to reporters. I'm tired of talking to washed-up detectives. I just want to find Grace."

Holly sniffled and swiped at her nose. A tear tickled her cheek, but it couldn't put a smile on her face.

She said, "The woods... She's not out there."

"I don't know where she is, but–"

"She's *not* out there," Holly interrupted with a stern but pained voice. "If you found anything out there, you'd find... you'd find a body. I don't want you to look for a dead body. She's alive, Andrew. I feel it. Right here, in my heart. As long as her heart's still beating, my heart will, too."

Andrew gritted his teeth, held his breath, and nodded. He wanted to fall into Holly's arms and cry in her bosom.

Holly sniffled again, then she said, "Grace needs us. And we need each other. I know things haven't..." She closed her eyes and put her hand over her mouth. She took a moment to compose herself. She said, "I know things haven't been the best between us. I know you hate me."

"I don't hate you."

As if she didn't hear him, Holly continued, "And maybe I hate you, too. But that doesn't mean we can't be there for each other. I can't force you to be in our videos or do interviews with reporters, but... please don't block me out. Don't let it end like this. Please."

Andrew couldn't find the words to express himself. He kept thinking about Grace and Diego. He saw a small, cold, pale dead body and a slender, bloody, mutilated body.

He said, "I'm going to find her. And everything's going to be okay. I promise." As he walked past her, he said, "I'm going to bed. I love you, Holly."

Holly didn't say another word or spare another glance. She listened to his footsteps. As soon as the bedroom door closed behind her, she leaned against the wall and sobbed into her hand. Depression poisoned her mind and crippled her resolve. She didn't realize Andrew was fighting his own inner demons as well. He cried himself to sleep without making a sound.

***

Five days had passed since Andrew attacked Diego. The home invasion was reported on the news. The downstairs neighbor, Lupita Espinoza, had called the police shortly after Andrew departed from the apartment. Diego was found unresponsive. Thanks to the officers' first aid, he survived the drive to the hospital. He was placed in a medically-induced coma after multiple surgeries. The doctors were expected to awaken him in two weeks.

Andrew marked his calendar and counted each second. He expected Booth to question him about the home invasion sooner or later. The day after the attack, while Holly and Max were at a news station, he buried his bag of bloodstained clothing in the backyard. But he didn't touch the bag of tools in the storage container. He hated himself for attacking Diego, but he wasn't ready to end his investigation.

He spent those days trudging through the house in a bathrobe, depressed and high-strung. He barely spoke to Holly or Max, and he avoided every visitor.

He didn't get out of bed until he heard them leave. Home alone, he sat in the living room and watched the news while keeping his eyes on the front and back doors. He expected Booth to knock. If not, he expected stun grenades to smash through his windows and SWAT members to kick his doors down, like something from a movie.

But no one ever knocked.

His neighbors united around Holly and Max. They cared about Andrew, but they didn't know how to help him. *How can you help someone who isn't seeking help?*

Andrew flipped through the channels. The mainstream news outlets discussed the ongoing impeachment trial of the President of the United States. Some fearmongering organizations spoke about the Chinese coronavirus, counting each death with a sense of faux sadness. *'Oh, there goes another one. Boo-hoo. Are you next?'* The news also covered the typical celebrity gossip and daily outrage.

The local news channels focused on traffic, weather, crime, and politics. But Grace wasn't mentioned. She was last week's news, brushed under the rug like a charismatic actor's dirty deeds.

Andrew said, "My girl is still missing. My wife, my son... They're begging you for help. Instead, you're talking about the same old *shit* every day. You'll talk about her for five minutes, right? Between the *bullshit* politics and the *fearmongering*, right? But... But when she shows up, you'll act like you saved her, huh? No, no. If she turns up... turns up de... If she turns up dead, you'll find a way to blame us. You trade blood for ratings. You're monsters. You're monsters!"

He threw the remote at the television. The remote hit the wall above the entertainment center. It shattered, batteries and plastic flying through the room. The news kept playing. A reporter talked about this year's Superbowl commercials, something about a dead 'peanut' causing controversy on social media.

Andrew huffed and smiled. The absurdity of life struck him. In his bathrobe, he went to the store to buy a new remote.

Chapter Sixteen

Devastation

Andrew and Holly sat at a conference table, side-by-side. Andrew's unkempt beard stuck out in every direction. He finally showered and dressed himself. Like his daughter's heterochromia, his eyes differed from each other. One eye was bright and hopeful, the other was lusterless and dejected. Beads of sweat glimmered on his forehead, but the room was cool.

Holly shuddered. She repeatedly tapped her feet against the floor and her fingers against the table. She stared at the door—waiting, waiting, *waiting*. It had only been ten minutes since they were escorted into the conference room, but it felt like ten long, dreadful days. Every second mattered when it came to finding Grace. And every second in that room was wasted.

Andrew was afraid of being questioned about the home invasion. Holly feared they were called to the station to identify a body—a cold, dead body.

Andrew grabbed her hand and said, "Everything's going to be okay."

Holly kept her eyes on the door. Andrew felt her fingers moving in his hand. She was still trying to tap the table. She acted as if she didn't feel him. It was only her and the door. Andrew sighed and released her hand. Their love had withered away. They couldn't find any comfort in each other. Another three minutes passed at a snail's pace.

Detective Booth entered the room with a thick folder. He said, "Sorry to keep you waiting. You arrived sooner than I expected."

"You said it was about our daughter, of course we're going to rush down here," Holly said.

"I understand," Booth said as he sat at the end of the table near the couple. He tapped the folder in front of him and said, "So, let's not keep you waiting any longer. I have photos in this folder. I'm going to ask you to–"

"Oh God," Holly interrupted, rivers of tears flowing down her blushed cheeks. "Did you find her? Was she hurt?"

"The photos are–"

"Did–Did he kill her? Please, don't tell me she's dead. Not now, not like this. She–She's alive, isn't she? She has to be. She has–"

"Let him speak, Holly," Andrew interrupted.

Booth noticed the anger in Andrew's voice. He figured they were having marital issues. He had seen it all before. Missing kids either strengthened a family or destroyed them. He saw a couple crumbling before his very eyes. But he wasn't there to act as a marriage counselor.

Holly took a handkerchief out of her bag and wiped her face. Andrew nodded at Booth, signaling him to continue.

Booth said, "These are photos of evidence we've discovered since Grace's disappearance. We're talking clothing, accessories, and the like. You may be alarmed by some of these images, but I need you to examine them thoroughly and I need you to tell me if any of it belongs to Grace. It's very important that you take your time and you answer honestly. Are you ready?"

Holly stammered, "I–I–I'm ready."

Andrew just nodded.

Booth opened the folder. He placed a photo on the table and slid it towards the couple. The image showed a child's blue baseball cap, tattered and stained with dirt.

Holly said, "No."

Andrew shook his head and said, "No."

Booth placed the photo beside the folder—*the 'no' pile*. He slid another photo towards the couple. The picture showed a long-sleeve striped shirt. Again, the garment was threadbare and dirty.

Holly swallowed loudly, then she shook her head and said, "No. She was wearing a… a long-sleeve shirt, but it didn't have any stripes on it. There was a small unicorn on the front. It was… It was small, you know? Like the Ralph Lauren logo on their shirts. But it was a unicorn. She loved unicorns and princesses and all that stuff."

Booth said, "Mr. McCarthy?"

Andrew pushed his tongue against the side of his mouth as he examined the photo. He couldn't remember what Grace was wearing on the day of her disappearance. *I'm an awful father,* he thought. He trusted Holly's memory and her motherly instincts. He couldn't remember ever seeing Grace in a striped shirt anyway.

He said, "No. No, it's not hers."

Booth placed it in the 'no' pile. He slid the third photograph towards them. Their eyes widened. It was a baby blue backpack. It was covered in mud and dirt, as if it had been buried in the woods. Holly blinked rapidly while Andrew leaned closer to the photograph, as if their actions would somehow make the image clearer. They stared at it for a minute, speechless.

Holly said, "N–No..."

"Are you sure about that, ma'am?" Booth asked.

"I–I'm positive."

"Do you want to take another minute to–"

"*I'm positive,*" Holly interrupted with a loud but shaky voice. "Grace has a blue backpack, but it–it's darker than that. This is baby blue. Grace likes blue. Regular. Blue. That is *not* her backpack. I'm positive."

Booth looked at Andrew and said, "Mr. McCarthy?"

Andrew lifted the photo from the table. He scanned it again and again—*and again.* He knew Grace's favorite colors were pink and blue. But, in that picture, he couldn't tell the difference between baby blue and 'regular' blue.

Bottom lip shaking, he said, "I don't know."

"It's not hers, Andrew," Holly snapped as she glared at him.

"I don't know…"

"It's not! Look at it again! It's–"

Booth raised his hands and yelled, "Okay, okay!" He placed the photograph beside the 'no' pile. He said, "I'll put it in the 'maybe' pile. We'll examine it again."

Holly rolled her eyes and rubbed her forehead, frustrated by Andrew's answer. Andrew wrestled with his emotions, fighting the urge to sob. He sucked it up and nodded at the detective—*keep going.*

The couple looked at pictures of socks, earrings, sweaters, and jeans. They were even shown a broken Nintendo Switch console. They didn't recognize any of it. The truth was: most of the belongings came from another missing child in the area—*Liam Hansen.* The police hadn't connected the pieces yet.

Andrew leaned back and drew a sharp breath. A photograph of a dirty pink shirt sat before him. It was the same shirt from Diego's apartment. Holly answered Booth with confidence—*no*—but Andrew didn't hear her. He was deafened by the shock. An image of Diego's mutilated face flashed in his mind.

Booth asked, "Mr. McCarthy, do you recognize this garment?"

Andrew opened his mouth to speak, but he couldn't say a single word. So, he clenched his jaw and shook his head. The detective slid a picture of a girl's underwear towards them. Again, Andrew recognized it from Diego's apartment.

"No," Holly said. "That's not hers."

"N–No," Andrew croaked out.

Booth said, "Okay. Those are all of the pictures I have for you today. I know it was tough, but you did great."

Holly asked, "Where did you find all of that? Do you have a suspect? Are you getting close to finding Grace?"

"I can't get into the specifics."

"Oh, come on. *Please,* detective, it's been over two weeks since I've seen my baby. Give me hope. Give me something."

Booth sighed, then he said, "Mrs. McCarthy, some of this clothing was found in the woods near Rolando Hills. If you remember correctly, we combed through the area several times with volunteers. I'll admit: some of this clothing appears to be years old. Some of it might not have been worn by any children at all. We needed it in the pool to get reliable, honest responses from you—to get your memories working."

"So, this was all just a test? In other words, it was all a waste of time?"

"No, I wouldn't say that. Some of the clothing— and I won't say which so don't ask—was found in multiple crime scenes throughout the city. You helped us narrow down our search."

Diego's apartment, Andrew thought. *Diego was telling the truth. There are other active child molesters. There are other victims. Someone else took Grace.*

"Crime scenes?" Holly repeated, eyes big and fearful. "What does that mean? Is she okay?"

Booth responded, "We have no reason to believe she's been harmed. We haven't found any signs of foul play. We're searching sex offenders who are in violation, those who received high scores in the Static-99R, and other potential suspects. So far, we haven't found a trace of Grace. It's not the best sign, but it gives us hope. And we're not done looking. She's alive. I know it."

Holly thanked him for his work, then she spoke about her reward offer. Andrew replayed Booth's words in his head—*sex offenders, in violation*. Someone knocked on the door. Another detective entered the room.

Booth said, "This is my partner, Detective Tara Duffy. Mrs. McCarthy, would you mind stepping out with her? She has a few questions for you, and I'd like to talk to your husband alone."

Holly glanced at Duffy, then at her husband. Head down, Andrew twiddled his thumbs. Holly cooperated. She exited the conference room and followed Duffy into another office down the hall. Booth and Andrew sat in silence for a moment.

Booth said, "Mr. McCarthy, I should start by saying you're not under arrest. You aren't being detained, either. You are free to leave anytime. The door is open and you know your way to the exit. *But* it would be beneficial for you and your family if you stayed and answered all of my questions honestly. Understood?"

It's about Diego, Andrew told himself. *He suspects me. He knows something. What am I supposed to do? Walk out? No, if I do that, he'll know I'm guilty. Play it cool, Andrew.*

Andrew said, "I understand. What can I help you with?"

"I want to ask you about Grace and your family. We're rewinding this whole thing and starting from the beginning, you understand? Some of these questions may sting, but you have to answer *honestly*."

"Shoot. What is it?"

"What were you doing during Grace's disappearance?"

"I told you already."

"Tell me again."

Andrew said, "I left work early that day. You can ask my boss, Douglas Greenberg. I went to Best Buy on Rose Street and purchased a home surveillance system. Ask 'em and they'll tell you. I had a little back-and-forth with one of their 'geeks' about some home installation service they tried to sell me. Then I went home and installed it myself. That's when Holly called me."

"Okay. How was Holly's school life?"

"What do you mean?"

Booth shrugged and said, "Good grades? Poor attention span? Any bullies?"

"She was... She *is* a bright girl. Her grades were fine. I don't know about her attention span in school, but her teacher never complained. Maybe you should ask her about it. And bullies... She never mentioned it. I mean, I never asked and she never mentioned it. I *should* have asked. I could have done more. But I didn't. That's the truth."

The room became silent again. Booth gave Andrew a minute to calm himself. He didn't want to push him too far.

The detective asked, "How's your relationship with your extended family?'

"Fine, I suppose."

"No angry in-laws? No vengeful brothers? No jealous cousins? Nothing like that?"

"No, no. Believe it or not, my in-laws are great. They love us. They're pouring all of their savings into Holly's reward offer. My mom lives in New York with my older sister, my brother is an expat, and my dad is dead. If you think they had something to do with this, you're wrong."

"And I'd be glad to be wrong," Booth responded. "How was Grace's home life?"

Andrew narrowed his eyes and asked, "What?"

"These are the questions that sting, Mr. McCarthy. Was there ever any abuse in your household? Between yourself and your children or your wife and your children or yourself and your wife?"

And the question stung. Andrew was disgusted and offended by the insinuation. Mouth ajar, he shook his head in disbelief.

Booth said, "Please answer the question."

Andrew said, "There was never *any* abuse in our home. *None.* We... We might look rough now, but we love each other and we love our children. I've never laid a finger on Grace or Max and neither has Holly. This is just... This is sick. Our daughter is missing and *this* is what you're doing?"

"It's part of the job."

"It's bullshit. Get off your ass and find my daughter."

"We're–"

"Are you done with your questions? Because I think I'm done here," Andrew interrupted. He stood up and said, "Get out there and find our daughter, asshole. And *don't* waste our time again."

Booth could only sit there and watch as he marched out of the room. He had been called worse names in the past. Although Holly didn't storm out of the room or insult her, Detective Duffy didn't fare much better with her interview. Holly was just as insulted by the detective's insinuation. The couple didn't share a word during their drive home. They sensed each other's anger, so they knew they were both subjected to the same offensive questions.

At home, Holly went straight to the kitchen and told her father about their meeting at the police station. Annette watched Max and his friends in the backyard. They could hear Holly's shouting, but they tried to ignore it.

Andrew went to his bedroom. Desperation transformed into determination, fear into courage, regret into anger. He sat down at his desk. He compiled a list of sex offenders in violation. He highlighted the sex offenders convicted of exploiting and harming children. There were six names on his new list. One of them was a transient.

"I can find you," he whispered. "I won't let you hurt her..."

The first name on his list read: *Adam Woods*. He was thirty-eight years old. He was convicted of possessing child pornography and attempted kidnapping. (The victim of the latter crime was nineteen years old, although she looked younger to Adam.) Thanks to a plea deal, he only served ten years in prison. He was forced to register as a sex offender for twenty years.

Andrew began researching torture methods. He read about the US government's enhanced interrogation techniques, which were authorized by the George W. Bush administration. As far as he knew, sex offenders didn't have any political or religious goals, but they were *very* good at terrorizing women and children around the world.

He searched for examples of torture in the Bible. He researched torture methods from the Middle Ages and Ancient Rome and *all* of history. He even researched several historical sadists: Vlad the Impaler, Tiberius, Nero, Caligula, Shirō Ishii and Unit 731, Adolf Hitler and the Nazis. Since the beginning of mankind, people had always been awful to each other.

Andrew thought about Diego again. But he didn't feel any remorse or shame for his actions. Instead, he thought about his mistakes. He reconsidered his approach.

"They're not just going to let me walk into their homes," he muttered. He searched 'how to use a lockpick' on YouTube. He said, "I can break in. A cheap lock or an open window. I'll need some practice, but this is... It's doable."

In his notebook, Andrew wrote down a list of supplies. He was ready to spill blood for his family. He was ready to kill for Grace.

Chapter Seventeen

Adam Woods

"I just got home," Adam Woods said as he opened his front door. He held an old but functional flip phone up to his ear. He said, "I already clocked out. You want me to go back, clock in, and work the night shift? I ain't a slave, man... Jerry... Jeremiah, hey, you know that's not what I meant. I just need some sleep, pal."

He closed and locked the door behind him. He pulled the phone away from his ear. His boss, Jeremiah Crews, raised his voice at him.

Adam said, "Okay, okay. Sorry. I... I know... Hey, I know we're not pals. It was just, like... what do you call 'em? A figure of speech? Whatever, I'm sorry. Listen, let me sleep six or seven hours and I'll get back there before sunrise. How does that sound?" He stood in silence and listened to Jeremiah's rant. He said, "And I appreciate you giving me this job. I really do. Come on, Jeremiah, give me a break."

Jeremiah spoke about Adam's performance and referenced his criminal past. He threatened to fire him if he didn't show up by sunrise.

Adam said, "I got it... I got you... Thank you very much, boss. I'll be there and I'll give you a hundred and ten percent. Have a nice night, Jer–" Jeremiah hung up. Adam sneered at his phone and muttered, "Asshole."

In the living room, Adam turned on a lamp and the television. An episode of SpongeBob SquarePants was playing. He smiled at the TV, then he went into the bathroom to his left. He took off his orange vest and his blue flannel shirt. Then he washed his large, calloused hands and acne-scarred face. Water dripped from his graying mustache.

He ran his wet fingers across his smooth, bald scalp and said, "Ahh, Adam, you're getting too old for this shit. You can't let this asshole treat you like shit. You got caught with your hands dirty *once*. Not twice, not three times, *once*. You deserve better than this, pal. You should be the boss, not that dumb motherfucker."

He sighed in disappointment, then he smiled at himself in the mirror. He strolled into the kitchen. He took some pans out of the oven and placed them on the stove. He grabbed some uncooked chicken from the refrigerator and a bag of frozen vegetables from the freezer. He turned the knobs while laughing at the show. In the rerun, Squidward was forming his own marching band.

Adam stopped upon hearing a creaky floorboard in the living room. He gasped and staggered as he glanced over his shoulder. A man stood in the archway leading into the living room. He wore coveralls, steel-toe boots, gloves, a ski mask, and a utility belt for security officers—black from head to toe. A large duffel bag was slung over his shoulder. He aimed a stun gun at Adam's abdomen.

Adam stammered, "Wh–Wh–Who a–are you? I don't got any mon–"

The intruder shot him. The prongs penetrated his stomach under the right side of his rib cage. The jolts of electricity surged across his entire body. Adam felt his abs cramping under his fat. His muscles tightened and ached. He leaned back against the stove and glared at the intruder. He slid down to his ass, back against the oven door.

He tried to open his mouth, but his jaw was locked in place. He could only hear the grinding of his teeth. The intruder marched forward. He pulled a wrench out of his bag. Adam raised his arm, palm facing the intruder—*please, don't.* The intruder struck the side of his head with the wrench. The *clank* echoed through the house over SpongeBob's high-pitched laughter. Adam fell to his side, unconscious.

The intruder turned off the stove, then he dragged Adam away from the oven.

***

Adam awoke, vision blurred. He squeezed his eyes shut. A throbbing headache accompanied the stinging pain from the cut on his temple. He felt his warm blood trickling down his cheek. He opened his eyes again, eyelids twitching like a drug addict itching for another hit. He found himself sitting on a dining chair, stripped down to his underwear.

'Hmmm! Hmmm!'

His screaming was muffled by a strip of duct tape over his mouth. He tried to stand up, but he was attached to the chair. His arms were bound at the wrists behind the backrest with zip tie handcuffs. At his ankles, his legs were restrained to the chair's legs with zip tie handcuffs as well. And a piece of thin but durable rope tied his thighs to the seat.

'Hmmm! Hmmm!'

He tried to scream again, but SpongeBob SquarePants and Patrick Star were louder than him. His neighbors couldn't hear him. They were eating dinner or watching television. It would take gunshots to alarm them. He jerked to his left, then to his right. He almost tipped the chair over. Then he heard someone *click* his tongue. He finally looked ahead.

Andrew sat on a dining chair in the archway in front of him with the duffel bag on the floor beside him. He had removed his mask before he moved Adam's body. He wasn't afraid of exposing his identity to him. He wore it in case Adam had arrived with unexpected company. But, like Diego, Adam lived alone—no girlfriend, no wife, no children, no roommates. He was outcasted by society.

Adam tried to say something along the lines of: *who are you?*

Andrew stood up. He walked behind Adam's chair and approached the stove. The pans and pots *clinked* and *clanked* as he rummaged through the oven. Adam yelled again, but his words were incomprehensible. Andrew pulled a saucepan and a stock pot out of the oven. He placed the stock pot on one of the burners and turned a knob on the stove. He returned to his duffel bag and grabbed a gallon of water. He dumped the water into the stock pot.

Muffled by the tape, Adam yelled something like: *what are you doing?!*

Andrew took a box cutter out of his utility belt. He crouched in front of Adam. He grabbed the sex offender's ankle, then he sliced the side of his foot open. He cut him from his big toe to his heel. Adam screamed and convulsed in his seat. The chair screeched across the linoleum tiles. Blood spilled out of the wound in waves, like puke from an infant's mouth. The blood pooled under Adam's foot. Some of it flowed down the grooves between the tiles.

Andrew tightened his grip on Adam's ankle to stop him from moving. He cut the other side of his foot from his heel to his little toe. Adam tapped his foot against the floor. His blood splashed on Andrew's sleeves. The cuts on his foot widened with each frantic tap. His bones were visible in the gashes. Andrew grabbed his foot and pushed it up, forcing his toes to point up at the ceiling. He cut his sole down the center from his hindfoot to his toes.

The wound on his sole stretched instantly, exposing his pulsing muscles. Whites and blues and purples and reds were visible in the cut. Adam felt the skin around the cuts crawling and tingling. He swore he could *see* the screaming nerves in each wide laceration. The puddle of blood under the chair grew, reaching his other foot and the chair's rear legs. The bottoms of his feet were painted red. Some of the blood landed on the top of his feet, too.

Adam screamed, and his shout was intelligible: *God, no!*

Andrew paid him no mind. He saw the steam rising from the stock pot. He heard the water sloshing and bubbling as it boiled. It was time. He placed the pot in front of Adam, then he returned to his seat. He crossed his legs and waited for Adam to stop his sobbing. Adam saw the boiling water in the pot, but he couldn't comprehend the situation. One thought ran through his hazy mind: *is he going to boil me alive?*

Adam stopped screaming after a minute. He breathed deeply through his nose to catch his breath. His mutilated foot trembled in the puddle of blood.

Andrew said, "To you, I bet this looks like a pot of regular, boring boiling water. That, in and of itself, may be frightening to a man in your position. You're probably imagining all of the awful, nasty things I can do to you with this pot. Dip your hands in it, pour it on your bald head or your genitals, force you to swallow it to melt your insides... But it gets worse for you, Mr. Woods. You see, this is not a pot of regular, boring boiling water. This is a pot of regular, boring boiling *salt* water. You ever swim at the beach with a cut?"

Adam's eyes stuck out of their sockets. It didn't take him long to connect the pieces. His feet slid from side-to-side. He jumped, lifting the chair an inch into the air. He groaned in pain as he landed. He unintentionally aggravated the long cut on his sole. But the adrenaline flowing through him helped him fight through the pain. He jumped again, dragging the chair another inch to his right. More blood dripped from his sole. He knew he couldn't get away. He looked at the kitchen window to his left and screamed.

'Hmmm! Hmmm!'

Andrew rushed forward. As if he were sitting on a toilet, he sat on the man's lap to stop him from moving. He felt him shaking and panicking underneath him. He cut the zip tie handcuff around Adam's right ankle. He lifted his leg, then he dragged the pot closer to the chair. He dunked his mutilated foot into the boiling salt water. He nearly lost his balance as Adam writhed violently under him. He felt like he was riding a mechanical bull.

The pot wobbled as Adam's foot shook in the water. The water overflowed, spilling on the floor and mixing with the puddle of blood. Plumes of blood billowed out in the swashing water. The boiling water burned his skin up to his shin. It turned red, then patches of petechiae began to spread, and then his skin blistered. The salt water flowed into every cut. He felt the sting in his muscles and bones. The burning pain followed his veins up his leg, across his abdomen, and straight into his heart.

Two minutes passed. By then, Adam couldn't feel parts of his foot. The partial numbness was terrifying. After three minutes, he felt like his foot had been dismembered. Andrew lost his grip on Adam's leg. Adam managed to pull his foot out of the water and kick the pot over. The bloody water spilled out, rippling like a wave towards the archway. Andrew released his leg. Adam's foot hit the floor. He felt some pain in his leg, but he couldn't feel much in his foot.

Adam's head fell back over the chair's backrest. He gazed at the ceiling, hypnotized by the light. *Why me? Why me? Why me?*—he thought.

Andrew pulled a new zip tie handcuff out of a pocket on his utility belt. He restrained Adam's ankle to the chair's leg again. He walked over to his seat, blood and water splashing with every step. He sat down with his legs crossed. He waited patiently for Adam to recompose himself. The man's red, bloody, sliced, swollen, blistered foot didn't bother him. The violence was now normal to him. This was what he came to do.

***

While Adam snorted, Andrew said, "I'm here to talk about my daughter, Grace McCarthy. I thought you would have seen her on the news, but considering that you seem to watch cartoons all day, that might not be the case. So, let's start from the beginning. My girl, Gracie, she was abducted from her school over two weeks ago. I don't believe my girl— my *beautiful* girl—would have followed an ugly bastard like you. But I believe you know something. You people talk to each other. You share pictures and videos and... and clothing... and all that shit. You must have heard or seen something. You're going to tell me everything you know. If you don't... Well..." He pointed at Adam's scalded, mutilated foot. He said, "Don't scream when I take that tape off your mouth. You already know I mean business."

Andrew moseyed over to him. He grabbed the corner of the tape, then he yanked it off his mouth. It stayed attached to his cheek, dangling down to his shoulder. Patches of his mustache were torn off in the process, stuck on the tape. Adam gasped for air. Eyes tightly shut and lungs full, tears racing down his red face, he opened his mouth as wide as possible. A dry croak escaped his throat. Veins stuck out from his neck and forehead. The vein on his forehead slithered across his bald scalp. He did everything in his power to stop himself from screaming. He sighed loudly.

"Good boy," Andrew said. "Now tell me about Grace."

"I–I–I need a–an ambulance."

"You do. What does that have to do with my daughter?"

"Wha–What? He–Hey, man, my–my foot. I can't feel... parts of my foot. Holy shit, wha–wha–"

"If you can feel parts of it, then what's the problem?" Andrew interrupted.

"I *can't* feel parts of it! My foot! What did you–"

"*Hey,*" Andrew hissed as he leaned forward in his seat. He jabbed his finger at Adam and said, "We're done talking about your damn foot. If you mention it again, I'm going to cut it off and shove it up your ass. You understand me, motherfucker?"

Adam opened and closed his mouth repeatedly. He was shocked by the threat. And he believed it. He pissed himself. The puddle under the chair was now comprised of salt water, blood, and urine. His boxers were soaked.

Andrew said, "I'll take that as a yes. Now, what do you know about Grace McCarthy?"

Teeth chattering, Adam shook his head and stuttered, "I–I never he–heard of her."

"You've never seen her before?"

"N–No, sir."

Andrew opened his wallet and took a picture out. He showed it to Adam. The picture showed Andrew and Grace at a park. He had a picture of himself and Max, and another with the entire family in his wallet, too. But those didn't matter at the moment.

"This girl," Andrew said. "Her left eye is hazel and her right eye is brown. Have you seen her in any of your disgusting pictures? Or videos? Have you heard any of your perverted 'friends' talking about a girl like this?"

"Pic–Pictures? Vi–Videos? What are you talking about?"

"Don't play stupid with me, Adam Woods. You're a pedophile. People like you don't change. You *can't* change. This shit's in your DNA and you know it. Have you seen her in any pictures or videos?"

"I–I don't know what–"

Andrew slapped the tape over Adam's mouth. Adam tried to scream again, but it was too little, too late—*hmmm! Hmmm!* Andrew turned on the stove and started heating up a saucepan. He searched through the kitchen cabinets until he found a bottle of cooking oil. He poured it into the saucepan, filling it to the brim.

He stood in front of Adam and said, "You have until *that* boils to speak. If you don't give me something to work with, I'm going to hurt you again. If you scream or try to get away, I *am* going to hurt you again." He took the tape off his mouth and asked, "Where's my daughter?"

Panic in his eyes, Adam stammered, "Un–Until wha–what boils? What are you–you doing? I don't know anything!"

"Where is she?!"

"I don't know!"

"What did you do to her?!"

Adam cried, "Oh God, man! I–I didn't do anything... I watch porn, but–but I didn't hurt nobody. I don't know tha–that girl, man. You have to believe me."

"Give me a name or a website or something to work with," Andrew demanded. "Who's your source? Who gives you this shit? Does he live in town?"

"I don't have a fucking source, man. I just use the forums and shit. You can find some of this crap on Twitter and Tumblr and... and Facebook and anywhere, man. Please, please, please. Don't hurt me anymore. Please, man, I'm begging you."

Andrew didn't know how to search Twitter or Facebook—or any website for that matter—for illegal pornography. He couldn't believe it could be found on mainstream websites anyway. He needed an exact name or a link. The cooking oil boiled on the stove, popping and spattering.

He slapped the tape over Adam's mouth and said, "That's not enough."

Adam screamed in fear, but to no avail. He hopped forward with the chair. A twinge rocketed through his leg as his butchered foot hit the floor. He moved less than an inch. He couldn't escape the kitchen.

Muffled by the tape, he shouted the same thing over and over: *Please! Please! Please!*

***

Andrew took the saucepan off the stove. The boiling oil *crackled* and *popped*, landing on his chest and sleeves. He felt the heat from the boiling oil on his neck and face. He stood behind Adam. He placed one hand on Adam's shoulder and pressed down on him, trying to pin him down to the floor. The chair kept *screeching* across the tiles as Adam squirmed in his seat.

Andrew said, "You *will* give me a name or you *will* die tonight."

He poured some oil on Adam's right forearm. From his elbow, it flowed down his arm and cascaded across his hand. Then it dripped from his fingers.

Hmmm!—Adam screamed at the top of his lungs. He heard his skin *sizzling*, like meat on a frying pan. His arm went from pale and lean to red and swollen—then puffy and pink. His arms shook involuntarily. His body couldn't handle the pain, which inadvertently led to *more* pain. Some of the oil on his arm flew onto his back because of all of his shaking.

Andrew repeated the process on Adam's left arm. He watched the boiling oil flow down his forearm, following his thick, protuberant veins down to his hands. The calloused skin was burned off his palms. His discolored arms began to peel. Some blood oozed out from the second-degree burns. Some of the remaining cooking oil fell from his skinless fingertips and plopped on the puddle under the chair.

A puddle of blood, salt water, urine, and cooking oil.

Andrew sidestepped to the front of the chair, careful not to slip on the puddle. Adam's eyes rolled back and he drew fast, panicked breaths through his nose.

Andrew slapped him and said, "Stay awake. It will only get worse for you if you fall asleep. Where is Grace?" He took the tape off Adam's mouth and repeated, "Where is Grace?"

Adam gasped for air, then he yelled, "Help! I'm burning! Oh my–"

Andrew placed the tape over his mouth again. He slapped him and asked, "Who sells you your shit? Where's my daughter? Tell me... Tell me something, Adam."

He took the tape off his mouth. Adam bellowed in pain. He couldn't form the most basic words—*Please! Help! Hey! No!* The pain wiped his vocabulary.

Andrew covered Adam's mouth again. He slowly poured the rest of the oil on Adam's chest, as if he were carefully pouring syrup on a stack of pancakes. The oil flowed from his collarbones down to his waist, leaving large patches of thick, pink skin across his torso. His skin peeled and blistered. He felt the burning pain *in* his torso, too, as if his organs were melting. Sweat, from the heat and pain, covered his body.

Andrew yelled, "Tell me! Tell me!"

He pressed the bottom of the saucepan against Adam's kneecap. It was still hot enough to burn his skin. Adam's head spun. His pupils were dilated. He stared at Andrew in disbelief. He heard Andrew's voice, but he didn't recognize his language. He heard Russian—or was it Spanish?

'*Rasskazhi mne! Dígame!*'

The sex offender fell unconscious.

***

Adam coughed as he awoke. A bright light blurred his vision. After a few blinks, he realized he was staring at the ceiling. He lay on the floor next to the puddle. He felt the cool tiles on his ass, so he knew his soiled underwear was removed while he was unconscious. His right arm, stretched out above his head, was restrained to one of the dining table's legs with a zip tie handcuff. His hands, swollen and red, were useless due to the second-degree burns. He couldn't stand up because of his mutilated foot, either. Even with one free arm, he couldn't fight back or escape—no way, no how.

"Help me," he squealed in a soft, raspy tone. He was surprised to hear his own voice. There was no tape over his mouth. He croaked out, "I'm sorry... I'm sorry. Somebody help..."

"You're awake," Andrew said, leaning against the archway with his back to the kitchen. He had changed the channel to the local news—not a *peep* about Grace McCarthy. He said, "I was afraid you went into shock. I'm not a paramedic, but I tried my best to keep you alive. I laid you down and held your legs up. I heard that helps. I hope you appreciate that. Now, let's continue our little chat."

"Pl–Please, man. Don't do this. Don't... Don't hurt me. I–I didn't touch your girl. I never seen her in any pic–pictures or videos."

"But you have pictures and videos, don't you?"

Adam's bottom lip quivered. Layers of tears covered his eyes. He felt throbbing pain in all of his extremities, except his left foot. He couldn't escape by screaming or lying. He understood that now.

He stuttered, "I–I do. But I didn't make it. I haven't touched a–anyone since... since before I went to prison. I–I swear."

"Where do you get it from?"

"The internet."

"*Where?*"

"I–I told you already. I met... some people on Twitter. They're called, um... They're MAPs."

"Maps? Like a fucking... a fucking map, Adam? Are you kidding me?"

Adam said, "No, no, no. It's a–a... an acro... What do you call 'em? An acra–"

"An acronym?"

"Yeah!" Adam yelled, wide-eyed. "It stands for... for minor, um... what was it? Minor attracted person. Tha–That's it. Some of 'em, they have pictures and videos, man. Talk to them. Talk to..."

He hissed, then he moaned. He couldn't lay still, writhing in pain on the floor. He cried and begged incoherently. Andrew repeated the acronym in his head: *MAP, minor attracted person; MAP, minor attracted person.* He memorized it for future research. He crouched beside Adam. He showed him a red stiletto high heel.

He asked, "Does this actually fit you? I found it in your closet. Now you're lucky I didn't find any children's clothing in there. You should see what I did to the last guy hiding a girl's shirt and panties in a shoebox..."

The last guy—Adam whimpered upon hearing those words. He was facing a man with experience. His chances of survival declined. He had only thought about death during one other period of his life: his prison sentence. Some sex offenders didn't last long in the joint. He thought about death again.

'Does it hurt? Does it just go black? Will I see it coming? Do heaven and hell really exist? Was I forgiven? When was the last time I confessed?'

Andrew said, "I'm getting tired of this. This is your last chance to help me. Give me a *specific* name. Hell, it can be a username, too. Just give me something I can use to find Grace. Please, Adam."

Adam blinked erratically as he dived into his memories. He had seen thousands of illegal pictures and videos. He couldn't remember seeing Grace in any of them. He thought about his contacts. Sex offenders didn't use their real names on websites, so they relied on aliases. But he couldn't remember their exact usernames.

He said, "I don't know... It's just... Everything hurts so much." He began to hyperventilate. Between breaths, he said, "I... think... I'm... dying."

Andrew sighed, then he said, "Not yet."

He placed another strip of duct tape over Adam's mouth, then he swung the heel at Adam's genitals. The pointy heel hit his scrotum. Adam sat up and gasped. The pain was surreal. His balls ached, as if his testicles were suffering from the worst cramps imaginable. The pain shot into his stomach. He felt a sudden urge to simultaneously vomit and defecate.

Andrew placed his free hand on Adam's chest and pushed him down to the floor. He swung the high heel at him, hammering away at his genitals. The heel ruptured one of his testicles. It struck the shaft of his penis, then the glans. Most of the glans turned red, resembling a fly agaric—*a red mushroom*. His battered scrotum was hit again. It turned purple and pink because of his internal scrotal bleeding.

The heel hit his thighs a few times, too, leaving red circular marks on his legs. It even punctured his leg once.

Adam couldn't handle the pain in his stomach anymore. He vomited. The brownish-green puke landed on his face. He had eaten enchiladas and beans for dinner. Some of the vomit flowed back into his mouth. He coughed and retched as he choked on it. Explosive diarrhea shot out of his ass. The kitchen floor was now flooded with blood, salt water, urine, cooking oil, and feces.

The high heel broke in Andrew's hand. With the final blow, Adam's scrotum was torn open. Andrew could see *inside* his scrotum. He saw Adam's off-white testicle, covered in blood, as well as a tint of blue. The glans of his limp penis fell into his scrotum through the wide gash. Blood appeared to be leaking out of his urethra.

Andrew breathed deeply. He held the broken shoe over his head, as if he were contemplating striking him again. But he couldn't do it. He was disgusted by the genital mutilation and the bodily fluids. He threw the shoe aside. He pulled the box cutter out of his utility belt. He held the blade up to Adam's neck and leaned over him.

He said, "Look at me. Look at me, you perverted bastard."

Adam could barely see him through his fading vision. His eyes rolled back and he hacked, like a cat choking on a hairball.

Andrew said, "This is for all of those kids you hurt. All of those kids in those pictures and videos... This is for *my* daughter."

He gritted his teeth and screamed as he slit his throat, dragging the blade from one jugular to the other. He severed his trachea and cut into his esophagus. Fountains of blood gushed out of his jugulars. Some vomit oozed out of the cut on his throat. Croaking sounds came out of his mouth and his neck. It was like he had two mouths.

Adam reached for his neck with his free hand. He stopped breathing after fifteen seconds, but he continued twitching for a minute.

Andrew put on his ski mask and gathered his supplies. He washed the blood and other bodily fluids off his gloves and clothing at the sink. He checked the clock on his cell phone: *10:46 PM*. He was late for his next appointment, so he didn't have time to clean the crime scene. He scanned the kitchen one more time. He watched as Adam's vomit ran down his cheek and finally touched the kitchen floor.

Blood. Salt water. Cooking oil. Urine. Feces. Vomit.

What a sight to see.

Andrew was unnerved by the experience, but he learned to bury his emotions. *For Grace,* he told himself. He exited the house through the back door. He hopped over the brick partition in the backyard and landed in an alley. His minivan was parked behind a dumpster. He took off his ski mask as soon as the coast was clear. He cruised out of the neighborhood and headed towards the city's outskirts.

Chapter Eighteen

Caleb West

The clock on the car stereo read: *11:25 PM*.

Andrew sat in the driver's seat of his van, parked on the side of the road. He watched the homeless encampment under the freeway to his right—tents and tarps as far as the eye could see. The ground was littered with trash: plastic bottles, oyster pails, foam food containers, pizza boxes, plastic bags, sheets of paper, torn clothing, used syringes. Fires burned in rusty steel drums. Music played from someone's battery-operated pocket radio—*In the Air Tonight* by Phil Collins.

Andrew thought about wearing his ski mask, but it was too conspicuous. He decided to keep the utility belt around his waist, though. He figured no one would notice or the homeless would mistake him for a police officer. He saw a homeless man wearing a tattered trench coat, soiled boxers, and old boots pushing an empty shopping cart towards the encampment. No pants, no shirt, but the man wore a leather belt over his underwear's waistband.

"Caleb West," Andrew whispered as he opened his notebook. There was a folded mugshot inside. He said, "Black, six-foot-two, a hundred fifty pounds, brown eyes, born December 17, 1964. That makes you fifty-five years old. Rape by force... lewd acts with a minor child... You're a real monster, Caleb. Let's see where you're hiding."

He checked the stack of cash in his wallet. He withdrew one-thousand-five-hundred dollars from an ATM before heading to Adam's house. In the real world, everything was for sale—information, integrity, drugs, guns, *people*.

He hopped out of the van. He walked past the drooping fence. Over the song's explosive drums, he heard cars zooming down the freeway above him. People were driving home, delivering products in massive semi-trucks, or heading out on road trips while the homeless struggled to survive underneath them—almost like an underworld of poverty under a bridge of wealth. It was an interesting thought.

Andrew approached the man in the trench coat. He showed him Caleb's mugshot and asked, "Have you seen this man?"

His words slurred, the man sneered and muttered, "Have I seen this man? Have *I* seen him? *Me?* Have I seen that man? What'd I look like? Huh? Do I look like I seen that man? Oh, sorry, *'this'* man? What kinda name is 'This Man' anyway? Shit, crazy motherfuckers... Where'd I put my water?" He scowled at Andrew and asked, "You take my drink?"

Andrew was speechless. He had volunteered at homeless shelters before. The guests at the shelters were usually kind and appreciative, fighting through the negativity in their lives in search of a brighter future. In the homeless encampment, most of the transients were sick—mentally and physically—or drugged out of their minds.

Why isn't anyone really helping them? What happened to our taxes? Where the hell is our money going?—he thought.

The homeless shelters in town also functioned as domestic violence shelters, so transient sex offenders weren't allowed to stay. Andrew visited the most notorious homeless encampment in town in search of Caleb West.

He said, "I didn't take your drink. Take a look at the picture. Have you seen him?"

The skeletal man leaned closer to the picture. Andrew could see his bloodshot sclerae, the black bags under his eyes, the pitted acne scars on his cheeks, the scabs on his forehead and neck and chest. The homeless man turned his head slowly, then he gazed into Andrew's eyes. His expression said something along the lines of: *oh my God.*

Andrew leaned closer to him and asked, "What is it? You know him?" The man nodded slowly. Andrew asked, "Where can I find him?"

The man smirked and said, "That's me. Yeah, that's me right there. Before the government abducted me... before they took everything from me..."

"Goddammit."

"Before they changed me... Are you here to pay me, mister? What do they call it? Reparations? No, condensation. No... What? *Compensation.* You gonna compensate me for my troubles?"

Andrew said, "No, I don't–"

"Then get the fuck away from me, dog-fucker!" the man barked.

Andrew staggered back, startled. He buried his right hand in his pocket and grabbed the utility knife. He was ready to draw it at the first sign of trouble. He walked backwards, retreating while keeping his eyes on the unstable man.

The homeless man slipped on the mud and fell to his ass beside his shopping cart. He yelled, "Dog-fucker! Drink-stealer! Get away from me! All of ya, get away! I don't need your help! Hey! Don't... Don't touch me!"

There was no one there.

Andrew hurried to the first set of tents around a concrete pillar. He reached for the zipper on the mesh entryway of a blue tent. He stopped and took a second to think, then he shrugged.

He knocked on the entryway and asked, "Anyone home? I need help finding someone. Hello?" There was no response. He approached the tent to the right. He tapped the tent and said, "Hey, I'm looking for someone. I have cash. Hello? Anyone there?"

Again, there was no response. The third tent was open, so he peeked inside. A woman appeared to be sleeping under a torn, dirty blanket. Her skin looked gray. A bundle of tangled black hair covered her face. Her breathing was slow and shallow, one breath every fifteen seconds. He couldn't extract any information from her, and he couldn't save her.

He went around the pillar, knocking and asking for help. He found a bearded man sleeping under a table with a blue tarp on top. He growled and kicked at Andrew.

Andrew approached two young women—a redhead and a brunette—standing next to a fire in a steel drum, hands out in front of them. They were short and thin—skin and bones. Their teeth were yellow, decaying and riddled with cavities. The redhead was missing two incisors at the top of her mouth. They were covered in sores, acne, and track marks.

Meth-heads, Andrew thought. *They've been around. They've seen enough. They can help. They just need a little 'motivation.'*

Andrew said, "Hello, ladies. I was wondering if I could ask you for a little favor."

The redhead said, "I ain't fucking you."

"I'll do it," the brunette shrugged. "How much you got?"

Andrew smiled and said, "I'm not looking for company. I need information."

"Information? What do we look like? Teachers? This look like a school to you? Go to a library or something, dude."

"Maybe 'information' was the wrong word. I'm looking for a person. Have you seen this man around here? Or maybe in town?"

Andrew showed them the mugshot. The brunette furrowed her brow and cocked her head to the side while the redhead smirked.

The brunette said, "Isn't he... No, that was Jayden... Well, maybe I sucked his dick, too. Yeah, I think he's no good. Limp and dirty. Stay away from that guy."

"He's definitely dirty," the redhead said. "Why you lookin' for that dirty motherfucker anyway?"

Andrew considered his responses: *I just want to talk to him about some money he owes me; I'm his parole officer and he hasn't checked-in; I want to torture him until he tells me about my missing daughter.* The first option wasn't bad, but he didn't want any of his friends to warn him. He immediately eliminated the second option. He assumed the transients wouldn't react well to a police officer disrupting their 'peace.' Honesty seemed like the best option.

He said, "He's a convicted sex offender. My daughter—my five-year-old girl—has been missing for over two weeks now. The cops can't find her because they're looking in the wrong places. I'm here looking for the right people. I'm going to hurt him until he talks. That's the truth. Now, will you help me find him?"

The women stared at him with deadpan expressions, then they giggled. They stopped laughing as soon as they realized Andrew wasn't laughing with them. They saw the sincerity—the raw *anger*—in his eyes.

The redhead asked, "How much?"

"How much?" Andrew repeated.

"For his head."

"Yeah, how much?" the brunette asked.

"Oh, shut up, girl. You can't tell Caleb from Jayden. You can't help this asshole."

"Fuck you, bitch. He probably trusts me more than you."

Motivation, Andrew thought. While the women argued, he pulled two one-hundred dollar bills out of his wallet. He held the money out in front of him. He felt the heat from the fire through his glove. The women stopped insulting each other. Dollar signs in their eyes, they saw enough money for an 8-ball of meth in the stranger's hand.

Andrew said, "You can split it or you can fight for it, but I'm giving you two-hundred dollars for his head... and your silence. Can you take me to him?" The redhead grabbed the money, but Andrew tightened his grip on the cash. He repeated, "Can you take me to him?"

The redhead said, "Yeah, yeah. You can trust us. Hey, you don't even gotta go far."

The brunette said, "He sleeps over there, near those–"

"*Hey,*" the redhead hissed. "Don't just tell him."

"Oh, yeah. The money first. Give us the money."

Andrew examined them. They were clearly addicted to drugs—they were scratching and twitching and tweaking—but they seemed trustworthy.

He said, "No games. And you don't tell a soul."

"We promise," the women said in unison.

Andrew released the money and said, "Take me to him."

***

Andrew followed the women through the homeless encampment, cars zooming down the lanes on the freeway above them. The music grew louder—*La Bamba* by Los Lobos now played from the radio. It came from a blue tent, which appeared to be propped up with sticks. They slogged through another heap of garbage, pushing past bags of trash, cardboard boxes, and broken bicycles.

The makeshift homes were sparser as they reached the end of the camp. They approached two tents surrounded by shrubs. A bonfire burned in a ditch in front of the tents—a tire, some wood, *garbage.*

The redhead pointed at the blue tent to the right and said, "He lives there. If he ain't home, he's probably at that Kmart downtown. You know, the one that's closed."

The brunette said, "I think I seen him at Walmart, too. He stands out there with his cup and his lil' sign. *'Vet needs money for family.'* He ain't no vet and he ain't got no family. But that's his sign and that's the guy you're looking for."

Andrew asked, "Are you two positive about that?" The women nodded while scratching their necks and squirming. Andrew said, "If you're wrong, if someone else is in there... I'll kill them and then I'll kill you. So, you better be positive. Okay?"

The women knew he wasn't bluffing. They saw bloody murder in his eyes. They glanced at each other, then they nodded at Andrew.

Andrew said, "Get out of here. Don't look back. Don't call the police. Don't tell anyone about this. Just get far away from here. Can you do that for me?"

"Yeah, yeah," the redhead said. She grabbed her friend's arm and pulled her away from him. She said, "If ya need anything else, you know where to find us. She's really good at sucking dick."

"I am," the brunette said, walking backwards beside the redhead. "Thanks for the cash. Good night! I love you!"

"Oh, shut up."

"What? They like sweet talk."

"He ain't no John."

"How do you..."

Their chitter-chatter was drowned out by the speeding cars on the freeway as they wandered away. The music barely reached the bonfire. Some of the transients drank and ate together, others slept in their tents and under tarps, a few argued with the voices in their heads, and at least three of them shared a needle to shoot black tar heroin.

Andrew turned his flashlight on and opened the red tent to the left. He flashed the light at a homeless black man sleeping under a pile of coats and pants tied together—a homemade blanket.

Eyes closed, blinded by the light, the man asked, "Whatchu doing, man?"

"I need you to leave."

"*What?*"

"Don't cause a scene. I have–"

"Whachu talking about, man?!" the homeless man yelled, his jaundiced eyes bulging in surprise and anger. He was sick—and he probably didn't know it. He asked, "Who the hell is you? What is you doing here, man? You tryin' to–"

"I have money," Andrew interrupted with a stern voice. He pulled a fifty dollar bill out of his pocket. He said, "Take it and leave. Don't come back until tomorrow morning. Do we have a deal?"

The man puckered his lips and moved them from side to side. He asked, "You got more?"

"Take it or leave it. The easy way or the hard way. Either way, I'm taking you out of this tent. What's it going to be?"

As he dressed himself, putting on a coat, a beanie, and his boots, the transient said, "We got a deal, man. I'm outta here. Just... one... second." He stumbled towards Andrew. He took the money out of his hand and said, "Don't touch my shit, man. You know how long I been–"

"I won't touch a thing. Get out of here."

"I'm gone, I'm gone."

The transient struggled to his feet outside of his tent. He staggered away while flicking the cash with his finger and mumbling to himself—*fifty whole dollars! Hell yeah!* He hid the money in his pocket and hurried out of the homeless encampment. He needed a fresh meal.

***

Andrew kicked dirt into the hole and extinguished the bonfire. The tents were swallowed by the darkness. Only some dim light from the cars on the freeway reached them.

He entered the blue tent to the right. He found a black man in a sleeping bag, snoring and groaning. He flashed his light at the mug shot, then he examined the man's face. The top of his head was bald, but his thick, uneven beard connected to the gray hair at the sides of his head. Andrew peeked into the sleeping bag. The homeless man's clothing was loose—two sizes too big—and his feet stuck out from a hole at the bottom of the sleeping bag. He was tall and skinny, cadaverous and gaunt.

"You are Caleb West," Andrew whispered. "You grew a beard, you lost some hair, but... this is you, Caleb."

Andrew placed his flashlight in the corner of the tent. He peeked outside. He saw the fires around the pillars, but he didn't see or hear anyone. He stood on his knees and watched the transient's lips flutter with each snore. He removed his right glove, then he raised his bare hand. He hit the ceiling, causing the tent to wobble. Another snore ripped through the area.

He swung down at him with as much force as possible. The *whoosh* of the swing and the *whack* of the hit came in the blink of an eye.

Caleb grimaced and groaned in pain as he awoke. He squirmed in the sleeping bag and mumbled to himself. He was dazed by the slap to the face as well as his natural drowsiness. Just as he reached for his face, Andrew slapped him again. Caleb finally realized he was being attacked. He kicked and swung his arms, but he was trapped in the sleeping bag.

Andrew squeezed his neck with enough pressure to stop him from screaming, but not enough to strangle him. He pressed his knee into Caleb's stomach, pushing the rest of the air out of him. *He can't fight if he can't breathe,* he thought. He slapped him a third time—then a fourth, then a fifth, and then a sixth time.

Caleb's nose broke. His cough sent a string of gooey blood out of his right nostril—a bloody snot rocket. It landed on his lips, beard, and Andrew's hand. His cheeks swelled and turned purple. With the sixth slap, his teeth cut his bottom lip open. Blood flooded his mouth and painted his lips red. The blood dyed the gray hairs on his beard, too.

He couldn't escape from underneath him, but he managed to squeeze one of his arms out of the sleeping bag. He dug his long, dirty fingernails into

Andrew's wrist, but it wasn't enough to stop Andrew from choking him. He stared at Andrew with a set of fearful puppy eyes—*why are you doing this to me?* He didn't recognize his attacker. He wasn't a loan shark, drug dealer, or pimp. He looked like a regular man.

A regular, *angry* man.

Andrew said, "When I let you go, you will *not* scream or fight. You will answer my questions. You *will* cooperate. Are we clear?"

Caleb could only croak. He tried to nod, but he could barely move with Andrew's fingers firmly wrapped around his neck. He was lightheaded from the lack of oxygen, too.

Andrew said, "Blink twice for yes."

Caleb blinked twice. Andrew released his grip on Caleb's neck. Caleb gasped for air and tried to sit up, but Andrew pushed him back down.

Andrew said, "Don't move."

"I–I can–can't breathe," Caleb said in a raspy tone. "You–You're… fucking up… my stomach. Oh, shit…"

"I'll take my knee off your stomach in a second. If you get up, I'm going to knock all of your teeth out and force you to swallow 'em. Clear?"

Blood frothing on his lips, Caleb nodded and blinked twice. Andrew took his knee off the transient's stomach. He took a knee beside the sleeping bag. He gave Caleb thirty seconds to catch his breath.

"What's your name?" Andrew asked.

"Na–Name?"

"Don't make me ask twice."

"It's, um... My name is... John... Davis."

"John Davis?" Andrew repeated.

"Ye–Yeah, you got a prob–"

Andrew lunged forward. He grabbed Caleb's neck in one hand and slapped his face with the other—*whack, whack, whack!* He struck him six more times. Caleb thrashed, swinging his limbs in every direction. The sleeping bag slid off him. He looked to his left, then his right, and then his left again, trying to dodge Andrew's hand. But his efforts were fruitless. The slaps stung his red and purple cheeks. His jaw ached and his nose burned. Tears welled in his eyes.

Andrew had learned the tactic from the CIA. It was considered an enhanced interrogation technique, used to startle, humiliate, and hurt suspected terrorists. A punch could cause more damage, but it wasn't as disrespectful as a slap. It didn't have the same psychological effect. A punch said: *I'm going to kick your ass!* A slap said: *You're my bitch, you pathetic coward!* And Caleb felt like Andrew's bitch in that tent.

"Pl–Please, stop," he croaked out. "Co–Come on, m–man."

Andrew thought: *if my daughter said that to a guy like you, would you have stopped?* The answer was obvious to him. He slapped him again and again.

Between slaps, he said, "What... is... your... name?!"

He stopped with his hand raised over his head, blood smeared on his palm. His hand trembled, he broke some bones in his palm, but he refused to show any weakness around the sex offender. He took his other hand off Caleb's neck.

Caleb gasped, then he rubbed his neck and stuttered, "Ca–Caleb... Caleb... Caleb West."

"Good, good," Andrew said as he slowly lowered his arm. "Caleb, you're a sex offender, right?"

"Y–Yes, sir."

"I have some questions for you. Take a look at this picture for me."

He took Grace's picture out of his wallet and showed it to him. Caleb stared at it for a few seconds, shuddering and sniffling.

Andrew said, "Her name is Grace McCarthy. Have you seen her?"

"No, man. I–I don't know that girl."

"You didn't take her?"

"*Take?* What the fuck, man?! I didn't do nothing! I ain't–"

Andrew lifted Caleb's baggy shirt up to his chest. There was a thick, vertical scar at the center of his torso. The black scar was about three inches long. He had survived a stabbing. Although they weren't visible, there were two gunshot scars on his left thigh from a shooting that occurred when he was in his twenties. The scars, his current living situation, the blood on his face, the desperate screaming—none of it bothered Andrew.

He slapped Caleb's stomach with the back of his hand. He struck him until his fingers hurt. Rosy imprints of his fingers were scattered across his abdomen. Caleb raised his knees as an awful stomach cramp tore through him. The aching sensation in his abdomen was unbearable. The excruciating pain stopped him from screaming. He covered his stomach with his arms and rolled to his side, curling into the fetal position.

So, Andrew slapped his face again. He hit everything from his right ear to his chin. Caleb was disoriented by the blow, seeing double and then triple.

Andrew said, "Don't raise your voice at me, motherfucker. I know you know where to find my daughter. Now, *talk.*"

Caleb mumbled, "I–I, um… hmm… huh…"

"Caleb, I need you to talk to me. My girl, my five-year-old daughter, is missing. Have you heard anything? Have you seen her with any of your fucking pedophile friends?"

"I don't… have any…"

Andrew pulled the box cutter out of his utility belt. Caleb was familiar with the *clicking* sound. His eyes widened as Andrew held the blade up to his face. Andrew pressed the blade against Caleb's neck, nicking his skin and shaving a few hairs off.

The transient said, "Wa–Wait."

"I've done this before. I'm not afraid to kill you. Who's going to miss a homeless sex offender anyway?"

"*Wait.*"

Andrew tilted his head and asked, "You have something for me?"

"Gra–Grace… You said her name was Grace, right?"

"Yeah. Yes, I did."

Caleb spit a blob of blood at the tent, then he swallowed another mouthful of it. He said, "I heard that name today. Some guys, some fellas, they… they–they shoot porn in an apartment. A–A condemned apartment, you know? They said they… they had a girl named 'Grace.' That's what they said. 'A girl.' I don't know nothing else. Goddamnit, I think I swallowed my tooth…"

Andrew ignored his complaints. He felt like his heart had plunged into his stomach. His mind ran wild with the awful possibilities—*they're taking her picture, they're raping her, they're killing her.* He fell back on his ass and gazed at the transient.

He said, "Take me to your friends."

"They're not my friends, man. I swear, I ain't got nothing to do with 'em."

"You said they shoot porn at a condemned apartment, so you *know* where they are. Take me to them and you'll walk away with some teeth in your mouth, Caleb."

Tears and blood on his face, Caleb shrugged and said, "Okay, okay. Let me just–"

Andrew dragged him out of the tent. They sprang to their feet outside. Caleb turned and pushed Andrew. Andrew drew his stun gun and aimed it at Caleb's chest. The fight ended before it could begin.

Caleb sucked his teeth, then he said, "Fucking asshole... What the fuck is this? I can't even grab my shoes?"

"You don't need your shoes. We're just going for a drive. As soon as I get my daughter, I'll drive you back here or to a hospital. Start moving. I'm parked on the street. And don't try anything funny or I'll gut you in front of your neighbors. In fact, put your hands up. Do it."

Glaring at Andrew, Caleb swiped at his mouth and nose. He smeared his blood on his cheeks and hands. Fresh blood came out of his busted nose and sliced lip. He spit another blob of blood out, then he raised his hands over his head. He marched forward.

Andrew escorted him to the van while aiming the stun gun at the small of his back. To the other transients, they looked like a cop and a perpetrator. They didn't bother to help Caleb. If they were correct, he was heading to prison where he'd have a roof over his head and a meal in his belly.

Lucky bastard.

Chapter Nineteen

Amateur

"They're in there," Caleb said, holding a piece of tissue up to his nose.

Through the passenger window, he looked at a building to their right. The five-story apartment complex was condemned after a fire broke out in a kitchen. The fire roared through the first and second floors, killing seven tenants and injuring many more. The exterior of the building was stained with soot, dappled with bird shit, and decorated with gang graffiti. The windows were either broken or boarded up.

The building next door—a bakery with an apartment on the second floor—was also abandoned. There was a gas station across the street. A young man worked the cash register, dozing in and out of sleep.

Andrew asked, "How many are there?"

"No idea."

"They're your friends, aren't they?"

"Fuck no. I seen 'em around. I talk to 'em sometimes. But we ain't buddy-buddy or anything like that."

"Are they armed? Are they gangsters? Drug dealers? Human traffickers? I need something to work with, Caleb."

Caleb looked at his reflection in the rear-view mirror. He hissed in pain as he rubbed his swollen, bruised cheeks.

He said, "They're just guys. They smoke. They slang. They fuck. I don't know if they kill, but they fuck. Yeah, they fuck a lot. They make amateur porn, you know? That good stuff."

Andrew sneered at him. *Amateur porn*—he didn't want to think about his daughter and porn at the same time. He holstered his stun gun. It was useful against a single target, but it wouldn't have been effective against a group of people if they all rushed him at once. He checked the canister of pepper spray in his utility belt—*ready to use.*

He said, "Let's get in there."

Caleb responded, "Come on, man. Let me go home. I'm too old for this shit. And I didn't do nothing to your–"

"I'm not going in there alone. If my daughter's in there, if they're holding her hostage or anything like that, I need someone who can talk to them— someone who can negotiate."

"I told you: they ain't my friends."

"But they'll recognize you. They'll trust you more than they trust me. Besides, I'm not asking you, Caleb. My offer is still on the table: I can knock your teeth out, make you swallow 'em, cut you open, and take 'em out of your stomach while you're still breathing. What do you think about that?"

Caleb's eyes widened and his mouth hung open. He thought: *this motherfucker is crazy!* He climbed out of the van. He led Andrew to the entrance of the apartment building. The door was missing. A sheet of plywood covered the doorway instead. He pushed the plywood aside and made his way into the building.

In the hallway, they heard a *squelching* sound and a man's muffled voice. It was coming from the end of the hall.

Andrew turned on his flashlight. A rat scampered across the hallway, exiting one apartment and entering another. The walls and ceiling were black from the fire. Some of the doors leading into the apartments appeared to have been chopped by an axe during the rescue effort. Used syringes, broken glass pipes, and other drug paraphernalia stood out amongst the heaps of garbage in the hall. The building was used as a drug den by the local addicts.

The *squelching* accelerated and grew louder. Then a man's grunt and a female's stifled moan joined the squelching. Andrew couldn't tell if it was a girl's cry or a woman's moan. He only thought of one name: *Grace.*

He pushed Caleb and said, "Start moving."

"Where am I going?"

"Down the hall. Follow the noise."

Caleb kept his eyes on the floor. He stepped around the syringes and broken glass while trying to keep his balance. And those same syringes and shards *crunched* under Andrew's boots. Andrew was solely focused on the noise at the end of the hall. Images of Grace flashed in his mind with each step.

From the last apartment to the right, a man said, "Make her gag on it. Yeah, yeah, like that. I wanna see her deepthroat it."

Andrew grabbed the back of Caleb's shirt and pushed him down the hall. They entered the last apartment to the right. Caleb huffed, then he laughed in relief. Andrew was taken aback by their discovery.

In the living room of the small, one-room apartment, they found a group of people filming a pornographic movie. The director-slash-cameraman, Zack Walsh, stood in the corner behind a digital SLR camera on a tripod. He was shirtless, but at least he wore a pair of jeans and boots. In the opposite end of the room, two burly men had sex with a woman on a shabby, moist three-seat sofa.

The men only wore white socks and sunglasses, although the room was only illuminated by a single lantern. The woman, short and petite, was nude. Her face was decorated with too much makeup, like a child who had just found her mother's lipstick for the first time and smeared it all over her lips. Her brown hair was long, frizzy, and dirty.

She sat on one of the men, Clark Baxter, riding him in the cowgirl position. The other man, Paul Bender, stood on the sofa, thrusting his thick, veiny dick down her throat. She gagged and retched, saliva and pre-ejaculate dripping from her mouth. Paul forced his penis past her uvula. A lump protruded from her neck. Then he pinched her nose and slapped her a couple of times.

He said, "You like that, don't you? Oh yeah, you like it... Eat that dick, bitch. Take it all, girl. Oh God, that's so good."

The woman's face turned blue because she couldn't breathe and purple because of the slaps. She slapped his thighs, she tried to push him away, but she couldn't overpower him.

Clark grabbed fistfuls of her ass and spread her cheeks. Crusty feces ringed her anus. The area around her anus was stained green and brown. He pounded away at her from below, his scrotum smacking her ass with each rapid thrust. He didn't wear protection. And there were scab-like sores across the shaft of his penis—*genital herpes.*

Paul released her throat, allowing her to gasp for air. He backhanded her, then he slapped her face with his dick.

Andrew could connect the pieces. The woman's name was 'Grace.' She was addicted to drugs and coerced into filming porn with the men. He was angered by their treatment of her, the violent sex was shocking, but he knew he couldn't save her. Even with their dicks out, he couldn't win a fight against three strong men.

While scratching the sores on his bare chest, Zack asked, "Who the fuck are you guys?"

Caleb stuttered, "He–Hey, man, I was just–"

"I remember you," Zack interrupted, grinning. "You couldn't get your dick up last time, right? Oh, man, what the fuck are you doing here? We need nigger dick, but we don't need *limp* nigger dick."

Without stopping his thrusting, Clark leaned to his right and asked, "Is that Washington?"

"It's Caleb. Keep fucking, I'll deal with them," Zack said. He approached his visitors. He wagged his finger at Caleb's chest and said, "You owe me money. We paid you to fuck and you couldn't do it. Then you ran out on us. That's called 'stealing,' boy."

Caleb said, "I–I thought we were finished."

"You *stole* from us."

"I didn't mean to. It–It was an accident, man. I'm sorry, Zack. Alright?"

"You *owe* us."

"I ain't got no money, man. I just brought this guy to you. That's it. I'll get outta here and–"

Zack drew a five-round revolver from the back of his waistband. He pushed Caleb against the wall and held the revolver up to his neck.

"You're not going anywhere," he hissed. He nodded at Andrew and said, "Neither are you. Who the hell are you? Who is this guy, Caleb? Your bodyguard? Who is he?"

From the couch, brow furrowed in concern, Paul said, "Hey, Zack, need help over there?"

"I got it. Keep fucking. Don't worry, the camera's still going. We're good."

Grace dug her fingernails into Clark's shoulders as the man shoved his penis into her ass. She yelled, "Oh my God! Oh my–"

Her screaming was interrupted by Paul's penis as he thrust it into her mouth. Hands up, tears racing down his cheeks, Caleb begged for mercy. His words were jumbled together. Holding his breath and shaking like a wet puppy, Andrew stared at the camera in the corner and thought about the director's name—*Zack, Zack, Zack*. It was funny how things worked out. Coincidences happened every day. He stood in a room with a 'director' named Zack and an amateur pornstar named 'Grace.'

A name and an inanimate object could unlock a person's most forgettable memories. A coincidence could change everything. The revelation hit him like a drunk driver crashing head-on into oncoming traffic.

He remembered the photographer from the park and diner. He remembered hearing his name while they spoke to the police officer. Detective Booth had investigated Zachary Denton, but he didn't find any evidence linking him to Grace's abduction. He didn't release Zachary's name to the family, either. He wanted to stop Andrew from making a mistake and he wanted to protect the integrity of their investigation.

Vigilante justice didn't look good in a court of law.

Andrew thought: *But what if they missed something? They're not using techniques like me, are they? The kid's a professional liar. He lied his way out of it again, didn't he?*

"Where'd you get that camera?" Andrew asked.

Zack glared at him, then he smiled and chuckled. He asked, "Are you joking? I got your boy here with my *gun* on his neck and you're asking about the camera?"

Andrew asked, "Did you get it from a young guy? Curly hair? Brown eyes?" Palm facing the floor, he raised his hand up to his chin. He asked, "About yay high?"

Zack said, "No. I bought it. On the internet. Got it?"

"Got it... You selling that gun?"

"*What?*"

Andrew said, "I want your gun. I'm going to need it."

Zack laughed again, but then he stopped. He could see Andrew was serious. Caleb continued to cry and beg in front of him. Grace vomited on Paul's dick and Clark's shoulder. They slapped her around. Without cleaning his dick, Paul mounted Grace in the doggystyle position. Clark knelt on the sofa in front of her and jammed his dick in her mouth. Her teeth scraped the scabs off his penis.

Zack smirked and asked, "How much you got?"

Andrew checked his wallet. He said, "A thousand-two-hundred-fifty dollars."

"Yeah? And what's stopping me from robbing you?"

"Then you'd have to kill me. And, *look at me*. I'm not homeless. I'm not a drug addict. People will care when they find me dead. Then they'll find you and... Well, they'll probably shoot you down like dogs. And if you don't die like dogs, you'll go to prison and get fucked like 'em. Kinda like what your buddies are doing to that poor girl over there. So, do we have a deal?"

Zack's grin revealed his decaying teeth. He said, "Maybe, maybe. I can sell you the gun, but... but then you can't take this nigger with you. He's ours now."

Caleb cried, "No! I ain't part of this! I was sleepin' when he–"

"Shut the fuck up!" Zack yelled. "It ain't so bad anyway. We're just going to make you work off your debts. Like a... Like a slave. Your people know all about that, don't they? So, what do y'all say?"

Andrew didn't like Caleb. He was a rapist and a child molester. But he didn't like Zack and his crew, either. They were violent, racist, and misogynistic psychopaths. Considering Zachary Denton escaped from the authorities unscathed, he assumed the young photographer was helped by a network of child kidnappers. And to dismantle that network and find his daughter, Andrew needed a gun.

He said, "He's yours."

"No! No!" Caleb shouted. "I did what you said! That's Grace! That's your girl!"

Zack said, "Then we got ourselves a deal. Paul, get strapped."

Paul took a handgun out from under the sofa's cushion. He continued thrusting into Grace from behind, moaning with pleasure while occasionally insulting her—*'you dirty bitch.'*

Zack pressed his forearm against Caleb's neck, silencing him while pinning him to the wall. He opened the cylinder of the revolver. He tilted the gun, allowing the cartridges to spill out. *Clink, clank, clink*—the cartridges bounced on the floor like Mexican jumping beans.

He said, "Get your own bullets."

He handed Andrew the revolver, and Andrew gave him the cash. Andrew closed the cylinder. He glanced at the woman. His conscience said: *what if she really was your daughter?* He looked away before he could catch a glimpse of her eyes. He couldn't face her. He looked at Caleb. The homeless man reached for him, his fingertips barely caressing Andrew's sleeve. He begged with his eyes—*'please, don't leave me with them.'*

Andrew walked away. He strolled down the hallway, listening to the men's laughter and the victims' sorrow. Unfortunately for the woman and Caleb, he killed his conscience and buried it in his mind. His daughter was his only concern.

As he rushed to his van, he growled, "*Zachary Denton,* I remember you."

Chapter Twenty

A Prime Suspect

Andrew parked in the garage. He hid the revolver under the driver's seat, then removed the utility belt and his gloves. He checked the clock on the car stereo: *3:13 AM*. He washed his hands and face at a sink next to his workbench, then he entered his home. It was dark and quiet. He went upstairs, straight to his bedroom. He grabbed his laptop from his desk.

Click—a lamp on the nightstand was turned on as he headed to the door. He stopped in his tracks, but he didn't look back.

Rubbing her eyes, Holly sat up in bed and said, "Andrew? Andrew, what are you... What are you doing?" She checked her phone on the nightstand. She said, "It's three in the morning. Where were you?"

"I was out."

"Out?"

"Yeah. I was looking for Grace. I went to a support group for parents with missing kids. Then I went and grabbed a drink. Maybe two or three. Can't really remember."

The room was dead silent for fifteen seconds. They couldn't even hear a gust of wind or a creaky tree outside.

Holly said, "I got a notification on my phone. Someone withdrew a thousand-five-hundred dollars from our checking account today."

Andrew licked his lips, then he said, "It was me."

"Why? You *know* that money is for the reward."

"I know. I'm sorry, Holly. I needed it for... for something."

"For what, Andrew? What have you..."

Violence had a scent—a pungent, metallic odor. It ingrained itself into Andrew's skin and clothes. He smelled like he had rubbed coins on his sweaty skin. Death brought an air of sadness and tragedy along with it. Holly smelled the violence and she saw the black cloud of death hanging over Andrew's head. *What have you done?*—she didn't want to know the answer to that question.

Andrew said, "I was looking for leads. I thought the money would help. I can deposit it again if you want."

"N–No. Keep it if you need it. I can find the money somewhere else. Just, um... Just tell me something, Andrew. Did you find something about Grace?"

Andrew didn't know what to tell her. *'I killed someone. I tortured several people. I left someone with a gang of psychopaths. I saw a girl being raped and brutalized on camera. I think our daughter's in trouble.'* He didn't want to traumatize his wife with stories of violence and abuse and exploitation.

He said, "I'm going to keep looking for her. I'm just retracing the police's steps to see if they missed anything."

Holly swallowed the lump in her throat. She asked, "Do you think she's okay? Are you looking for her? Or are you... are you looking for revenge?"

"I'm... I'm looking for her."

"Then why can't you look at me?" Holly asked, teary-eyed.

The dead silence returned. Holly started sobbing. Andrew held his hand over his mouth. A single tear rolled down his cheek.

Holly said, "Whatever you're doing, you do it because she's alive, Andrew. Because she *is* alive. Don't do it for any other reason. I feel it in my gut, in my heart, in my... in my soul. My baby, our daughter... she's still out there. Don't forget that. Don't forget her."

Andrew wiped the tear from his cheek and said, "I'm going to withdraw more money tomorrow. If you don't want me to, call the bank and cancel our cards. If you trust me... let it be. Give me time, don't tell anyone about any of this, and I'll bring something back. I have to go now."

"Andrew, please, say it. Say she's alive. Andrew. Andrew!"

Andrew marched out of the room, laptop in hand. He rushed downstairs before Max could get out of bed. Max heard the rumbling floorboards downstairs and his mother crying. He thought about chasing his father, but he was more concerned about his mother. He went into the master bedroom. He teared up upon finding his sobbing mother. He ran to Holly's side. He hugged her and cried with her. They apologized to each other—and they didn't know why. It just seemed appropriate during times of confusion and distress.

Andrew returned to the garage. He opened his laptop on the workbench, then he opened the web browser.

"Zachary Denton," he said. "Yeah, that cop, he called you 'Mr. Denton.' I saw your name on your website. *Zachary Denton.* I know how to find you."

He searched his name on Google. He found 2,300,000 results. He searched dozens of Facebook and LinkedIn profiles, he checked out some YouTube accounts, and he browsed a few personal websites, including websites by doctors and lawyers. He even searched the local obituaries.

He used quotation marks to refine his search: *"Zachary Denton."* The search engine brought back 4,250 results. The first page was filled with the same results as his previous search. So, he added another word to his search query: *"Zachary Denton" photography.*

Nine-hundred-and-twenty results.

He ignored the first link. It was too difficult for him to track someone down on Facebook. He checked an Instagram profile. The account was private, but he could see the user's profile picture. It wasn't him. Then he clicked on a personal website.

Andrew felt like his heart had stopped. His vision turned black for a second, then he found himself teetering. He almost fainted.

The website was elegant, black and white with a simple, intuitive design. There were five pages: Home, About, Commissions, Gallery, Contact. He opened the 'About' page. He found a picture of Zachary Denton and a short biography revealing his upbringing, his education, and his current work. He recognized him from the park and the diner.

"It's you," Andrew whispered. "I–I found you..."

Finger shaking, Andrew clicked on the 'Gallery' page. He discovered pictures of weddings, sport events, and nature. He gritted his teeth upon seeing a picture of the park. He didn't find Grace on the website, though. He clicked the 'Contact' page. Since Zachary provided a service, he was required to provide a phone number, an email address, and a mailing address.

Andrew searched Zachary's address. He lived in a large, 1,240-square-foot loft in the downtown area. He guessed the rent was around three thousand dollars.

He muttered, "A twentysomething twerp like you can't afford to live in a place like this. Not with 'photography.' No fucking way." He narrowed his eyes and bit his lip. He said, "Unless... Unless you're taking pictures of kids and selling them online. Unless you're kidnapping kids and trading them for cash. You took her, didn't you? It was always you."

The idea sparked a fire of rage in Andrew's eyes. He searched the neighborhood with Google Maps and devised a plan to enter and escape from Zachary's apartment. Then he gathered his supplies. He took the hacksaw and some rectangular sheets of sandpaper from the workbench. He filled his bag with household items—weapons of torture.

Chapter Twenty-One

The Face of the Company

The doorbell rang.

Zachary Denton stood in front of his stove, grating goat cheese onto a veggie omelet on his skillet. Cheese already oozed out of the omelet, but he couldn't get enough of it. The table behind him was set with a plate, a glass of orange juice, and a mug of coffee. There was a basket of fruit at the center of the table, filled with fresh oranges, apples, and bananas.

The doorbell rang again.

Zachary turned off the stove and yelled, "One second!"

He wiped his hands on a towel, then he strolled towards the front door. He walked past pillars surrounded by shelves filled with books and vases with beautiful flowers. The local news played on mute on his sixty-five-inch QLED 8K television. The red sofa in front of the TV looked like something out of a castle—*Victorian.*

His workstation was in the farthest corner. The iMac was open to Adobe Lightroom. He was in the process of editing a couple's wedding photos.

He opened the front door and said, "Can I help–"

He was hit with what felt like the most powerful jab to ever be thrown by a person or animal. The sound of his jaw *popping* was louder than the doorbell. He staggered away from the door, bent over, and grabbed his jaw. It was dislocated. Gums bleeding, his front teeth were loosened by the blow. A string of blood dangled from his bottom lip.

He looked at the door. His eyes widened in horror. He immediately recognized his attacker—*Andrew McCarthy*. Lip curled, Andrew snarled at him. Zachary could see his warpath and the trail of carnage behind him. He stumbled forward to shut the door.

He yelled, "No!"

Andrew rammed the door with his shoulder before Zachary could close it. The edge of the door hit Zachary's forehead, tearing his brow open from his hairline to his left eyebrow. He stumbled back, legs like wet noodles. He was overcome with nausea. He fell to his hands and knees, blood dripping from his forehead and mouth.

Andrew marched into the loft and locked the door behind him. He threw his duffel bag on the floor. The floorboards creaked under the weight. Zachary crawled towards the living room. His cell phone was charging near his iMac. Andrew followed the trail of blood. He kicked Zachary in the ass, pushing him down to his side.

Zachary rolled onto his back and raised his hands up. He stammered, "Wa–Wa–Wait! Pl–Please–"

Andrew punted Zachary's head like a football. His steel-toe boot clashed against Zachary's jaw. Another *pop* echoed through the spacious loft. Three of

Zachary's lower incisors were ejected from his mouth. The bloody teeth bounced across the floorboards. A tooth rolled under the sofa. Zachary's arms stiffened up, but they didn't fall to his sides. His stiff arms stayed in the air for ten seconds.

It was called the 'fencing response,' and it was the body's natural reaction to a concussion.

Zachary unleashed a ghastly groan, then he snored and moaned. His eyes rolled back as he twitched. Blood spumed on his mouth and flowed down his cheeks.

Andrew grabbed the collar of Zachary's shirt, then he dragged him into the living room. He threw him onto the sofa. Then he went back to the front door to grab his bag. Zachary regained consciousness for a few seconds, then he fainted again. Andrew zip-tied his ankles, then he zip-tied his wrists in front of him. He wiped the blood off his face with a towel, then he slapped a strip of duct tape over his mouth.

***

Zachary awoke to the *clinking* and *scraping* of silverware. Ten minutes had passed since Andrew's arrival, but he felt like he had slept for a day. His head throbbed with pain, his gums stung, and his jaw ached. He lay on his side, facing the television. He felt the hot blood on his forehead. The cut on his head was still bleeding. But he wasn't concerned about his injuries. The intruder terrified him the most.

Andrew sat on a dining chair between the television and the coffee table. He ate Zachary's veggie omelet and drank his coffee.

Zachary sat up. He mumbled something indecipherable. He was too weak to fight or scream. The room spun around him. The floor was the ceiling and the ceiling was the floor. He could have removed the tape over his mouth, but that thought didn't cross his mind. Fear changed a person's ability to think rationally.

With a full mouth, Andrew said, "You're a great cook." He swallowed the food—*gulp.* As he walked to the kitchen, he said, "A great cook, but a terrible person."

He placed the plate and mug in the sink. He grabbed an apple, then he returned to his seat across from Zachary.

He took a bite of the apple and said, "I'm going to get... straight to the point. I'm going to kill you, Zachary Denton." *Hmm*—the sound escaped his lips. He said, "Wow, that is one juicy apple. I've never tasted one like this. It must be fresh. Like, straight-from-an-apple-tree fresh."

Zachary's face sank with a horrified frown. *I'm going to kill you*—he believed Andrew's words and he was terrified by his nonchalance. And that was exactly what Andrew wanted. He acted casual to build tension. The suspense—*the fear*—was a form of psychological torture. Zachary tried to say something again, but the tape muffled his voice.

Andrew continued, "Anyway, I'm going to kill you because I know—*I know*—you took my daughter from her school. I'm going to ask you about her in a minute, but first I'm going to hurt you. You want to know why? Because I know you're going to lie to me. You think I'm bluffing or I don't know a thing about pain. So, let's skip the first lie and get straight to the torture. Then maybe—*maybe*—you can tell me the truth."

Zachary cried hysterically and fell to his side. Andrew turned up the volume on the television. A local reporter discussed the pothole-riddled roads while criticizing the government's response—or lack thereof. Andrew took the titanium shears out of his bag. He placed one knee on the sofa in front of Zachary's stomach, stopping him from rolling off.

"No!" Zachary screamed in a stifled voice. "No, no, no!"

Andrew punched down at him. His glove cut Zachary's cheek below his right eye. Some blood trickled into his eye, causing it to burn. He was dazed by the punch.

Andrew opened the shears over Zachary's right index finger. Then he squeezed the handles. The finger was severed with a *cracking* sound. It was cut off at the base of his finger—above the metacarpophalangeal joint. Zachary's eyes widened. He was revitalized by the electrifying pain. The pain shot up his arm. He sat up and held his hands up to his face. He screamed in terror as a geyser of blood shot out from his exposed knuckle.

Andrew punched him again—one, two, *three times.* Zachary's nose was broken by the punches. Blood dribbled out of his nostrils. He was stunned, but he kept whimpering and groaning.

"Please!" he cried, although it sounded like baby-talk from behind the tape: *pwease!*

Andrew snipped at Zachary's right thumb. He cut through the webbing between his thumb and index finger, and he severed the proximal phalange bone at the base of his finger. The thumb was still attached to his hand, though, dangling from a thin piece of flesh. Andrew severed it with another snip of the shears. The amputated thumb fell on the couch cushion beside the index finger.

'Hmm! Hmm! No!'—Zachary tried to scream.

Andrew silenced him with another jab to the jaw. He stabbed the back of Zachary's left hand to pry his fist open, then he repeated the process. He severed the photographer's left index finger and left thumb. A piece of his left thumb's proximal phalange bone stuck out from the remaining nub. His hands were covered in blood.

Zachary was pale and sweaty. He snorted, struggling to breathe through his nose. Andrew picked up the amputated fingers.

He held the fingers up to Zachary's face and said, "They say opposable thumbs separate us from the animals. That, and consciences. And now that you don't have either of those, I guess you're just another animal waiting to die."

'Please! God!'

Andrew threw the fingers at the floor. He sat him up and pushed him back against the backrest. Then he wrapped the towel around Zachary's mutilated hands.

He said, "I'm going to take the tape off your mouth. You're going to answer my questions. I hope you understand one thing: you *can't* change the outcome of this. It would be beneficial for you to cooperate immediately. No games, no screaming. I'm done playing, Zachary. Are you ready?"

Zachary shook his head. He couldn't stop whimpering. He peed himself due to the pain. His urine soaked the cushion and ran down his legs. He was willing to cooperate, he was happy to confess, but he didn't want to die.

In a soft voice, Andrew said, "Make it easy for yourself, kid. It'll all be over soon."

***

Andrew slowly removed the tape from Zachary's mouth. Zachary's lips parted, jaw shaking from side to side, but he couldn't say a word. Tears sprinkled out of his eyes with each rapid blink. On the verge of panicking, he gasped for air. He couldn't draw a deep breath, so he couldn't scream. For the first time since he moved into the loft, he wished he lived in a smaller home with thinner walls. He wished he lived near that one nosy neighbor lurking in every apartment complex.

He raised his hands. He watched as his blood soaked through the thin towel. He tried to move his index fingers, as if he were squeezing the triggers of a pair of guns, but he couldn't feel any movement.

Only pain.

"I–I don't want to die," Zachary croaked, hiccupping and sniffling.

Andrew said, "Tell me about my daughter. Tell me about Grace."

"Pl–Please don–don't let me die. It–It hurts so much. I–I'm sorry. I'll do… I'll do anything."

"Talk."

"Will–Will you let me live? P–Please?"

Andrew sighed in disappointment. He covered Zachary's mouth with the tape again. He marched into the kitchen while Zachary screamed. He grabbed the stainless-steel cheese grater from the countertop. Before Zachary could stand, he pushed his knee into his crotch and crushed his testicles.

"N–No! No! No!" he shouted from behind the tape, striking Andrew's stomach with the bottom of his fists.

Andrew pressed the cheese grater against the right side of Zachary's face, pushing his head back against the sofa. He dragged it downward. His forehead was sliced open. The cut on his cheek widened, stretching down to the center of his cheek.

His skin was peeled off his face. Some strands, thin but durable, were jammed in the cheese grater.

The intruder wiggled the grater up and down until the skin was torn off his face. Pieces of skin were stuck in the large holes. Other strings of bloody skin dangled away from Zachary's face. His right cheek was mushy. The remaining skin was pink and inflamed.

Andrew pushed the cheese grater against Zachary's face again, but he used a different side this time—the side with the medium-sized holes. He grated Zachary's face. He tore the remaining pieces of skin off. He ripped his eyebrow off his face. The hairs spiraled down to Andrew's knee. Although his eyes were clenched shut, blood flooded Zachary's eye socket. A tear seeped out, too.

Zachary heard his voice in his head: *'Please let it end. It's too much. Help me. Someone help me.'*

The grater made a loud *screeching* sound as it scraped part of his frontal bone and cheekbone. Andrew stopped. The strings of bloody skin piled on the cushion beside Zachary's trembling thigh, like cheese drenched in hot sauce atop an omelet. In that room, at the hands of a vengeful father, Zachary Denton became Harvey Dent. He was a real-life Two-Face.

Andrew threw the cheese grater aside. He grabbed Zachary's chin and looked at his sealed eyes. He felt the young man's slightest shudder. He felt each panicked breath from Zachary's nose against his face. He saw true fear in him. He was a bigger coward than the other sex offenders he had tortured.

"I'm going to give you another chance," Andrew said. "Considering what I just did to your face, I'll try to be patient. But I haven't seen my daughter in weeks, Zachary. I'm running out of time... if I'm not out of time already. So, forgive me if I run out of patience. Desperate times call for desperate measures. You know the saying? So, the same rules apply. You'll tell me what you know and I'll give you the easy way out. You won't scream, either. Do you understand me now?"

Zachary nodded reluctantly.

***

Once again, Andrew removed the tape from Zachary's mouth. Zachary's teeth chattered, like a Chattery Teeth wind-up toy. Thanks to the tape, the lower half of his cheek wasn't shredded off. Yet, he felt tingling, debilitating pain across his entire face, as if a colony of fire ants was marching across his skin and stinging him every step of the way.

Andrew asked, "Do you know who I am?"

Zachary's eyelids flickered because of the blood in his eyes. His vision was blurred and red, but he recognized the man sitting on his coffee table. He nodded.

Andrew asked, "Do you know my daughter?" Zachary nodded again. Andrew asked, "What's her name?"

"He–Her... Her name is... G–Grace."

"Last name?"

"Um... Mc–McCarthy."

"And how do you know that?"

"She... told... me."

Andrew lowered his head and sighed. He was conflicted. He wanted to find his daughter and he expected to discover something about her in Zachary's apartment. On the other hand, he was hoping he was wrong and he'd receive a phone call from Holly claiming they found Grace safely in someone's underground apocalypse bunker.

'She went in there by accident and the door locked behind her. She had plenty of food and water. She's scared, but she's okay. Come home, honey, we're waiting for you!'—he imagined Holly saying.

Andrew asked, "Did you take her from her school?"

They stared at each other for a minute. Andrew was calm and steady while Zachary was scared and shaking uncontrollably. The reporter on the television spoke about a pile-up on the freeway. No one reported Caleb's disappearance. As predicted, most people didn't care about the homeless.

Zachary said, "Yes."

Andrew breathed deeply, then he said, "You're doing good so far. Don't fuck it up. Now, tell me: where is she?"

"I–I can ex–explain, but–but you need to... give me a chance."

"I'm listening."

Zachary explained, "I don't... know exactly... where she is. I took her, then I passed her on to... to someone else."

"You sold her?!" Andrew shouted.

"No, no, no," Zachary whined as he winced. His tears rolled over the open wounds on his cheek, causing his face to twitch. He stammered, "I–I–I did my–my job."

"And what's that?" Andrew hissed through his gritted teeth.

"I'm not... I'm just the... the bait. I'm the–the face of the company. They picked me be–because I look trustworthy. I–I meet kids and I, um... I lure them away."

"You *abduct* them."

Zachary nodded, then he groaned in pain. He raised his shaking hands to his face. He didn't want to see his butchered hands under the towel. Instead, he pressed the towel against his mutilated cheek. A jet of blood squirted out. He moaned and whined. He couldn't soothe the pain.

Andrew asked, "Where is she? Who did you give her to?"

"His name is... Em–Emilio Padilla. He works at a... um... a workshop. He–He's a mechanic."

"A mechanic? You're saying a mechanic has my daughter?"

Zachary could only nod.

Andrew asked, "Where can I find him?"

"Google it."

"You little punk, I'll beat the–"

"Wa–Wait! I mean, just Google it!" Zachary said as he recoiled in fear. He lifted his knees up and curled into a ball. He nearly rolled onto his side again. He said, "It's called Santiago's Auto Repair. I–I don't know the address, I swear. You can find it on Google. I–I don't know anything else. Oh, fuck, ow... Oh, shit... Please, can we... can you let me go? I'm s–sorry for e– everything. I don't want to die. Please, I really don't want to die. I'm scared and I'm hurt and... and I'm scared. Please don't do this. I–I did everything you said. I didn't hurt your girl. I'm just... I'm an idiot, but I'm not e–evil. Please..."

Andrew searched for *Santiago's Auto Repair* on Google on his cell phone. He found the auto shop about two miles away from Zachary's home. There were only two reviews averaging three-point-five stars, but it had been open for over a year. The company's website stated that they only accepted cash. His wild imagination told him it was used to launder money or as some sort of transportation hub or as a secret studio for them to shoot pornographic films. He found his next target.

He looked at Zachary and, interrupting his begging, he said, "I can let you go. Your quality of life won't be the same, you might be trading a loft for a prison cell after this, but *sure,* I can let you live. But I need the truth. And I need to believe it. Did you hurt my daughter? Did you touch her?"

Eyes wide and bloodshot, Zachary shook his head and yelled, "No! I would never! I swear!"

"Did you take her picture? Or video?"

Zachary closed his mouth. He grimaced as he swallowed a mouthful of blood. He didn't trust Andrew. At the same time, he didn't see any other way out. He was missing four fingers, three teeth, and half of his face. He couldn't punch, headbutt, or even bite Andrew. *Gulp*—he swallowed another mouthful of blood.

He said, "I–I'm a... I'm a NOMAP."

"No... map?" Andrew repeated in a confused tone.

"It stands for non... non-offending... minor..."

"Minor attracted person," Andrew finished the sentence with him.

"You–You know it?"

"Something like that."

Zachary cracked a nervous smile while tears of relief welled in his eyes. He said, "Good. Tha–That's good. Then you know... you know I'm just sick. I like... I like kids. But... *But,* I don't hurt them. I *never* hurt them. I don't have a record or anything like that. I just take their pictures. They're like products, you know? You've shopped online before, r–right? You've seen pictures of products, right? I take their pictures like that. So, people can see..."

Finishing his sentence again, Andrew said, "Your product, your inventory, your kids."

"Exactly. I took Grace's pictures. A lot of pictures and I'm sorry for that—I know you don't think it's right—but I *didn't* hurt her. People like me, we–we just want love, you understand? We care about kids. And we are sti–sti–*stigmatized* because of it. I mean, we… *we* are the victims! We're normal, just like the gays and trans, but no one sees that! No one's listening to us! We just want to love without being judged or hated or… or fucking crucified. I'm a normal kid, man."

Andrew stared at him with a steady, emotionless face—no remorse, no anger. Zachary held his bloody hands out in front of him, clasped together as if he were praying in a church. Andrew leaned closer to him. Only the television blared in the loft. They couldn't hear the cars or pedestrians outside. Their neighbors were as quiet as mice.

Andrew lunged at Zachary. He sat on top of him. He covered his mouth with the tape, disrupting his bloodcurdling shriek. And he kept his hand over Zachary's mouth.

He said, "You're not a 'kid' or a 'victim,' and you're not 'normal,' Zachary. There are no such things as MAPs or NOMAPs. A pedophile is a pedophile. And you deserve to die."

***

Andrew pulled a canister of pepper spray out of his utility belt. He sprayed it at Zachary's face. At close-range, some of the spray wafted back to Andrew's face. He felt it land on his beard. Yet, he felt a burning sensation in his eyes, nose, and mouth. He jumped off of Zachary, covered his mouth with his elbow, and coughed. He teetered into the kitchen. He washed his face with cold water at the sink.

Zachary fell to his side on the sofa, screaming and convulsing in pain. The blood on his cheek fizzed while bloody mucus launched out of his broken nose in spurts. His eyes were as red as cherries. A coughing spell interrupted his bawling. It sounded like he had a whooping cough. The tape crinkled as he coughed and retched. Under the tape, his lips darkened into a shade of purple.

He was blinded by the pepper spray. He couldn't open his eyes anyway. He couldn't hear the television over his coughing, either. He only heard his inner voice.

Do something, you're dying, save yourself, that inner voice said.

But he couldn't move. He could twitch and shake, he could slither like a snake, but he couldn't control himself. It was as if his motor cortex—the part of his brain responsible for planning, controlling, and executing voluntary movement—had been damaged. In reality, the overwhelming pain paralyzed him. He felt like his head, inside and out, was on fire.

Andrew drank some tap water, then he spit into the sink. He muttered, "Fuck this. I need to find Grace."

He drew a chef's knife from the knife block on the counter. He walked back to the living room. He stood behind the sofa and stared down at Zachary. He despised him, his hatred was unquestionable, but some doubt started to cloud his mind.

He's the first person I hurt who's younger than me, he told himself. *He had his whole life ahead of him. He's not a registered sex offender, but that just means he was never caught, right? He is evil, right? He's not sick. He can't be sick. Don't let him fool you.*

He thrust the blade into the side of Zachary's neck. Blood sprayed out of Zachary's severed jugular as he wiggled the knife's handle and widened the wound. Zachary hacked and groaned again. He became stiff for ten seconds, then his limbs loosened up. The duct tape crinkled one more time as he let out his final breath. Yet, his body kept spasming.

Andrew said, "You should have stayed away from my daughter."

He glanced around the loft. He thought about looking through Zachary's computer, but he was afraid of stumbling upon his trove of pictures and videos. He couldn't see his daughter like that. He didn't think he could control himself, either. A part of him wanted to destroy the computer—to destroy the deviant content hidden inside—but he knew the police would need it for their inevitable investigation. The families of the other victims deserved closure, too.

He gathered his supplies, then he walked out of the loft. He closed the door behind him, but he couldn't lock it. He didn't expect anyone to visit anyway. He headed to his next destination.

Chapter Twenty-Two

Santiago's Auto Shop

Andrew sat in the driver's seat of his van in the parking lot of Santiago's Auto Shop. He stared at his cell phone. He found Emilio Padilla in the sex offender registry. He was a forty-two-year-old man convicted of aggravated stalking of a fifteen-year-old girl and lewd or lascivious battery. According to his registered information, he stood five-eight and weighed a hundred and seventy pounds. His mugshot showed a man with olive-green eyes and wavy, grizzled hair.

Andrew glanced around the parking lot. There were two other vehicles in front of the shop. Through the storefront windows, he could see someone standing behind a cash register. There were two garage doors to the right. One of the doors was open halfway, the other was closed. He couldn't hear anything inside of the shop because of the zooming cars on the streets around him. He waited for five minutes to see if any customers would walk out or show up.

Aside from the cashier, the place looked deserted.

He grabbed his duffel bag and climbed out of the van. He took one final glance around as he approached the entrance. The store was located on the corner of a busy four-way intersection. In the other corners, there was a gas station, a Burger King restaurant, and a strip mall. The other businesses were busy, as usual. A police cruiser drove by the shop. The police were still oblivious of Andrew's plot.

The door chime rang through the shop.

Andrew walked past some shelves of motor oil, antifreeze, and wiper fluid. He approached the cash register. A middle-aged man in coveralls worked the register. His coveralls were unbuttoned, the sleeves tied around his waist. Sweat stains turned the collar and pits of his white shirt yellow. He didn't resemble the man in the mugshot, but Andrew had to be sure.

"What's your name?" he asked.

The clerk stopped scribbling on a sheet of paper. He smiled and said, "Excuse me?"

"I'd like to know your name."

"Well, that's a little odd. Do we have a problem here? Is this about a past–"

"Please, sir, just humor me."

The clerk raised his brow at Andrew. He didn't feel threatened, but he was surprised. Most customers initiated their business transactions with different variations of the same message: *good morning. How much does this cost? And that? Can you check my oil here? How much? Great!* They usually didn't start by asking for a name.

The clerk said, "Jeremy Evans."

Andrew's eyes darted to a door to his right. The door led to the garage. He heard *clunking* and *clanking* tools. They weren't alone.

In a soft voice, just above a whisper, Andrew asked, "Are you working with Emilio Padilla right now?"

Jeremy said, "I am. Is there something you need?"

"I need to talk to him—*in private.*"

"Well, uh… I can let him know you're here."

Andrew said, "I want to surprise him. Do you mind stepping out for an hour or so?"

Jeremy chuckled. It was a nervous laugh. He ran his eyes over the mysterious customer. He didn't look like he was related to Emilio. He had never met any of Emilio's friends, either.

He said, "Listen, I would love to take an hour off— it beats standing around here doing nothing all day— but I can't. I'm on thin ice already. My boss would fire me if he found out."

"Thin ice? Why?"

Jeremy began to laugh again. In disbelief, he asked, "Does it matter?"

"Humor me."

Jeremy tipped his head to the side. His confused expression said something along the lines of: *what the fuck? Who is this guy?* He looked at Andrew's duffel bag. He thought: *what's in there? A gift? A gun? A bunch of cash?* Andrew's enigmatic aura made his skin crawl. Yet, he felt compelled to answer him.

He said, "I'm a felon, okay? It's tough to get a job when you have a criminal record."

"What did you do?"

Jeremy planted his knuckles on the desk, leaned forward, and said, "Grand. Theft. Auto."

Andrew believed him. He opened his wallet and pulled five one-hundred dollar bills out. He slapped the money on the counter, then he slid it towards Jeremy.

He said, "You're not the only felon in here. Give me one hour with him. No one will come in." Andrew saw the temptation in Jeremy's eyes. He placed another hundred-dollar bill on the counter. He said, "Put it in the cash register. That's more money than you'd make in a normal hour, right? Keep the rest for yourself. It's more than you make in a week, isn't it?"

He's right, Jeremy thought. He glanced at the surveillance camera in the corner above the garage door. It didn't work, he knew that, but he still believed his boss was watching his every move. But five hundred dollars was a lot of money. It could pay his bills, it could finance a guilt-free trip to a casino, it could help him live like a regular human. He put one of the bills in the cash register.

He said, "Don't break anything, don't steal anything. I'm going to be at Burger King for *one* hour. I'm watching this place like a *hawk*, you hear? If I see you walk out with anything, I'm calling my boss and the cops."

"Deal."

Jeremy flipped the OPEN sign hanging on the door over to CLOSED. As he walked out, door chime ringing through the store, he said, "One hour."

Andrew locked the door behind him. He whispered, "I only need thirty minutes."

***

"Another customer?" Emilio asked.

He lay on a plastic creeper under a red 2009 Honda Civic hoisted on an auto lift. With a flashlight, he checked the undercarriage for any signs of leakage. He heard some footsteps in the garage. From under the vehicle, he saw a man's steel-toe boots and pants.

He said, "I don't know if I told you, but I'm leaving early again. I have a meeting with my, you know... my business associate. If you put 'em in for today, I hope you can handle it on your own." The footsteps wandered to the rear of the vehicle. He said, "Hey, man, don't be a bitch about it. The boss knows. He's cool with it."

The garage door started closing. The sunshine disappeared, leaving only bright, artificial light in the garage. One last breeze swept into the room, then the air conditioner automatically turned on.

Emilio asked, "What are you doing, bud?" He heard the footsteps again and he saw the man walking beside the auto lift. He stopped in front of the vehicle. Emilio said, "Hey, Jeremy, what's–"

He was pulled out from under the car on his creeper. Andrew towered over him. He took a zip-tie out of his bag and threw it at Emilio's chest. Then he grabbed the five-round revolver in his bag and aimed it at him. Emilio's eyes widened upon spotting the gun.

He stuttered, "The–The money's in the re–"

"Put them on your wrists," Andrew demanded. He wagged the gun at him and said, "The zip-tie, moron. Zip-tie your wrists together, like if you were handcuffing yourself. Do it or you get a bullet through your ballsack."

"Oh, fuck. O–O–Okay."

Emilio did as he was told. He didn't recognize Andrew. He guessed it was a regular robbery. He had been at the other side of the gun before, so he knew things could go wrong at any second. Andrew leaned over him. He tugged on the strap and tightened the zip-tie.

He threw another zip-tie at him and said, "Your ankles."

"Ye–Yeah, sure, bu–buddy."

Emilio zip-tied his ankles together, then he lay back down on the creeper with his hands up to his chest. Again, Andrew pulled on the strap and tightened the restraint. He placed his revolver in a pocket in his bag. If things went wrong, he didn't want Emilio to overpower him and take the gun. He pulled a claw hammer out instead.

Emilio said, "Hey, you don't need to do any of that. There's a key for the cash register in the–" Andrew swung the hammer at Emilio's left knee. Emilio screamed, "Ow! Oh! Fuck! What are you–"

Andrew swung it at his knee again. The sound of the hammer hitting his bone was unnerving. It was louder than Emilio's screaming. The creeper rolled across the floor as he squirmed on top of it. Andrew grabbed his belt and pulled him back towards him. He hammered away at his kneecap until he heard Emilio's patella shatter under his skin. Although muffled by his flesh and pants, it sounded like a windshield cracking.

Emilio sat up and placed his hands over his busted kneecap. It was his natural reaction to pain, but it didn't help him. Andrew turned the hammer around. He swung the hammer's claw at Emilio's hand. The first hit broke the metacarpal bones on his right hand. The second swing tore a chunk off the top of his hand and exposed his broken bones. The third swing broke the middle and ring fingers on his left hand as he attempted to pull away from the hammer.

Howling in pain, he fell back against the creeper. He grabbed the car's bumper and tried to roll away from Andrew, but Andrew kept a firm grip on his belt. There was no escape.

Andrew struck Emilio's busted kneecap with the claw five times. The claw ripped his pants. His bruised skin—purple and blue—was visible through the hole. There was a small cut on his knee, too. Emilio's screams echoed through the empty garage. His shouts barely seeped past the garage doors. Outside, his weeping was masked by the traffic.

Jeremy sat at a table in the Burger King across the street, watching the auto shop with squinted eyes as he waited for his order.

With a strong, angry voice, Andrew said, "I'm tired of running around this town. I'm tired of meeting people like you. I want to find my daughter, Grace McCarthy, and I want to take her home. Where is she?"

"Wha–What are you talking about? You're a fucking psycho, man," Emilio cried. Drops of blood fell from his hand and plopped on his chin and neck. He said, "I'm a mechanic. I don't–"

"*Don't* play stupid with me. I know about your little side business. Zachary Denton told me everything. He transferred my daughter to you. A five-year-old girl with dark brown hair and heterochromia. One hazel eye, one brown. There's no way you could have forgotten her already. *Where is she?*"

Tongue-tied, Emilio stammered incoherently. He was awed by the truth. He expected the police to catch him sooner or later—even white-collar criminals couldn't evade the authorities forever—but he never expected a vigilante father to hunt him down and torture him in an auto shop. The most unlikely scenario was occurring before his very eyes. It was a jarring experience.

Andrew muttered, "Goddammit. You bastards love the hard way, don't you?"

He sat on top of Emilio, mounting his stomach to stop him from rolling away on the creeper. He pulled a vise-grip out of his bag.

Emilio stuttered, "Wa–Wait, we can–"

"Too late, motherfucker."

Andrew pushed Emilio's arms down. He closed the vise-grip over Emilio's nose. He twisted the adjustment knob until the jaws were tight over his nose. Emilio swung at Andrew's forearms with his broken hands while begging for mercy. The pitch of his voice rose sharply. Andrew squeezed the handles until he heard a loud *click* and a moist *crack*. Blood trickled out of Emilio's nostrils and leaked into his throat.

Emilio squeezed his eyes shut while hacking and gasping for air. The creeper moved like a broken shopping cart, jerking every which way, but he couldn't slip out from under Andrew.

"Pl–Please," he croaked out in a squeaky, nasally voice.

Andrew turned his wrist. With a loud *popping* sound, blood erupted from a cut under the bridge of Emilio's nose. He twisted his wrist in the other direction. He cut Emilio's nose in half, but both halves were still attached to his face. One of his nostrils was detached from his nasal septum, dangling over his upper lip. Blood covered the center of his face, mouth, chin, and neck. His nasal septum was twisted into a bloody nub. Bloody snot bubbles popped over his nostrils.

Pop, pop, pop!

Andrew pressed a towel against Emilio's butchered nose. He said, "Now, let's try this again."

***

Jeremy ate a Whopper and fries while drinking a frozen Coke. He played Tetris on his phone while occasionally glancing over at the auto shop. He didn't notice anything out of the ordinary.

Sitting on top of Emilio, Andrew said, "Zachary said he handed my daughter to you. And you know what? I believe him. You're a sex offender. You stalked a teenager. You molested a girl. You have my daughter."

In a throaty, nasally tone, Emilio mumbled, "What did you... do to me?"

Ignoring him, Andrew asked, "Where is she, Emilio? You have her in a closet? A trunk? Some sort of secret room?" He glanced around and shouted, "Grace! Gracie, sweetie, are you here? It's daddy! Daddy's here, baby! Give me a sign! Say something!"

There was no response.

Emilio said, "You fucked... my nose. I can't feel... I can't feel my face."

"Well, I'll tell you what you will feel: *pain,*" Andrew said. "I'm going to make you suffer if you don't start talking. Where is Grace?"

"Oh, fuck... my nose."

"Your balls are next. Where is she, goddammit?"

Emilio frowned and cried, "I don't have her. I just... I transferred her. I help out sometimes, but I just transferred her!"

"You've got to be fucking kidding me. You too? You transferred her?"

"Yeah, yes... yes... I'm the middleman. Just the middleman..."

Andrew sighed in disappointment. He felt like he was on some sort of wild-goose chase. Zachary claimed he transferred Grace to Emilio, and now Emilio claimed to have transferred her to someone else. But it made sense. If they were operating a human trafficking network, if they were moving children from one place to another, it made sense to use a middleman to muddle their trail.

Every business had a hierarchy. He was working his way up to the CEO while searching for a special product.

Andrew asked, "Who did you transfer her to?" Emilio mumbled incoherently, as if he were fading out of consciousness. Andrew slapped him and said, "Stay awake. Answer the question, you nasty bastard."

Emilio answered, "My boss."

"Who's your boss? It wasn't Zachary, was it? Did he lie to me?"

"No, no... Zachary gives me the kids and... and I take 'em to Cheese?"

"Cheese? What kind of stupid name is that?"

"My nose," Emilio whimpered.

Andrew grew impatient. He reached into his duffel bag. He pulled an ice pick out. He thought: *not yet, he needs to talk.* He threw it back into the bag. He pulled out a wrench and wagged it at Emilio's bloody face. *You already beat him with a hammer so it's too similar, you can do better,* he told himself. He grabbed the hacksaw. He slapped Emilio until he opened his eyes.

He said, "You're going to start losing pieces of yourself. Who the hell is 'Cheese' and where is he?"

With fearful eyes, saliva and blood bubbling out of his mouth, Emilio said, "He calls himself 'Cheese.' His real name is Damian Hall. This is... He's the boss, okay?"

"And who are you? You're just a delivery boy? Huh? You never hurt a kid with him before?"

"I–I'm just... I'm... I'm a..."

"Tell the truth, Emilio. I already left a bloody mess in your little buddy's loft downtown. Don't make me tear you to pieces, too."

"O–Okay, bro, okay," Emilio said with a shaky voice. "I'm a... I'm Damian's expert. He hired me because I... I have experience, you know? I taught him and Zachary how to get those kids. Zachary was better at it because... because he's handsome. He... He *was* handsome. Then I helped move 'em. I took the kids to his house. I shot the videos. I helped him... make the mess and clean it up. He handled the distribution and everything else. I am... I was... I did whatever he paid me to do."

The mess—Andrew's eyes welled with tears as he listened to those words. He didn't need it spelled out for him. He made a 'mess' in Zachary's apartment—Adam's apartment, Diego's apartment, Caleb's tent. He thought: *they hurt kids for movies, they hurt Grace, I'm too late.*

Emilio continued, "Listen, man, I was fucked by the system. I was set up to do it again and again. They made me register as a sex offender, you know that already, but that doesn't mean shit. They make it easy to cut your bracelet and move in silence. I'm not even wearing one right now. They don't care. Every jail is… full already. They don't have room for the same old people. And no one ever bothered to 'help' me. You know why? Huh? Because I'm just a normal guy. Everyone else is just too ashamed or too stupid or too brainwashed to admit it. I'm a–a product of my environment. Kids are getting more mature every day. Just look at 'em, man, and you'll see. And I'm…" He chuckled, then he groaned in pain. He said, "And I'm nothing in the bigger picture. If you kill me, someone else will just take my place. At the end of the day, right or wrong, it's just business, man. The millionaires and billionaires and fucking *trillionaires* and whatever, man… They're going to keep paying for this. They're just lucky. People like me don't have private jets to escape with and private islands to hide in. I'm nothing, man… You got the wrong guy… Wrong guy… You should be going after them… not me. Shit, my fucking nose. I can't breathe. I–I can't move."

Only Emilio's cries echoed through the shop. Andrew sat on top of him, stunned. He clenched his fists and gritted his teeth.

He said, "That was quite the speech. I've heard it all before. 'You're the victim, we're the bad guys, yadda yadda yadda.' The problem is: I don't remember asking you for your opinion."

"Come on, man…"

"Since Grace isn't here, I'm going to assume she's with your buddy. Damian Hall, right? That's what you said?"

"Yeah, but–"

"Where can I find him?"

"Just forget about–"

Andrew pinched the nub on his face that used to be his nose. Emilio screamed and writhed on the creeper. Blood rolled down his cheeks and onto his ears.

"An address, Emilio. *Now,*" Andrew said.

"Okay! Okay! Oh, fuck!" Emilio yelled. Andrew released his nose. Panting to catch his breath, Emilio said, "223… Sunset… Drive."

"Good boy. Now, don't move."

"I–I can't… breathe. Help… me."

Andrew searched the address on his cell phone. The house was located in the Rolando Hills neighborhood. *That's where Booth found the bloody clothes,* he thought. He remembered combing through the wooded area with a group of volunteers and cops. He wondered if he had missed any signs.

He said, "Emilio, I'm not going to kill you."

"You–You're not? Oh my God, tha–thank you!"

"No, I'm not going to kill you. You deserve much worse. You deserve a life in prison. You deserve to get fucked until your rectum is hanging out of your body. And the doctors will stuff it back in only for it to get fucked out of you every night. You deserve to choke on dick until you fall unconscious every night—until your stomach is so full of cum that they have to pump it out of you. You deserve to be… footless."

Andrew planted vivid images of extreme violence in Emilio's mind—the seeds of eternal terror. But only the last word reverberated through his head.

"Footless?" he repeated.

***

Jeremy checked the clock on his cell phone. He had already finished his meal. He had twenty minutes to kill before Andrew's time was up.

"What's going on in there?" he whispered as he watched the auto shop from afar. "What the hell did I do?"

Sitting on Emilio's stomach, Andrew turned around. He scooted forward and sat on Emilio's thighs to stop him from kicking. Emilio shrieked until his vocal cords stung. He grabbed the vehicle's front bumper and pulled with all of his might. He rolled a few inches under the car, the vehicle wobbled and the auto lift screeched, but then his bloody hands slipped off the bumper.

"No! No! No!" he cried. "Help! Help me! Jeremy, oh my God! Mr. Hall! Help!"

Andrew rolled Emilio's pants legs up. He scowled as he examined his bare ankles. *He really isn't wearing an ankle monitor,* he thought. His rage was fueled by the police's failure to monitor the city's criminals, especially those known to recidivate. He grabbed Emilio's shin with a firm grip, then he sawed into his right ankle with the hacksaw.

'Ahhh! Ow! Ahhh!'

Emilio couldn't say a word. He could only scream—blurts of pained noise. He grabbed at the front bumper again, but his fingers slipped off. The vehicle wobbled again and the auto lift groaned. He sat up and reached for one of the tires. His fingers caressed the grooved rubber, then he fell back against the creeper.

He slammed his fists against the floor as the blade tore through his bone. The pain pulsed through his leg, synchronized with his heartbeat. He heard his bone cracking and skin shredding. His foot shook violently, boot and sock drenched in blood. His foot continued to shake even after he lost voluntary control of it.

The blade snapped inside of Emilio's ankle, trapped in the splinters of bone, severed veins, and mutilated flesh. His foot was barely attached to his leg by his Achilles tendon. His white heel cord was visible through all the blood and flesh. His foot swung until it was twisted 180-degrees, the front of his boot touching the floor.

Andrew jumped up to his feet and shouted, "Goddammit! Look at what you–"

Spasming and jerking in pain, Emilio rolled a few more inches under the suspended vehicle. He rolled off the creeper and hit the floor. The creeper struck the lift securing pad, causing the securing lifting arm to move. The car fell from the auto lift—*front bumper first.* Laying on his back, Emilio saw it in what felt like slow motion. One-point-twenty-five tons of steel fell towards him.

His eyes, pupils dilated, said: *I don't want to die.*

The front bumper hit Emilio's head. And the top half of Emilio's head exploded. It *cracked* like an egg falling on the kitchen floor. It *burst* like a watermelon being thrown off a building for a science experiment. It *popped* like a cyst in a dermatologist's office. Like a broken water hydrant, blood shot out of Emilio's head. Bits of crushed brain rode the wave of blood like trash in the ocean. Shards of his shattered skull swam in the blood, too. His eyes were crushed under the bumper.

His limbs continued shaking for about fifteen seconds. A *crackling* sound came out of his gaping mouth.

Andrew turned pale. He had committed acts of unspeakable violence, he had watched videos of torture to prepare for his investigation, but he wasn't prepared to watch someone's head explode. It was like something from a movie, but this was *real*. Emilio's head wasn't a prop full of fake blood. He could smell the death. He could *taste* it at the back of his mouth.

Pennies.

So many pennies.

He grabbed his bag and exited the garage, fighting the urge to vomit. He sped away in his van and headed towards Rolando Hills.

At Burger King, Jeremy said, "*Finally.*"

The clerk hurried back to the shop. He called out to Emilio as he rushed through the store, but there was no response. He only heard a liquid dripping. He entered the garage and found the bloodbath. Watching someone die or finding a dead body in person was different from watching someone die on the internet. It was terrifying—*paralyzing*. It was worse for him because it was personal. He knew Emilio. He worked with him every week. The human mind couldn't protect him from that. It couldn't tell him: *it's just a movie, it's just a picture, it's nothing*.

He took a step forward, arms away from his body as if he were about to hug someone. Then he fainted and landed face-first near the entrance of the garage.

Chapter Twenty-Three

The Hall Residence

Andrew was parked in front of an iron gate. He leaned out his window and pressed the 'Call' button on the intercom.

"Hello?" he said. "Anyone home?"

No one answered. The sun was beginning to set, rays of golden sunshine penetrating the leafy branches at each side of the road. A Tesla Model 3 cruised down the road behind Andrew's van, heading to one of the other fancy homes in the neighborhood.

Through the intercom, a woman said, "Good evening. May I help you?"

Andrew said, "Hello, ma'am. My name is…" He hesitated for a second. He lied, "My name is Matthew Chambers. I work for a Mr. Fred Fields from Fred's Insurance. Maybe you've seen our commercials."

"Um… maybe so."

"Great. I'm glad the marketing team finally got something right. Now, I'm here to talk to you about your homeowners insurance. Are you insured, ma'am?"

"Yes, I believe so," the woman responded.

"Believe so?" Andrew repeated, laughing warmly.

He knew the woman was watching him from a camera on the intercom. He put a big, toothy smile on his face. The woman giggled, too. She bought it—hook, line, and sinker.

Andrew said, "Listen, ma'am, with the recent fires and earthquakes, the heavy rain and mudslides, it's very important that you're insured. And, even if you are insured now, it's important for *you* to have the best coverage at the best price. I'd like a couple minutes of your time to talk to you about some of our insurance plans."

"Oh, I'm not sure about–"

"It won't take more than ten minutes. And, I can tell by just listening to that sweet voice of yours, it would absolutely make my day to have this chat with you. *And*, on top of all that sweet-talk, you can save yourself *thousands* of dollars a year. That's a nice vacation, isn't it? Save that up for a couple of years and you got yourself another house. How about it?"

Andrew stared at the lens on the intercom. His eyelids began to twitch as he fought to maintain his smile. He sat still, but his heart raced in his chest, as if he had just run a marathon. Plan B was far more daring: ram the gate, crash through the front door, and kill everyone before the police arrived.

The woman said, "You can park in front of the garage. My husband's almost home, but I'm sure he won't mind."

"I'm sure he won't mind after he realizes he's married to a clever businesswoman like yourself. Thank you very much."

"Hush, now," the woman blushed.

The gate rolled open. Andrew drove up the driveway. After about one-tenth of a mile, he discovered a large two-story mid-century modern home with a flat roof in the woods. Decorated with nude walls and orange bricks, it had tall floor-to-ceiling windows with beautiful views of the woodland, the creek, and the city down below.

The driveway dipped into a garage under a deck. A luxury SUV was parked in one of the parking spaces. The other space was reserved for the man of the house.

Andrew parked in front of the SUV. He gazed at the front porch with a set of cold, vengeful eyes and pursed lips. *This is it, this is the end of the road,* he thought, *she has to be here.* He was determined to find Grace. Yet, he was unable to move. He was afraid to turn the page, afraid to end his investigation. He didn't know what he would do if Grace wasn't in the house—or if he discovered a dead body instead of a living child.

"Damian Hall," Andrew whispered. "Whoever you are, if you hurt her, if you touched her... God, please let her be okay."

***

The front door swung open. Andrew was greeted by a woman in her mid-fifties. Teeth like pearls, skin like silk, short hair like chocolate, she did everything in her power to retain her youth. Her eyes, dim and tired, gave her age away, telling tales of a life of hardships and triumph, love and loss, pain and glory. She seemed welcoming, though.

Andrew said, "Hello, ma'am, um... I'm sorry, this is a little embarrassing or perhaps unprofessional, but I was expecting to talk to your husband, so I don't have your name..."

"Oh, I understand. All of the bills are under his name. He's a wonderful provider," the woman said. "My name is Dawn Hall. And you said your name was..."

"Matthew Chambers."

"Well, it's nice to meet you, Matthew."

"The pleasure is all mine, Mrs. Hall."

"Oh, please call me Dawn. 'Missus' is too formal," Dawn said. She looked at the duffel bag slung over Andrew's shoulder. She pointed at it and asked, "And the bag?"

Andrew responded, "Paperwork. I'm a traveling salesman, so this bag is like my office."

"I see. You should really think about getting a briefcase. It looks much more professional," Dawn commented. She stepped aside and said, "Well, come in. You can take a seat in the living room. I'll get you some tea."

Andrew smiled and said, "Thank you very much."

He walked into the foyer. He noticed a red button on the wall beside a light-switch. He was surprised by the minimalist interior. An archway to the left led to the kitchen. The opposite archway opened up to the living room. In front of him, an L-shaped glass staircase led to the second floor. He didn't hear anyone upstairs.

He entered the living room while Dawn scurried into the kitchen. He was welcomed by a soft classical tune—*Molto Allegro* by Mozart. The music played from speakers installed in the ceiling. Two recliners and two sofas surrounded a glass coffee table at the center of the room. Behind one of the recliners, a fire burned in a fireplace, crackling and popping.

The walls were decorated with bookcases. Most of the books were works of nonfiction—memoirs, self-help, and philosophy books. A few novels stood in the shelves, too—mainstream stuff, books Oprah would recommend to bored housewives after getting a paycheck from a big publisher. Encyclopedias on criminology and criminal justice occupied the bottom shelf of one of the bookcases.

Behind one of the sofas, the sliding glass doors opened up to a beautiful deck with a pool and hot tub overlooking the woodland. There was some grilling equipment out there, too, as well as an outdoor dining set. The patio was clean and the pool was calm. They weren't hosting any parties. It looked like they hadn't had a visitor in months.

Andrew stood in front of the glass sliding doors and shouted, "Nice home you have here, Dawn! Do you have any housekeepers?"

Dawn entered the living room with a tray holding two teacups on matching saucers. She placed the tray on the coffee table, then she took a seat on a sofa.

"No housekeepers, just lil' ol' me," she said. "Why do you ask?"

"It's a big house. I imagine it would take some time to clean it. Plus, you may be eligible for discounts if you employ any live-in housekeepers."

"Oh, we don't need any housekeepers. I'm a housewife, Mr. Chambers. Cleaning, cooking... It's what I do. Maybe my husband should start paying me."

Dawn giggled and waved her hand in front of her face, as if to say: *I'm so silly.* Andrew gave her a sympathy laugh—*ha-ha.* He sat down on the sofa across from her.

As he reached for his teacup, Dawn said, "Careful. It's very hot. Let's wait a few minutes." She leaned forward in her seat. Beaming, she said, "It's green tea, straight from Japan. It's very popular over there. You know, they say green tea is very good for your skin, your brain, and your heart. It can even lower your risks for cancer."

Andrew smiled and nodded. The woman loved the sound of her voice. She was a housewife desperate for attention. She was naïve, too. In the woods, alone in a multimillion-dollar house, she was sheltered from the horrors of the real world. She lived in a bubble and viewed the world through rose-tinted glasses. *Home invasions? Robberies? Murder? Rape?*— that only happened in third-world countries.

Dawn continued, "I visit my primary care physician, Dr. Lee, every six months. She thinks the tea is helping."

As she babbled on and on, Andrew opened his bag and took a gander at his tools. He was willing to hurt sex offenders, but he didn't want to torture Dawn. As far as he knew, she was innocent. *Collateral damage,* he thought.

Dawn said, "My husband is healthy, he really is, but he works too darn much. That's why I've been trying to get him into some holistic health programs. Dr. Lee isn't a fan, but they're really good for the body, the mind, and the *spirit.* My husband, that man, he's always running around town, buying businesses here and there. He thinks he's playing Monopoly. Do you know how many auto shops, laundromats, and car washes he's bought in the last two years?"

Andrew's eyes darted towards Dawn. The pieces were starting to fall into place.

He asked, "How many?"

"Guess, hun," Dawn said with a big grin.

"*How many?*" Andrew repeated.

"Oh, you're no fun. Well, to be honest, I can't tell you an exact number, but it's a lot. Two, maybe three of each? He's gone at sunrise and back at sunset. It must take a lot of energy to manage so many businesses. He needs to slow down, don't you think? Maybe hire a few managers or... I don't know, I'm not a businesswoman, but there has to be something he can do. By the way, do you insure businesses like that? I'm sure my husband would..."

Andrew stopped listening. He only heard Emilio's voice in his head: *his real name is Damian Hall. Damian Hall. Damian Hall.* He took the revolver out of his bag and aimed it at her. Dawn gasped.

The woman said, "Oh my goodness. What are you... I don't have any–"

"I'm not here to rob you," Andrew said. "If it's not obvious enough already, I'm not here to sell you insurance, either. We're here to talk about your husband. What time is he getting home?"

"I–I don't know. I guess, um... six-thirty? Almost seven?"

Andrew checked his phone. The clock read: *6:13 PM.*

He said, "I'm going to ask you a couple of questions. If you can answer them for me, you and your husband will survive this."

"My goodness," Dawn whimpered. Tears dripped down her cheeks as she closed her eyes. She leaned back against her seat and breathed through her mouth, puffing as if she were giving birth. She repeated, "My goodness."

Andrew said, "As long as you cooperate, everything will be fine. I don't *want* to hurt you, ma'am, but you have to understand what's going on here."

"And wha–what's going on?" Dawn asked, eyes still closed. "Why are you–you doing this to me?"

"Your husband kidnapped my daughter."

"N–No."

"He hired a punk named *Zachary Denton* to kidnap my girl from her elementary school," Andrew said, raising his voice. "And he worked with *Emilio Padilla* to transfer her to him. I know his system, Dawn. I know everything."

"No, he–he didn't. That's impossible."

"He did."

"He didn't!"

Andrew lunged at her. Dawn lowered her head, raised her hands, and quailed. She didn't want to see it coming. Andrew pushed her arms away, then he poked the top of her head with the muzzle of the gun.

He said, "*He did.* You don't have to protect him anymore."

Without looking up at him, Dawn cried, "Oh my goodness, oh my goodness, oh my goodness."

"Where's my daughter? What did he do to her?"

"Oh my goodness…"

"Answer me!"

"I don't know what you're talking about!"

Andrew grabbed her neck and pushed her back against the backrest. He squeezed her throat and stifled her scream. He pressed the muzzle against her chin and placed his finger on the trigger.

Through his gritted teeth, he said, "Your husband owns Santiago's Auto Shop where he employs Emilio Padilla, doesn't he? You said he owns auto shops across the city. He probably has other people transferring kids right now, doesn't he? At his laundromats and his car washes..."

"I–I don't know wha–what you're saying," Dawn croaked. "Pl–Please s–stop."

"Where's your husband? Where's Damian?"

"Dame... Damian?" Dawn said while clawing at Andrew's wrist. "Dame... is our... son. Harry... Harry is my... husband."

Andrew inadvertently tightened his grip on Dawn's throat. The theories flooded his mind. *'Damian Hall is the mastermind, Harry Hall is the financier, Emilio was the deliveryman and production manager, and Zachary was the bait.'* On the sofa, he saw a gullible, ignorant, simple woman. But he couldn't forgive her. It was a family business, and she was part of the family.

"You let this happen," he said as he tightened his grip on her throat. "You monsters, you bitch, you... *you cunt!*"

Ludwig Van Beethoven's 5th Symphony in C Minor played through the speakers. Dawn squawked like a bird while Andrew grunted. Then the sound of a humming engine seeped into the house. They glanced at the archway.

***

The front door swung open. The floorboards creaked in the foyer. Keys jingled on a keyring.

"He... Help," Dawn said in a low, husky voice.

"Dawn, honey, I'm home," Harry announced. "We got company? Hey, you in the kitchen?"

Andrew saw him peek into the kitchen—a middle-aged gentleman with slick gray hair and matching stubble. Harry stopped in the living room archway with an expression of dismay and befuddlement. He dropped his briefcase and put his hands up.

Andrew asked, "Where's my daughter? What did you do to her?"

Harry responded, "Wha–What are you doing to my wife?" He looked at Dawn and said, "She can't breathe. You're–"

"Don't move!" Andrew shouted as Harry took a step forward. He jabbed the revolver at Dawn's chin, practically uppercutting her with the gun, as Harry took another step towards them. He shouted, "Stay back or I'll shoot!"

"Dawn, hun… She can't breathe!"

Harry took a third step.

"Stop fucking moving!" Andrew yelled, desperation in his voice.

Harry said, "There's money upstairs. Money and–and jewelry. In the safe in the bedroom, the master bedroom. Take it. Take anything you want."

Another step.

Andrew said, "I'll kill–"

Harry screamed and rushed at Andrew. Caught by surprise, Andrew hesitated. He squeezed the trigger just as Harry tackled him. The bullet struck the ceiling. The loud gunfire left their ears ringing.

Andrew landed on the glass coffee table, and Harry landed on top of Andrew. The coffee table shattered into dozens of shards, glass crackling under Andrew's back.

Andrew was knocked out by the landing. Harry was dazed but conscious. Rocking from side to side, Dawn plugged her ears with her fingers and mewled—*ow, oh, ow.*

After a few seconds, Harry reached for the revolver in Andrew's hand. He crawled over Andrew's torso. He groaned as the shards sliced his palms open and dusted the gummy flesh under his fingernails. Andrew's eyes fluttered open. His vision focused after a few blinks. He stretched out as far as humanly possible to stop Harry from grabbing the gun.

He shouted, "Stop! I'll shoot her! I'll–"

"Damn you," Harry growled as Andrew squirmed under him. "Who do you... think you are?"

He grabbed Andrew's shoulder in his left hand, then he swung down at him with his right—*jab, jab, jab, hook, jab, hook.* He was an old but tough man. His hands were rugged and coarse, like bark from a tree. But he wasn't a trained fighter. He didn't know how to throw a knockout punch. He mimicked what he saw in the ring and the Octagon.

He slammed his elbow against Andrew's jaw. Under his beard, a small cut followed the dimple of his cleft chin.

Andrew grabbed Harry's throat in his free hand. He thought about shooting him and ending the fight, but he needed Harry to find Damian. He weaved and bobbed his head, trying to dodge Harry's punches, but to no avail. The cut on his chin widened. Blood soaked his unkempt beard and streamed down to his neck.

Harry grabbed a large shard of glass. The glass cut into his fingers and widened the lacerations on his palm. He swung the shard at Andrew's face. Across the left side of his face, a cut stretched from his temple down to his beard. Some bloody strands of hair fell beside him, shaved off by the shard. The cut was dark, almost black.

Andrew's survival instincts kicked in—*fight or die.* He swung the butt of the revolver at Harry's head. He pistol-whipped him until blood started gushing out of his scalp. The blood dyed his gray hair red and drenched his left ear. Harry, stunned by the blows, swung the shard at Andrew again. He cut his ear in half. The top-half of Andrew's ear, jagged and bloody, landed on the glass.

Screaming, Andrew grabbed a fistful of glass and threw it at Harry's face. The shards stabbed Harry's cheeks and the smaller glass particles irritated his eyes, temporarily blinding him. He covered his face with his hands and sobbed. Andrew struck the side of his head with the revolver again, knocking him off of him. They lay on the glass, writhing and hissing and screaming.

Andrew heard the floorboards. He lifted his head from the glass and looked at the sofa. Dawn stood up, weeping desperately with her palms pressed against her ears.

"Don–Don't move," Andrew warned.

Dawn couldn't hear him. She teetered away.

"Don't move!" Andrew shouted as he struggled to his feet.

"The panic button!" Harry yelled from behind his hands. "Run! God, please run, Dawn! Press it!"

"*Don't move!*"

Dawn lurched towards the archway. Andrew could only visualize the red button in the foyer. *The panic button,* he thought. He didn't see a frail, kind woman anymore. He saw a hindrance. He saw the end of his investigation if he didn't stop her. He closed his left eye and aimed the revolver at Dawn.

A gunshot roared through the house. Dawn collapsed near the archway. The bullet entered her back, went through her liver, and stopped in her large intestine. She curled into the fetal position, arms crossed over her stomach, and she gasped. The floorboards behind her were sprayed with a streak of blood.

"No!" Harry yelled as he stood up on his knees.

"I told you not to move!" Andrew shouted.

Harry stabbed Andrew's calf with another shard of glass. He tried to drag the shard upward, but the glass shattered in his hand. Andrew staggered, but he stayed on his feet. He turned around and punted

Harry's face. Harry fell back against the glass from the broken coffee table, knocked out cold with a broken nose.

Andrew wagged the gun at him and yelled, "It doesn't have to be like this!"

Finger twitching on the trigger, the thought crossed his mind again: *kill him, kill them all.* Yet, a part of him still believed Grace was alive. He couldn't jeopardize her safety. *What if she's locked up somewhere? What if he's the only one who knows where she is?*—he thought. He heard the floorboards again.

Dawn dragged herself to the archway, leaving a trail of blood behind her. Andrew was out of patience. He grabbed the back of her dress and lifted her up, pulling the neckline against her neck, like a garrote. The housedress started to tear due to the pressure. She walked in place while reaching for the archway. She only thought about pressing the panic button.

Andrew tugged on the dress again. He launched Dawn back into the living room. She lost her balance and stumbled towards the patio doors. Head-first, she ran through one of the doors. The *crashing* sound, like a glass chandelier hitting a floor, echoed through the woods, sending the birds skyward. Between the doors and the pool, she lay atop a patch of broken glass while smaller fragments were sprinkled on her back.

Some of the shards stabbed her stomach, cleavage, neck, and face. Blood pooled under her. Some blood cascaded into the pool, billowing out in the water like plumes of smoke.

"Where's Damian?!" Andrew barked. "Don't make me–"

Harry crept up behind Andrew and wrapped his tie around his neck. He pulled on both sides and choked him. Andrew dropped the gun and immediately clawed at the tie—a knee-jerk reaction.

As he pulled him back, Harry shouted, "Get away from her!"

He crashed into a bookcase behind him. A novel fell from the top shelf. Andrew tried to pull away, but Harry pulled him back. They collided with the bookcase again. Two more novels—thick Stephen King bricks—fell from the second shelf from the top. Harry held his breath and exerted all of his energy to choke Andrew.

Andrew scratched his neck until it was red and lacerated. He couldn't cut through the tie with his fingernails. He swung his elbow at Harry's stomach. Harry puffed and coughed, but he didn't release his grip on the tie. They teetered to the right, bumping into each bookcase every step of the way. Novels and textbooks plummeted to the floor.

Lightheaded, Andrew limped to the fireplace. He managed to squeeze his index finger under the tie, but he could barely gasp. He grabbed the first weapon he could reach: *a fire iron.* He ducked and swung the fire iron over his head. He struck the top of Harry's head. His scalp was split open vertically down the center. Most of his hair was now red with blood, and more blood cascaded over his brow.

The tie fell to the floor. Harry staggered back, arms outstretched, as if he were walking through a dark room in search of a light-switch. He heard the ringing again.

Andrew turned around and swung the fire iron at Harry's crotch, right between his legs. Harry crossed his knees and groaned. Andrew swept Harry's legs out from under him with a fast kick. The older man hit the floor, glass crunching under his body.

"I only wanted your son!" Andrew yelled, voice hoarse from the strangulation. "I would have let you go if you just… if you just gave me my daughter back!"

He grabbed the back of Harry's shirt and dragged him to the fireplace. He threw the fireplace screen aside, then he pushed Harry's head *into* the fireplace. The flames danced on his skin. The embers pricked his cheeks. On his right eye, his eyelids burned off. The liquid in his eye boiled. He lost half of his vision. His blood dripped from his brow and sizzled on the firewood.

Harry hyperventilated, drawing heavy breaths of heat and smoke. His skin reddened, then peeled, then tore, and then blackened—*charred*. The fire ate away at his face.

Andrew pulled him out of the fireplace. Harry rolled over the broken glass. He let out long, drowsy groans as he twisted and jerked, hands over his burned face.

Andrew muttered, "God... shit... Oh fuck... look what you're making me do..."

He grabbed his revolver, then he limped back to him. He shot him through his left kneecap. Harry sat up and shrieked, flakes of his burnt, crispy skin crumbling off his face. Then his eyes rolled back as he fainted. Blood squirted out through the hole on his slacks as his leg trembled involuntarily. The blood sparkled with the glass fragments.

"You fucking idiots," Andrew muttered. "You stupid, disgusting bastards—*animals!* I should have killed your idiotic wife. I should have blown her head off in front of you."

Andrew hobbled to the glass sliding doors. The cut on his calf stung with each step. He found Dawn where he had left her—bleeding out and sobbing on the broken glass. He glanced around and searched for another weapon. He didn't want to waste his ammunition on her. *Three bullets left,* he thought. He saw a garden hose attached to the back of the house. It was used to hose down the deck and the roof during the wildfire seasons.

As he unfurled the hose, he asked, "Mrs. Hall, have you ever heard of waterboarding?" Dawn just whined. Andrew said, "It's when a towel is placed over your face, then water is poured onto the towel. It's supposed to simulate drowning. Well, we're going to try something different today, ma'am. We're going to... improvise."

He rolled her onto her side. As she gasped for air, he forced the hose's cylindrical nozzle into her mouth. He chipped some of her fake teeth and even dislodged an incisor. He pushed the nozzle into her throat, forcing it past her uvula and tonsils. It entered her esophagus. A massive mound stuck out of her neck.

Dawn squeezed her eyes shut and grabbed her neck with both hands, as if she were strangling herself. Then she touched the hose. It was stuck inside of her.

Andrew limped to the hose bibb. He took one final glance at Dawn, then he turned the valve. He ran his eyes over the rubber hose as it inflated with the running water.

Dawn opened her eyes, then she closed them again. She looked like she was hacking, but only gurgling and sloshing sounds came from her body. She felt her esophagus expanding, pushing up against her spine and heart. Her stomach ballooned, filled with cold water. She felt it rubbing against her liver and spleen. But she believed all of her organs were growing.

Her abdomen swelled. Water squirted out of her nose and squeezed past the hose to escape through her mouth. Tears, warm and plentiful, dripped from her eyes—or perhaps it was more water from the hose. She convulsed as her stomach burst. Water, blood, and stomach acid flooded her abdominal cavity. Her spine cracked and her heart raced. Then her esophagus ripped. Water ran down her trachea and filled her lungs.

Andrew turned the valve to stop the water. He stepped over Dawn and watched her twitch. Her eyes had rolled back, revealing only her red sclerae. Around the hose, bloody water came out of her mouth. It took her a minute to die. He grabbed the back of her dress and dragged her across the deck, then he dumped her into the pool. The hose was still jammed in her throat, like a hook in a fish. She floated in the water face-down, clouds of blood surrounding her.

A rendition of *The Well-Tempered Clavier* by Johann Sebastian Bach played through the speakers. Harry lay on his stomach near the sofa. Half of his face was black, the other was ashen. He was drenched in a cold sweat. The pain in his shot kneecap was excruciating. His eyes were dim with grief. He tried to reach the panic button, but after witnessing his wife's gruesome murder, he lost his will to live.

Andrew crouched beside him and said, "I hope you saw *all* of that... because you're next. And you're suffering will be much, much worse. Tell me: where's your son? Or... Or where's Grace? I know you know." Harry chuckled and sniffled. Andrew said, "Don't make this any harder for yourself. She's here. Where is she?"

"Fuck you."

"What? Are you fucking kidding me? Huh? I'm going to *hurt* you. Don't you understand that?"

"Damian... My son... He's a bad kid, but he's *our* kid. And he... he knows how to make money. He knows... what the people want. You want him? He's in... his hole. He's a coward, but he's... he's *our* coward. Good luck... getting anything from him."

"Hole? Hey, talk to me. You care about your son, I care about my daughter. Help me find her."

"Yeah, I care about my kids. So, I can't help you..."

"Your... kids?" Andrew repeated in a whisper. "Damian and..."

Teary-eyed, Harry chuckled again, then he said, "They can't see me... like this. I–I can't ex–explain this... Let 'em know that I... that *we* loved 'em."

"What are you talking about?! Where's my–"

Harry rolled onto his back. He stabbed himself in the neck with a large shard of glass. He cut through his jugular. He dragged the glass until he cut through his Adam's apple. Then his limp arm fell to his side. Blood spurted out of his neck. He breathed sharply, then the back of his head hit the floor. More blood squirted out of the gash on his scalp. His hair was sopping wet. It looked like he had just showered in blood. He didn't breathe again. His vacant eyes were fixed on the ceiling.

"Shit," Andrew muttered.

The battle was over. An eerie sense of calmness hung over the house. Shards of glass floated in puddles of blood. Classical music clashed with the crackling in the fireplace.

Andrew stomped and shouted, "Shit!"

Chapter Twenty-Four

The Groomer

Toccata and Fugue in D minor, BMV 565 by Johann Sebastian Bach wafted softly down the empty halls. The furniture was overturned in every room of the house. Drawers were pulled out of dressers, nightstands and chairs flipped over, paintings yanked off the walls, sateen cotton bed sheets and designer clothing strewn on the floors. The walls and floors were scuffed during the frantic, thorough search. A hole was even punched into a wall in the home office.

In the master bedroom, a remote—now broken— was flung at a massive television, creating a web of cracks. A free-standing mirror in the corner was broken with a fist. In the kitchen, the cabinets were open. Pots, pans, broken dishes, and shattered cups covered the floor, joined by food from the refrigerator and pantry. Red wine, freshly squeezed orange juice, and other beverages flowed in the grooves between the tiles.

Andrew sat on a recliner in the living room, defeat written on his face. He stared at the speakers installed in the ceiling. The fireplace coughed up spumes of smoke and glowing embers—an accident waiting to happen.

"What have I done?" Andrew whispered. A vein stuck out of his forehead and his face reddened as he held his breath. Saliva spurting out from between his clenched teeth, he cried, "What have I done?! I killed them! I killed people! And I couldn't find her! All of this for... *for nothing!*"

He screamed and slammed his fists against the armrests. He screamed and he screamed and *he screamed* until he was lightheaded. He reached into the duffel bag between his legs. He grabbed a hammer and threw it at one of the ceiling's speakers. The hammer ricocheted off the ceiling and struck a bookcase.

Andrew muttered, "Fuck... Damn it... Grace... Gracie, I'm sorry. I don't know what to do anymore. I failed you, baby. I fucked everything up." He leaned back and covered his face with his hands. He said, "Oh fuck, Holly, Max... Why did I do this? Why didn't I go to the police? I ruined everything."

He spent a few minutes sobbing in the living room. A cool breeze from the broken glass door carried his whimpers through the house. His anger transformed into sadness, and determination into fear. Although he murdered and tortured several people, he wasn't a cold-blooded killer. Violence wasn't in his DNA. He taught himself to hurt people in order to save the most important girl in his life. He thought about his options.

I can kill myself like Harry, he thought as he stared at the old man's sliced neck. *I can run away and forget this ever happened, just disappear or hide out with the homeless. I can go to my family and explain everything. Or I can go straight to the police and turn myself in. My family deserves closure, but I can't be the one to give it to them. No, I can't face them.*

"Booth," he whispered. "The police."

He grabbed his duffel bag. He walked over to his hammer, which landed on top of a criminology textbook. He stopped as he bent over to grab it. His eyes grew wider and wider. He pulled a book off the shelf—and then another and another.

He whispered, "No... It's impossible. No, no, no."

He pulled all of the books off the two shelves at the center of the bookcase, flinging them across the room. Some of the textbooks landed on the broken glass. A novel hit Harry's head, causing another squirt of blood to shoot out of his neck.

There was a door behind the bookcase.

A hidden door.

He tugged on the bookcase, but it wouldn't budge. He tried to move the bookcases beside it— *impossible*. He looked down and noticed the bookcases were installed on a set of tracks. He searched for a crank handle or lever. He pulled a few more books off the shelves, hoping to find some sort of secret switch, like in the movies and books.

"Fuck this," he muttered.

He knocked all of the books off the bookcase, then he destroyed the shelves with the hammer. Splinters of wood hit his face and spiraled through the air. He reached the door. It was a heavy, wooden door. He turned the knob—*locked*.

"The hard way. Always the hard way," he said.

He rammed the door with his shoulder twice, then he kicked it with his steel-toe boot five times. A sliver of wood snapped near the doorknob while a boot-sized crater was pushed into the door. He swung the hammer at the doorknob. After three swings, the doorknob detached, fell to the floor, and rolled away. A few loose screws followed it down.

He screamed as he tackled the door again, then he kicked it once more. The door burst open, splinters and chips of wood flying back against his face. He coughed and rubbed his irritated eyes while waving his other hand in front of his face. His vision focused after a couple of blinks. He took a flashlight out of his bag and aimed it at the door.

He whispered, "Holy shit. Grace... I'm coming."

***

The hidden door in the living room opened up to a small hallway. At the end of the hall, stairs led down to a basement. Andrew imagined a dungeon. And bad things happened in dungeons. He saw a lean man with a thick mustache, stubble on his jaw, and a set of evil, piercing eyes—a cliché sex offender—in his head.

His worst nightmare.

Andrew drew the revolver and walked through the doorway. He aimed the gun and flashlight down the stairs. He saw a concrete floor thirteen steps down. Duffel bag slung over his shoulder, he descended the stairs carefully. Halfway down the stairs, he heard a man whimpering and muttering incoherently. There was panic in his voice.

As he reached the bottom of the stairs, Andrew said, "You... You're Damian Hall, aren't you?"

A short, fat man stood in the farthest corner to the left beside a workbench with a vise. He cowered with his back to the stairs, sweat soaking through his large gray t-shirt. His matching sweatpants were soaked in piss. There was a small puddle of urine under his wet slippers.

"Turn around," Andrew said. The man continued whimpering and muttering. Andrew barked, "Turn around! Look at me!"

The man followed his orders. His cheeks were rosy, his eyes were bloodshot, and his face was flabby. He cried so much that his cheeks almost wrinkled, like fingers and toes in a pool. Sweat shined on his bald head, like a polished bowling ball. His fat breasts sat atop his large, round belly. His anti-androgen medication took a toll on his physique, but it had little effect on his temperament.

Andrew asked, "Are you Damian Hall?"

"Y–Y–Yes," Damian said, his voice nasally and weak.

"So, you... you are also... Cheese? Right?"

"Y–Yes, I–I am."

Tears in his eyes, Andrew smiled and said, "I've been looking for you for so long. You're the... the last piece to the puzzle. You have the answers. So..." He took a step forward. He asked, "Where's my daughter?"

"You... I don't... My mom and dad and... You killed..."

Damian couldn't finish a single sentence. Hiding in the secret basement, he had heard everything—the gunfire, the shattering glass, the screaming, the crying, *the murder*. And even when the chaos ended, he couldn't muster the courage to leave. He waited and hoped for the police to arrive, and he prayed no one would find his underground dungeon.

But his prayers weren't answered.

Andrew glanced around. In the opposite corner, he saw a desk and a computer. The computer was off. There was a stack of blank CD cases next to the mouse. DVDs were stored in the cases. A bin of USB thumb drives sat at the corner of the desk. There was a pile of laptops on the floor beside the rolling chair.

There were hundreds of thousands of pornographic images and videos on those discs, drives, and devices—from amateur porn captured through unsuspecting victims' webcams to the most violent images and videos ever shot.

In another corner of the room, there were boxes and cases filled with video production equipment. There were some iron chairs, patio chairs, and a metal highchair—as well as some cleaning supplies—in the other corner. The room reeked of blood and rotting flesh. The atmosphere was haunting, bleak and chilly.

Andrew stopped smiling. He noticed there were no other doors in sight. There were no vents, either. Grace couldn't fit in one of the cardboard boxes in the room. It was a dead-end.

He asked, "Where is she?"

"My mom and–and dad, did you... Are they alive?"

Andrew took another step forward and wagged his gun at him. He said, "You don't get to ask any questions, motherfucker. Where's my daughter? Grace McCarthy. A five-year-old girl, brown hair, one brown eye and one hazel eye, taken from Plaza Elementary. Don't make me ask you again. Let her go. Right. *Now.*"

"I'm sorry."

"What? Don't... Don't fucking apologize to me. Just tell me where you're hiding her."

Voice breaking and face scrunched up, Damian repeated, "I'm sorry."

"Stop it! I'll blow your brains out, you fat piece of shit! Where is she?!"

Damian yelled, "She's dead, man! She's in the woods! With the others!" He fell to his knees and clasped his hands in front of his face. He cried, "Please don't kill me! I–I'm sick, man! I don't know why I do this shit, I just do! I'll give you anything, I swear. Whatever you want, man, whatever..." His eyes widened. He shimmied forward on his knees and said, "The money... The money, man! I was moving in a few months. To Vietnam or the Maldives, but I don't need to do that anymore. I can give you the money instead. It's *a lot* of money, bro. And it's untraceable! You can have it! All of it! And I'll go to jail! I'll tell the police everything. Just please don't kill me. Please, man. I don't want to die."

Damian was happy to hurt children. He was tough around weak and vulnerable kids. He derived pleasure from torturing them. Around adults, he was a completely different person. He was a weakling. He was a sadist, not a masochist. Like most people, he was scared of dying, too. Death was scarier when it could be seen from a mile away.

Andrew heard Damian's voice overlapping itself. He heard an echo of his first shout—*she's dead!*—and he heard the rest of his begging at the same time. His legs rocked. His breathing accelerated. He felt nauseous. His face and lips became pale. He glanced at the desk in the corner. He frowned, then he scowled at Damian. He stepped forward with the revolver out in front of him. He aimed down at Damian's head.

Damian scooted back, but he could barely move. He begged, "No, no, no! Please! Please, man! I'm sorry! I won't do it again! I swear!"

Andrew asked, "Is she in there?"

"Wha–What?"

"Did you record her? Hmm? Is she on your computer? On one of those discs?"

Damian nodded.

Gun shaking, Andrew asked, "What did you do to her?"

"You don't... want to know. Take the money and go. I won't tell anyone you were here. It can't bring her back, man, I know that, but it can... Just take it. Please don't kill me."

"What did you do to her, Damian? I mean, maybe we can still save her, right? Maybe she's not dead, right?"

"Fu–Fuck," Damian whispered as he lowered his head. "I'm sorry, du–"

"Tell me!"

Andrew's bark echoed through the house. Damian lowered his head and groveled at Andrew's feet. Foamy saliva dripped from his mouth.

He said, "We... cut... her. It was... It was all Emilio's idea. You... You should go after him. He works at–"

"He's dead," Andrew interrupted.

"Sh–Shit..."

"What did you do to my Gracie?"

"She... She's gone. We hung her... from the ceiling... from her feet. Then we whipped her."

She could survive that, Andrew thought.

Damian continued, "We took her eyes out. We put them up for sale online. That was Emilio's idea. And someone actually bought 'em. Then... we took her apart." His voice shifted from fearful to monotone. He said, "We cut her into little pieces. And we used those pieces to decorate this room for another video. Her arms, her legs, her organs... they were like ornaments on a Christmas tree. Then we buried her near the creek with the others. She's gone. I wish I could change things, I wish I wasn't me, but I can't do anything to bring her back. But I *can* pay you. I can make you rich."

Andrew visualized Damian's confession. He saw his daughter's severed limbs hanging from the walls. He imagined a man holding her eyes in his hand in a dark room, lit up solely by a computer monitor. He was at a loss for words. He couldn't live in denial anymore. He accepted the truth: Grace was dead and gone. Tears trickling from his eyes, he pressed the muzzle of the revolver against Damian's forehead. He could see him weeping hysterically, but he couldn't hear him.

Then a feminine shriek ripped through his head. The men looked at the stairs.

"Hailey?" Damian said, concern in his eyes.

"Oh my God! Oh my God!" the woman cried upstairs. The sound of rumbling footsteps entered the basement. An alarm followed—*the panic button*. The woman whimpered, "Daddy... mom... Oh my God, no..."

Andrew wiped the tears from his cheeks and asked, "Who is that?"

"My sister," Damian said. "Don't hurt her. She just turned eighteen, man. She's still in high school. She doesn't know about this. I swear, she had *nothing* to do with any of this. You have to believe me. Please, let me pay you. Let me make this right."

"Get upstairs."

"*Millions.* I have millions, bro."

"I have two rounds left. I'll blow your head off, then I'll go up there and kill her if you don't follow my orders."

Damian had to use his hands and knees to boost himself up to his feet because of his weight. He walked ahead of Andrew with his hands up. He felt like a death row inmate marching to the electric chair. Fear stopped him from fighting back.

"Dame!" the woman shouted as Damian reached the top of the stairs.

"Hailey," Damian said, voice laced with fear.

Hailey Hall was Damian's eighteen-year-old sister. Her brown hair was tied in a ponytail. Her tears smeared her makeup. She knelt beside Harry with her cell phone in her hand. She was calling the cops.

"Oh my God," she said. It was her default expression of shock. She asked, "Dame, what hap–"

She stopped as Andrew emerged from behind Damian. The revolver struck just as much fear into her heart as the carnage in her home.

Andrew said, "Hang up the phone and turn off the alarm."

"Oh my God," she repeated.

"Do as I say and you won't get hurt. Hang up the phone, turn off the alarm, then come back here and take a seat. If it's not done in the next fifteen seconds, he's dead."

"N–No. My dad, my mom, you–you killed my-"

"One, two…"

"Just run!" Damian shouted. "Leave and don't come back!"

Andrew continued, "Three, four, five…"

Hailey was terrified and devastated, but she couldn't abandon her older brother. She disconnected from the call, then she lurched to the foyer. The world spun around her. She mumbled something unintelligible but predictable: *oh my God*. She punched their code into the alarm system's keypad. The ringing stopped.

She glanced at the front door. *Just run!*—Damian's scream rattled around in her skull. She shook her head and went back into the living room. She kept her eyes on the ceiling so she wouldn't see her dead father. From the periphery of her vision, she saw her brother sitting on the sofa with his hands up while Andrew stood on the glass from the broken coffee table.

Andrew said, "Sit next to your brother."

"Oh my God," Hailey whispered.

She raised her hands above her head and stepped forward. She shuddered as the glass crunched under her sneakers. She breathed shakily as she accidentally kicked her father's stiff arm, but she never lowered her eyes. She stepped over him, then she sat beside her brother. Grief left her depressed and woozy. The emotional pain associated with the loss of life crippled her.

Andrew walked backwards without taking the gun off the siblings. He sat down as soon as he felt the other sofa's cushions against his calves.

Andrew said, "Hailey. That's your name, isn't it?" Hailey sucked her lips into her mouth and nodded. Andrew said, "It's nice to meet you, Hailey. We have a lot to talk about, don't we? I'm going to need your cooperation and your undivided attention. The police are on the way, so if you work with me for a couple of minutes, you can get out of this alive. Think of it as… buying time. Can you do that for me?"

Hailey glanced at her brother, then she looked back at the ceiling. She had caught a glimpse of her father's blood-soaked pants leg. She nodded again, her entire face twitching.

***

A rendition of *Ave Maria* played through the speakers.

More tears flowing down his cheeks, Andrew asked, "Do you know what your brother did? Your brother and your father? Your mother, too? Did you know about that secret basement?"

Hailey glanced over at the busted door behind the broken bookcase. She stuttered, "It–It's a panic room. A–A panic room…"

"You've been in there before?"

"Years ago. When I–I was a little kid."

"And how old are you now?"

"Eight–Eighteen."

"Eighteen," Andrew repeated, amazed. "My daughter is... Well, she was five years old. The most beautiful girl in the world. She had this thing called 'heterochromia.' You know what that is?"

Hailey shook her head slowly.

Andrew swiped at a tear on his cheek before it could reach his jaw. He explained, "It's when you have two different eye colors. Grace—that was my daughter's name—she had a hazel eye and a brown eye. Now, it's not like she was walking around with a blue eye and a green eye, but she was still unique. She was special, you know? She loved Disney stuff. Her favorite was, um... *Frozen*. She wanted me to dress as Olaf next year for Halloween. I was going to do it, but..." The lump in his throat suffocated his voice. He grunted, then he said, "But our plans changed. My daughter was killed, you see? You're probably wondering: what kind of monster is capable of killing a five-year-old girl? Of torturing, dismembering, and *killing* a five-year-old girl?"

"Stop it," Damian said. "Please, she really doesn't know. She doesn't need to know."

Ignoring him, Andrew said, "Well, let me tell you." He pointed at Damian, then at the dead body at their feet. He said, "Your brother and your 'daddy.' They did it."

"No," Hailey said in awe.

Damian said, "It wasn't dad. He didn't do anything to anyone. Don't listen to him."

"Oh–Oh my God, oh my God..."

"Hailey, it was me. This is my fault. Fuck, I'm sorry. I'm so sorry. I told you I was sick. You know I'm sick!"

Andrew said, "And it wasn't just my daughter, darling."

"Shut up!" Damian yelled while Hailey sobbed beside him.

Andrew continued, "There are others. He said they were buried near a creek. He said he's made *millions* killing kids. And the sick fuck enjoyed every second of it! And now he wants to cry like a little bitch!"

"*Shut up!*"

The Blue Danube by Johann Strauss II started playing. The music was accompanied by heavy breathing and whimpering.

Andrew said, "Your brother doesn't want you to know this because he's a psychopath. He's not ashamed of his actions. He's embarrassed because he got caught. He had no intentions of stopping."

"That's not true, man," Damian said in a squeaky voice. "I'm really sick. The doctors said so. I–I have pills."

"He does," Hailey said.

"So what? So fucking what?!" Andrew yelled. "You know every single person in this goddamn country is sick, don't you? You know every fucking medicine cabinet is filled with pills from some busy, careless doctor, right? We're *all* sick—anxiety, depression, OCD, PTSD—but only *you* and *your* kind hurt kids over and over. Pills don't work for people like you,

Damian. They don't fucking matter. You need something else. And, before the cops get here, we're going to treat you."

"We?" Hailey repeated.

"Yes, *us,*" Andrew said as he pointed the revolver at her. "Take off your sweatpants, Damian."

"What? N–No, I–I can't do–"

"If the cops knock before we're finished, I'm going to shoot your sister. That's your only warning."

Damian stared at Andrew with his tearful, desperate eyes, but Andrew didn't budge. He glanced at his sister, but she didn't look back at him. He lowered his head in shame. He pulled his urine-soaked sweatpants down to his ankles.

Andrew said, "Underwear, too."

"No, come on. I was–"

"Tick-tock, Damian. Someone can knock on that door any second now."

Damian groaned as he pulled his underwear down. A stench of urine and feces rose from his soiled boxers. His penis wasn't erect, but it stuck out horizontally. It was too small to hang. His fat stomach covered his bush of curly pubic hair.

Andrew bit his lip and breathed deeply through his nose. He debated with himself about Hailey's innocence. He didn't *want* to hurt her, but he needed to use Hailey to torture Damian—to *truly* torment him. *No one is innocent in this home,* he told himself.

He said, "Give him a handjob."

"Wha–What?" the siblings said with the same stutter and tone.

"Hailey, give him a handjob. Make him hard."

"N–No, don't make her do that. Please," Damian begged.

Hailey closed her eyes and, in a hushed voice, she said, "What the fuck? What the fuck? What the fuck?"

Andrew said, "We're running out of time. So, from now on, you only have three seconds to follow my orders. If you don't, I'll shoot you."

"I said I was sorry!" Damian yelled.

"One."

"I'm sick, man!"

Hailey repeated, "What the fuck?"

Andrew said, "Two."

Damian yelled, "Fuck! I have money! I can–"

He gasped as Hailey grabbed his dick. He tilted his head back, gazed at the ceiling, and frowned. His face contracted with deep shame. He felt a mixture of embarrassment and sadness—and pleasure. He felt every groove of her small, soft fingers. He entered a state of ecstasy. This was a dream of his, and a nightmare for his sister.

Hailey kept her eyes closed and faced forward, a grimace of disgust contorting her face. She felt his dick hardening in her hand—two inches, three inches, *almost* four inches. She felt the thick veins and the mushroom-shaped glans. She was revolted by her own actions, but she was willing to do anything to save herself and her brother.

Andrew's rant was terrifying, Damian's confession was heartbreaking, but she trusted her family more than her family's killer.

"I can't believe this," Hailey said. "Oh my God..."

"I'm sorry," Damian said before inadvertently moaning with pleasure.

Ew!—Hailey exclaimed as pre-ejaculate began to ooze out of Damian's dick, glistening on the pink glans. His dick squelched with each stroke.

"Can I stop?" she cried. "Please? Can I stop?"

Andrew said, "Look at yourself, Damian. You're a real deviant. No amount of pills could have fixed your brain. You were hard as soon as she touched your dick. You're about to cum. I can see it in your face. You're doing mathematics in that big, stupid fucking head of yours, aren't you? One plus one equals two, two plus two equals four, four plus four equals eight, eight plus... You know what you're doing, but it's not over yet."

He reached into his bag. He retrieved a sheet of 40-grit sandpaper—used for heavy sanding. He approached the sofa and placed it in Hailey's hand. Hailey opened her eyes and found herself face-to-face with Andrew.

Andrew said, "Wrap it around his dick and keep stroking. Don't stop until I say so. If you stop, even for a second, I'm going to shoot you in the stomach. I'll shoot you through your kidney and you'll bleed out in five minutes. And, trust me, those will be the worst five minutes of your life. Get to work, Hailey. Save yourself."

Hailey glanced at her trembling hand. Tears ran down her cheeks. Damian was too scared to look. He was close to ejaculating. *Faster! Tighter!*—he wanted to say it, but the shame was overwhelming.

Damian asked, "What is it? Wha–What did he give you?"

"I'm sorry," Hailey squeaked out.

She wrapped the sandpaper around his dick, held it with a tight grip, then she started stroking him again. Damian gritted his teeth and screamed as he threw his head forward. He looked at his crotch in horror. He watched as the coarse surface of the sandpaper grinded against his dick. His glans went from pink to rosy and then dark red—as dark as blood. It was scratched, then sliced. The ultra-sensitive nerve endings on the tip of his penis were scraped off.

Petechiae spread across the tip and shaft. The red dots were dark and plentiful. With a quick stroke, the shaft was cut vertically. With another stroke, the crown of the glans began to bleed, sending jolts of burning pain into his pelvis. Yet, despite the unbearable pain, his dick remained hard and the pre-ejaculate kept dripping out of his urethra.

"Stop! Stop!" Damian yelled.

Andrew shouted, "Don't you dare! Keep going! Faster!"

"No! No!" Damian yelled as he grabbed Hailey's arm.

"Let her go or she dies!"

"Please!"

"Let her go, motherfucker!"

As she sped up her strokes, Hailey cried, "I'm sorry! God, I'm sorry!"

Damian flung his head back against the sofa and stared at the ceiling, shrieking and gasping. His body was covered in sweat. A burning sensation spread from the tip of his dick to his pelvis. Blood covered his dick and his pubic hair. The crown of his glans was sanded down, leaving his dick perfectly cylindrical. Strands of skin were detached from the shaft, hanging away from his dick like a banana peel.

The doorbell rang.

***

Damian grunted and wept. Hailey glanced over at the archway, eyes wide with hope. The bloody sandpaper swirled through the air, then landed near Harry's dress shoes.

"Police!" a man shouted from the porch.

Another cop shouted, "Open up!"

Andrew said, "Scream as much as you want, but *don't* move."

He hurried to the archway. He leaned back against the wall. He aimed the revolver at the sofa while peeking over at the front door. Through the sidelights, he could see the silhouettes of the police officers. He noticed the door was unlocked. *Shit,* he thought, *don't check the doorknob, don't let it end like this.*

Hailey shouted, "Help! Help us! Oh my God, please! Help!"

Damian screamed as he stared at his mutilated dick. The pre-ejaculate blended with the blood on his glans. It shone red, like a ruby glowing in the sunshine.

Andrew yelled, "You hear that?! I have a gun and two hostages in here!"

"Help us!" Hailey screamed again.

From the porch, a cop put his hand on his holster, stepped back, and said, "Sir, please–"

"I won't talk to you!" Andrew interrupted. "I'll only talk to Detective Martin Booth! He knows who I am and why I'm here! Andrew McCarthy! My name is *Andrew McCarthy!* If anyone else walks through this door, I'm going to shoot him *and* the hostages!"

"Sir, I need you to–"

"I'm not the bad guy here! Bring Booth to me!"

Andrew marched back into the living room as the cops called out to him. The beat cops weren't prepared for a hostage situation. One cop stayed on the porch while the other walked around the house and updated their dispatcher. From a hill on the right side of the house, he spotted a body in the pool. He requested a SWAT team, a crisis negotiator, and Detective Booth.

Andrew paced in front of the sofa for five minutes, mumbling to himself about his next step—*I could do this, I can do that.* The shards broke into smaller fragments, like grains of sand. The siblings sniveled and shuddered on the sofa. Damian's penis became flaccid, but the sharp pain continued pulsing into his pelvis and up his spine. He was afraid to move.

Andrew said, "We're out of time. So, here's how this is going to end. Detective Booth is going to come in here. Damian is going to tell him where he buried my... my daughter's..."

Body.

He couldn't say that word. He thought: *can we even call that a body?*

He said, "My daughter's remains. After that, you'll walk out of here, Hailey. You'll leave this awful house of yours and you'll... Well, I don't know what'll happen to you, but you'll be far away from this nightmare. I'm sure of that."

Hailey said, "My mom... My dad..."

"There's only one more thing you have to do."

"Oh no... Please, no more..."

"You're going to bite his dick off."

Hailey yelled, "No! No, I can't! Oh my God, no!"

Damian's childish whimpering evolved into a delirious chuckle. He felt the Grim Reaper caressing his face, tickling his skin with a cold, bony finger.

"I'm sorry, I'm sorry, I'm sorry," he mumbled.

Hailey stammered, "Pl–Pl–Please, mister, don't make me do this. I–I'm begging you! Oh my God!"

Andrew squatted in front of Hailey so they were on an eye-to-eye level. He said, "Believe it or not, some people in some dark, forgotten parts of the world train their dogs to eat their enemies. I've seen videos of gang members forcing pit bulls to eat their rivals' genitals. Now, we can't blame the pit bulls because, well, they don't know any better. You, Hailey, are the pit bull in this situation. You will bite his dick off because you don't know any better, because you don't have any other options, because you need to convince me that you knew nothing about Damian's actions or my daughter's presence in your home. So, you're either the clueless dog or a disgusting, conniving bitch like your brother. Choose wisely."

Hailey was horrified by Andrew's speech. She looked at the patio doors behind him, then at the archway behind her. *Where are the cops?!*—she screamed to herself.

Between breaths, Damian said, "Just... run..."

"You run, you die," Andrew said as he aimed the revolver at her chest. "Bite his dick off and end it."

Hailey's mouth hung open in awe. Thoughts of death poisoned her mind. She questioned her ability to survive: '*no one can survive a gunshot that close, right?*' And she knew Andrew wasn't bluffing. Her father's dead body lay at her feet, head doused in blood. Her mother floated in the water, a garden hose sticking out of her mouth.

She didn't want to die—peacefully or violently. She was only eighteen years old. She was supposed to go to college in the fall. She was in love with her boyfriend. She had fantasized about a fairy-tale life with him. She wanted to be a nurse. She wanted to help people. She had her whole life ahead of her. She hadn't even started to live yet.

She slowly bent over and lowered her head towards Damian's crotch. She closed her eyes upon spotting his bloody penis. It looked slimy.

"Just... run," Damian repeated.

Andrew grabbed the back of Hailey's head and pushed her down. Damian's flaccid penis entered her mouth. She gagged as she tasted his blood. She tasted a hint of his bitter pre-ejaculate, too. She moved her tongue in circles, trying to avoid Damian's penis, but to no avail. She let out a bloodcurdling shriek.

Police sirens wailed outside. A helicopter flew overhead.

Andrew yelled, "Bite it!"

Hailey kept screaming.

"Bite it!" Andrew repeated.

"I can't!" Hailey shouted, voice muffled.

Damian yelled, "Just do it if you're going to do it!"

"Oh... my... God," Hailey cried out as she coughed.

Damian squeezed his eyes shut as Hailey chomped on his dick, teeth sinking into the shaft. Hailey grunted as she swung her head left and right. Blood hit the back of her throat, causing her to retch, but she didn't release her grip on his penis. She bit down harder, trying to end the situation as soon as possible.

Andrew grabbed her ponytail and yanked her head back. Damian's penis was cut in half with a moist crackling sound. The glans hit the back of Hailey's mouth. She gagged, then she vomited as she fell back against the sofa. The orange puke—along with Damian's severed penis—landed on Harry's stomach.

Damian fell unconscious with blood spurting out of his dick. Hailey lay on the sofa and wept. Her brother's blood was smeared on her cheeks. Some puke clung to her bottom lip.

Andrew sat down on the sofa across from them. A frown pulled the sides of his mouth down. The look of disgrace on his face said: *what have I done?* He felt no sympathy for Damian, but he was disgusted by his treatment of Hailey. *'Bite his dick off'*—he couldn't believe those words came out of his mouth.

Just a few weeks ago, he was a meek insurance salesman with a loving family. He had never thrown a punch. He couldn't even argue with a clerk who gave him the wrong change. He wondered: *did she know about Damian's crimes? Was she innocent? Will she ever recover from this? Is she better off dead?*

His phone vibrated in his pocket. Despite all of the noise—the music, the plopping, the sobbing—he answered it without checking the caller ID.

"Hello," he said.

"Mr. McCarthy," Booth responded, police sirens in the background. "I'm outside. Whatever you're–"

Andrew's eyes sharpened. He stumbled towards the parallel sofa and aimed the revolver at Damian's face.

He said, "Come in. The door's open."

"Mr. McCarthy, please don't–"

"If anyone else walks through that door with you, I'll shoot both of the hostages. Don't keep me waiting."

He disconnected from the call. He gripped the revolver in both hands to stop himself from shaking. He counted the passing seconds. He heard voices in his head: *he's coming; he's not coming; you fucked up, Andrew.* He couldn't hear Hailey's cries. He put his finger on the trigger as Damian's eyes fluttered open.

Four minutes passed, almost five.

The front door swung open. Andrew looked at the archway without turning his head. He counted the footsteps—*one set*. Booth walked through the archway. He approached the sofa. His face tightened, as if in anger or disgust. He saw Harry on the floor, Dawn in the pool, and the siblings on the sofa. He didn't see any injuries on Hailey's face, but he noticed the blood around her mouth. He could see Damian's dick was severed, too, and it wasn't a clean cut.

This wasn't a regular hostage situation. This wasn't an everyday crime scene. This was a bloody massacre.

Booth raised one hand towards Andrew in a peaceful gesture while pushing his coat aside and reaching for his holstered pistol with the other.

"Help me," Hailey said as she curled into a ball.

In a soft, understanding voice, Booth said, "Mr. McCarthy... An–Andrew, put the gun down."

Teary-eyed, Andrew said, "You were right, Booth. My daughter was taken. *He* took her with his gang of pedophiles. He took her and he... he killed her."

"Andrew, we can–"

"She's dead. He told me everything. There's nothing you can say to stop this. He's going to tell you where to find her body, okay? You make sure my wife *never* sees Grace like... like that. Okay? Okay?!"

"You have my word, Andrew. I'll take care of her and your family. They need you, too. So, put the gun down and talk to me."

Andrew huffed, then he said, "They don't need me. Not after everything I did. I'm nothing to them."

"That's not true. We can still–"

Andrew said, "Tell him where to find Grace and the other bodies. Tell him, Damian!"

Damian said, "The creek... Two... big... rocks... Not far..."

"You hear that, detective? Search the creek. She's there. My baby's there."

Booth said, "We'll do that. We'll find her. Please, Andrew, put the gun down. No one else has to die. What would Holly think? Or Max? Or Grace? This isn't you."

They'd be ashamed, Andrew thought. *They wouldn't be able to look me in the eye. I'd become Max's boogeyman. Holly would leave me. I'd never see them again*. But he realized his path was set in stone. Sparing Damian and Hailey wouldn't change a thing. He was still a violent murderer.

He said, "Tell them that I did it for Grace. Tell them that I love them. Tell them that I'm sorry."

Booth said, "Andrew, don't you–"

Andrew squeezed the trigger. He shot Damian in the forehead at point-blank range. Chunks of Damian's brain and shards of his shattered skull burst out of the large exit wound at the back of his head. His head fell back over the backrest. A piece of his brain hung out of the exit wound, swinging like a pendulum—wet, soft, and squishy. After a few swings, it detached and hit the floor with a *splat.*

Booth drew his handgun. Without hesitation, he shot Andrew three times. The bullets entered his torso through his right side. The first bullet shattered a rib and punctured his lung. The second drilled through his intestines. The final bullet went through his liver. The bullets remained lodged in his organs. He collapsed near Harry's dead body.

Writhing in pain, Andrew could only think about his family. For the first time in his life, he welcomed death with open arms. He saw Grace standing on a fluffy cloud—*heaven*. And, in his mind, his daughter beckoned to him, inviting him to the most peaceful paradise he could imagine. In one swift motion, he pressed the muzzle of the revolver against his chin and squeezed the trigger.

"Jesus Christ," Booth said, wide-eyed.

The detective stood motionless for a moment. Hailey bellowed with her hands over her ears and her eyes closed. She cried for her parents, despite knowing they were already dead. An army of cops entered the house with their weapons drawn. A cop kicked the empty revolver out of Andrew's hand while aiming his pistol at him, as if he were expecting him to come back to life and attack him.

A group of cops tried to usher Booth out of the room, but he couldn't move on his own. His limbs were locked in place, eyes glued to Andrew's corpse.

He repeated, "Jesus Christ."

Chapter Twenty-Five

Epilogue

Dressed in a black suit, Max sat on a chair on a beautiful, lush lawn. His eyes and nose were red from his endless crying. Holly sat on a chair beside him, holding a handkerchief to her face as she sobbed. She leaned against her mother, Annette, who also cried her eyes out. All of the attendees—close friends and family from across the country—were dressed in funeral garb and sniveling.

There wasn't a dry eye in the cemetery.

Max watched as two caskets descended into the earth in perfect unison—a black casket for his father, a baby blue casket for his sister. It was a closed casket funeral. To Max, it was strange saying goodbye to someone he couldn't see, strange saying it to someone who couldn't say it back. He couldn't remember the last time he saw his father or sister.

But he remembered the love he shared with them. He remembered playing Mario Kart 8 Deluxe and Minecraft on the Nintendo Switch with his father. He remembered drawing, playing hide-and-seek, and watching Disney movies with his little sister. He was only eight years old, but he had enough beautiful memories of his family to last him a lifetime.

He didn't know why they held a closed casket funeral for his father and sister, but he knew it was bad. *Something happened to your sister,* that was all his mother told him while crying uncontrollably. He heard about his father's actions. It was all over the news—on TV and the internet—and kids loved to gossip just as much as their parents.

'Mr. McCarthy killed people!'

Max didn't see his father as a boogeyman. He didn't hate him for failing to save Grace, killing several people, or dying in another family's home. He missed Andrew, but he didn't feel abandoned by him. His father was a murderer just as much as he was a protector. He saw his father as a superhero—*a guardian*. He never stopped admiring him.

After the tragic events unfolded, Holly stopped talking about Andrew. She buried him with Grace out of respect for her family, but she couldn't talk about him. Max's grandpa, Rodney, who also attended the funeral, once told him: *don't hate your papa, sport. He did a bad thing, a very bad thing, but he did it because he loved you. He loved all of you so much.*

The media portrayed Andrew as a violent, psychopathic vigilante. His actions were denounced by politicians across the spectrum. Some groups even began advocating for more rights and protections for convicted sex offenders. Grace and the other murdered children faded into the background. Kids vanished and died all the time, but vigilantes didn't torture sex offenders every day.

A backhoe started filling the graves with dirt.

Max wiped the tears from his eyes and whispered, "I'll do my best, dad. I'm sorry, Gracie. I miss you guys so much. I love you... I love you..."

***

Bryan Kaiser sat in a dark room. His face was illuminated by the light from the computer monitor in front of him. He was a chubby fifty-two-year-old man with a bald head and a short, grizzled beard. He adjusted his glasses and narrowed his eyes as he scrolled through a folder on his computer—pictures, videos, *more pictures.*

"What to watch, what to watch," he whispered.

He opened another 'hidden' folder. The folder was named: *bad stuff.* It stored two hundred and thirty-four gigabytes worth of pictures and videos. The file names were vague, comprised of letters and numbers. The thumbnails revealed shocking images involving violence, women, and children—and even some animals.

"Huh," he said with a note of curiosity in his voice. "Haven't seen this one before."

He played one of the videos. The quality was subpar, fuzzy and blurry, but it was enough for him. A girl's cries came out of the speakers. He pulled his pants down, dripped some lube on his dick, and started masturbating. A tube full of formaldehyde sat at the edge of his desk. Two eyeballs floated in the tube, staring at Bryan as he masturbated.

One eye was brown.

The other was hazel.

Join the Mailing List!

Did you enjoy this disturbing journey into the world of child predators? Would you like to explore more of the dark side of humanity with me? Are you interested in the macabre? I regularly publish dark, disturbing, and provocative horror-thriller novels. My books blend true crime and splatterpunk, creating disturbing, unforgettable experiences. I've been known to dabble in other subgenres, too—supernatural, psychological, dystopian, body horror, and so on.

   If you'd like to learn more about my books and stay up to date with my latest releases, please sign up for my mailing list. By signing up, you'll also ensure you won't miss out on any of my massive book sales. (Seriously, I offer some *blowout* deals every now and then.) I usually send one email per month, but you may receive two or three during busier months—or none at all. Anyway, I promise you one thing: I won't spam you. This is strictly about the books. And it's all free! Visit this link to sign up: http://eepurl.com/bNl1CP.

Dear Reader,

Hello! First and foremost, thank you for reading! I believe *The Groomer* is my most disturbing novel to date, so I'm grateful that you made it to the end. I almost quit writing this book several times due to the nature of the subject matter. But I feel like it's an important story. I hope this letter will help you better understand *why* I wrote this book. (Spoiler alert: it wasn't out of sick pleasure.) I also hope you read and understood the content warnings plastered all over this book—in the front matter, on the product page, on the back of the paperback. If you stumbled upon this book by mistake, I hope this experience won't leave you scarred. It's based on reality, but remember: it's only a book.

I outlined *The Groomer* after reading about these so-called MAPs/NOMAPs on Twitter. To refresh your memory, MAP stands for 'minor attracted person' and NOMAP stands for 'non-offending minor attracted person.' In other words, these people are fucking pedophiles. And, on social media, on public accounts, these people attempted to justify their actions and preferences. They painted themselves as the victims. They tried to squeeze themselves into the LGBTQ+ crowd. They acted like they only cared about kids and they wouldn't do anything to hurt them. To be blunt, it pissed me off.

And it reminded me of the South Park episode 'Cartman joins NAMBLA.' NAMBLA being the 'North American Man/Boy Love Association.' It's like these people, these MAPs and NOMAPs, saw that episode and thought: *these pedos are onto something!* It was just such a bizarre discovery for me. This was after I had finished writing *Into the Wolves' Den*, which dealt with a similar subject while set in the 1990s. And a lot of readers loved that book. So, with all of the support I had behind me and my newfound anger towards this group, the idea for *The Groomer* was born.

Some of the scenes in this book were inspired by real crimes, real interrogation methods, and my research into 'hurtcore.' Don't worry, I didn't watch any videos. It didn't even cross my mind to do something like that. But I did read about some infamous videos and the notorious criminals responsible for them. There are some *evil* people out there. I'd name them here, but I'd rather not add to their infamy, but... holy shit, the things I read were just shocking. Although children *are* injured in this book, I ultimately decided to avoid filling this book with child torture. Grace's death, which was partially described by Damian near the end of the book, was originally planned to appear in this novel. But I just felt like it was *too* much even for me. And the book was already too long. The book is about 77,000 words long. That's almost unheard of in the extreme horror subgenre.

Anyway, if you enjoyed this book, I hope you can spare a couple of minutes to write a review on Amazon.com. (or your local Amazon store if you're one of my international readers!) You can also leave a review on Goodreads, Bookbub, your blog, your vlog, or even Twitter or Facebook. Word-of-mouth is marketing gold. With each review and shoutout, more people read my books. More readers equal more resources, and more resources equal more books! Your reviews also motivate me to improve and to continue writing. This book probably took you several hours to read, so I really appreciate you taking a few more minutes of your day/night to write a review or send me a message. Trust me, that pat on the back keeps me going.

Need help writing your review? You can try answering questions like these: did you enjoy the story? Would you like to read another story with similar themes/characters from me? Was it too disturbing, just right, or not violent enough for an extreme horror book? Were you satisfied with the ending? (This was my first time writing an epilogue!) Your review can be short and direct or long and detailed. It's very helpful either way.

I'm writing this letter on February 15th, 2020. I have *big* plans for this year, including longer novels with unique characters and settings. For example, *Kill Wu,* the final book in my Snuff Network series, will take place in Japan and feature characters from the first three standalone books in the series. I've been planning a book about a cult for a long time, too. I'm also planning on releasing the third book in my Heartless Heart-Ripper series by the end of this year. On a more personal note, it's also a big year because I'm getting married in March and I'm planning on moving to Japan by the summer—if all goes well with my visa applications, of course. Right now, I'm preparing for another month-long trip to Japan. I'll be there from February 28th to March 30th. (Scratch that. Turns out I'm staying until May 11th!) Let me know if you're interested in seeing pictures on Facebook or Twitter. I'd be happy to share more, but if you want me to keep it strictly business, I'm okay with that, too. None of this would be possible without you, so thank you!

If you enjoyed this book, please visit my Amazon's author page and check out my other horror novels. As I've mentioned before, I release new books frequently. Since I'm writing longer books these days, I'm aiming for six to eight new books per year. I might even publish more if I return to writing slashers or other shorter novels. Regardless, I'm *always* working on something. My writing focuses on 'human horror'—the type of stuff you read in the news, but with more grisly details and raw emotion. Inspired by crimes occurring all around the world, I write about the *evil* things people do to each other. I also write supernatural, psychological, slasher, and body horror. I'd like to experiment with extraterrestrial horror someday, too. My previous book, <u>*Damned from Birth*</u>, follows a serial killer's life in reverse. My next book, <u>*Lovelorn*</u>, focuses on a lonely man who is radicalized by an online community of anonymous misogynists and encouraged to hurt the people who hurt him. There's a lot more to come! Once again, thanks for reading!

Until our next venture into the dark and disturbing,
Jon Athan

P.S. If you have any questions or comments, or if you're an aspiring author who needs *some* help, feel free to contact me directly using my business email: <u>info@jon-athan.com</u>. You can also contact me through Twitter @Jonny Athan or my Facebook page. It might take me a while to get back to you, but I always try my best to respond. Thanks!

Made in the USA
Las Vegas, NV
11 October 2023

78963730R00203